CHRONICLES OF THE HOST 3

RISING DARKNESS

CHRONICLES OF THE HOST 3

RISING DARKNESS

D. BRIAN SHAFER

Destiny Image Fiction
An Imprint of
Destiny Image® Publishers, Inc.
P.O. Box 310
Shippensburg, PA 17257-0310

ISBN 0-7684-2177-2

For Worldwide Distribution
Printed in the U.S.A.

3 4 5 6 7 8 / 06 05 04

This book and all other Destiny Image, Revival Press, MercyPlace, Fresh Bread, Destiny Image Fiction, and Treasure House books are available at Christian bookstores and distributors worldwide.

For a U.S. bookstore nearest you, call
1-800-722-6774.
For more information on foreign distributors, call
717-532-3040.
Or reach us on the Internet:
www.destinyimage.com

Dedication

Many thanks to all my friends, family, and church family who encouraged me in the writing of this third book in the series. It's hard to believe that number three is a wrap! Thanks to my mom and dad, Andy and Mary Shafer; brothers Ron and Mike; and all the folks back in Texas.

Also thanks to Rob Belles and Dwight Davis for their inspiration and for allowing me to use them as characters in the book. Sorry they turned out to be bad guys, but what are you going to do about it?!

Thanks to my church family—Valley Christian Center—for supporting and encouraging me: Pastor Ray Noah, Connie Combs, Bryan Tebbutt, Phil York, and on and on and on.

And many thanks to my wife, Lori, and my beautiful daughters Kiersten and Breelin, who are growing up much too quickly— cut that out!

Most of all—thank You to the God and Lord we serve, whose willingness to die for all of us makes anything worthwhile possible.

"Some Thoughts About the Third Book From the Author"

Rising Darkness was born out of the idea of the intense warfare that had been waged against the nation of Israel during the years before Jesus was born. Although in the end light wins out, I chose this title to reflect the violent opposition to God's plan of redemption both in the hearts of men and of angels.

As I began book three I wanted to maintain the same energy and characters but from a different angle. I decided to tell the story in flashback fashion—as you read I hope it will make sense. The historical references are as accurate as I could make them, and the names of cities, historical characters, and such were researched for their valid spot in history.

I also added a timeline that places the reader for points of reference. Inasmuch as this book is not only a novel, but hopefully something of a teaching tool, I wanted the reader to have some sort of historical context. I used the date of 4 B.C. as the time around the birth of Christ, since that is how the calendars seem to work it out. Sounds weird that Jesus would be born four years "Before Christ"—but look it up sometime.

Finally, book three covers a huge segment of Bible history. Naturally I could not retell every detail that happened, particularly in the Kings and Chronicles section. I recommend that you read those Books again if you want to brush up on your Bible history. They are wonderful Books. Regarding the prophets, I tried to tell their message as directly related to any angelic involvement or messianic revelation, so this book is heavily weighted towards men like Elijah, Elisha, Isaiah, and Daniel.

I hope you enjoy the read. Please feel free to email me with your thoughts at dshafer@dublinvcc.org. God bless you.

Contents

Rising Darkness Cast of Characters:

Fallen Angels

Lucifer	chief of the fallen angels
Kara, Pellecus, and Rugio	Lucifer's chief rulers
Khasis	demon prince over Jericho
Jhara	a warrior assigned to Khasis
Berenius	an aide to Kara
Shawa	one of Kara's angels assigned to Samson
Aziel	a demon sent to torment Saul
Grolius	aide to Rugio; sent to harass Elisha
Nathan	chief aide to Rugio
Drezzan	aide to Pellecus in Babylon
Tinius	aide to Pellecus; formerly on Lucifer's council

Holy Angels

Michael	an archangel and Chief Commander of the Host
Gabriel	an archangel and Chief Messenger
Serus	an angel assigned to Bethlehem
Bakka	an angel assigned to Daniel the shepherd
Crillus	a warrior scout assigned to Michael
Crispin	wisdom angel and friend to Michael and Gabriel
Sangius	a chief aide to Michael
Dheer	an angel assigned to Samson
Romus	an angel in Bethlehem

Shepherds at Bethlehem

Eli
Elron
Joshua
Daniel
Jarod

Other Humans

Joshua	leader of Israel after Moses
Caleb	a leader in Israel; friend to Joshua
Jarez and Zogor	spies from Jericho sent to watch Israel's crossing of Jordan
Rahab	a prostitute in Jericho
Achan	one of Joshua's commanders
Zara	an aide-de-camp to Achan
Samson	a judge over Israel
Manoah	Samson's father
Dori	a priest of Dagon
Joseph and Mary	pilgrims to Bethlehem
Jesse	father of David
David	a shepherd; later king of Israel
Samuel	the last of the judges of Israel who anoints David king

Saul	Israel's first king
Goliath	the Philistine champion
Eliab	David's oldest brother
Solomon	king after David
Rehoboam	Solomon's son, ruler in Judah after the kingdom is divided
Jeroboam	first king of the Northern Kingdom of Israel
Zabud	an elder in Israel; former counselor to Solomon
Keriah	counselor to Rehoboam
Elijah	a prophet
Ahab	a king of Israel
Jezebel	Ahab's wife
Dobri	Jezebel's spy sent to watch Elijah
Elisha	a prophet after Elijah
Isaiah, Hosea, Micah	prophets in Israel and Judah
Sennacherib	king of Assyria
Kiriam	Sennacherib's envoy to Judah
Hezekiah	a king of Judah
Daniel	a prophet in exile
Ezekiel	a prophet in exile
Nebuchadnezzar	king of Babylon who destroyed Jerusalem
Ashpenaz	Nebuchadnezzar's chief advisor
Shadrach, Meshach, and Abednego	three Hebrews who are Daniel's friends
Arbo-kan, Divis, Bellesor	conspirators against the Hebrews in Babylon
Belshezzar	last king of Babylon
Cyrus	king of the Medes and Persians
Darius	ruler in Babylon after the Medo-Persian conquest
Kezzar-mar	conspirator against Daniel
Berza, Farsin, and Sheshbar	co-conspirators with Kezzar-mar

Chapter 1

"We lost our way—and then we lost our kingdom."

Bethlehem, 4 B.C.

The little fire crackled with delight as a few more pieces of very dry branches and sticks were thrown atop its dancing flames. Faces near the fire reflected a reddish sheen as they watched the wood being devoured greedily. One of the men stared vacantly into the light while watching his friend's efforts to keep the fire alive.

He looked at the others who sat around the flames. There wasn't much heat being thrown off, but then again it didn't really matter. This fire was not for warmth of body, but for warmth of spirit. The evening fields outside Bethlehem were bleak and boring for watchful shepherds, and this night was no different...or was it?

Not far from the shepherds, and unseen by them, stood two figures—angels of the Lord who had been assigned to watch over these humble men of the fields. And so they watched, enjoying the occasional banter of these who faithfully watched over their flocks. And they waited…

"Good Serus, why are we watching these particular men?" asked Bakka.

Serus, who had been apprenticed to Michael and was now mentoring Bakka in the ways and means of serving the Most High on earth, looked at his charge.

"We are watching these men because the Lord has ordered it so," said Serus.

Bakka stood silent for a moment more and then spoke again.

"But what are we to be doing in particular?" He finally managed to ask. "I thought I was sent to earth to engage the enemy—not to shepherd shepherds."

Serus smiled at Bakka's eagerness. He recalled all too well his first assignment with Michael. He too had been very zealous and had driven Michael to exasperation because of his desire to get in the war firsthand. Bakka was a good angel, recently released from the Academy of the Host where he had been trained in the art of warfare for the Most High. He was ready now to take the things he had learned and apply them in glorious battle for the Most High God.

"Every assignment is important, Bakka," said Serus. "The war is fought on many fronts and in many ways."

"Yes I know, good teacher," said Bakka. "But I wish to do something significant. Something that will make a difference in the war…"

Serus indicated the shepherds before them.

"Every decision that humans make, every action they take, every thought they think makes a difference in the war. Our duty is to uphold the Lord's authority in Heaven and on earth by serving these men made in God's image."

They walked over to the campfire where the men were enjoying a bit of meat cooked over the fire. Serus turned to Bakka.

"Look at these men, Bakka. They are poor and simple shepherds in the eyes of men. They have no real importance to anyone outside their families. And yet the Most High loves each of these as much as He loved the great kings of the past—even David himself. Our duty is to serve the Lord by serving them; to help them in their times of trial when they call upon the name of God in prayer; to protect them when we can from the enemy who seeks to devour them because he is jealous of the Lord's great love for them. The war is being fought here and now in the minds and hearts of men—even these simple shepherds who love God and look to Him for their deliverance. And you have been assigned to one of these men in particular—a man who has become discouraged of heart and mind."

"Which man?" asked Bakka. He eagerly surveyed the group, hoping that it was perhaps the brawny fellow who seemed to be more a soldier than a shepherd.

Serus coyly gave him a "you'll have to wait a bit more" sort of look, holding up his hand to stop their conversation. The words of a little boy of about eight, a son of one of the shepherds, had caught Serus's attention.

"Listen and hear how the minds of humans work," he said, smiling.

"But how old was King David when he killed Goliath?" the boy whose name was Joshua asked, continuing the line of questioning about his favorite hero, which had dominated the conversation thus far. The men smiled at the boy's curiosity about men and women of their past.

Joshua's father, a gentle man whose sunburned skin belied his age, smiled down at his little boy. He looked around at the other men, some of whom also had their sons with them. He then answered as if in deep thought.

"Well, Joshua, as I was saying, that was a long time ago. But I think he wasn't too much older than you when he killed the giant and saved Israel."

"But before that he had killed lions and all sorts of other animals, right?" said the boy, who made sure he could feel his little sling nearby. He kept a wary eye out for any intruding animals.

"Yes, that's true," said the father, Elron. "King David killed many wild animals before he met Goliath."

The men settled in around the fire. They enjoyed drinking in the stories they themselves had grown up with—there was comfort in reliving the glory days of Israel in the face of the present bitter occupation.

"But Joshua, you must realize that David didn't kill the giant," Elron said, taking the sling from the boy's fidgety hands. "The Lord Almighty killed Goliath. Just as He promises to destroy all our enemies."

As he finished speaking, the raucous sounds of drunken Roman officers roaring through the streets in chariots drifted up the hillside from the edge of town. The father turned toward the noise and then back to his son, who was still looking toward the sound of the disturbance.

"Yes, even the Romans will be defeated one day," he said resignedly. "The Lord will avenge us...someday."

"Not the Messiah, again," said Daniel, another of the shepherds.

"Yes, Daniel, the Messiah," said Elron. He gave them all a look of confidence. "He will come one day and save His people."

Daniel shook his head in disgust. He pointed toward the town and said, "The only thing the Romans will ever understand is violence. They killed my brother for some stupid senseless reason. They only understand blood. You know that!"

After a few moments of tense silence, the boy Joshua suddenly spoke up, sincerely puzzled by Daniel's statement.

"But don't you believe the Messiah will come some day?" he asked quietly.

Elron looked hard at Daniel as the man framed his answer. Daniel in turn looked at all the other men—particularly the fathers who held their sons close to them.

"I hope your father is right, Joshua," he said finally. "I hope that there is a Messiah, an Anointed One, who will come and save us." He then looked at the rest of the men. "But until that happens, we must be prepared to meet force with force!"

"We learned long ago that the might of men gains nothing," came the voice of Eli, an ancient shepherd whose wisdom was respected by all. "That is how we came to lose our freedom to so many...the Assyrians, the Babylonians, the Greek kingdoms and now the Romans. We lost our way—and then we lost our kingdom."

Daniel stood up, agitated now.

"We don't need a lesson in how many times we have been occupied, dear Eli," he said, throwing up his hands. "Surely you don't propose that we wait out the Romans."

"In the Lord's timing the Messiah will come," said Eli. "And when He does, He will set things right."

"When He comes...when He comes," said Daniel. He walked off, disgusted by the way the conversation had gone, as well as by the way he had handled it. As he walked he brushed up against Bakka, never knowing that he had touched an angel, and stood in the darkness, staring down at Bethlehem. The angel was amused at the man's reaction to such profound wisdom spoken by the old shepherd. He turned again to the conversation.

"But didn't we have to fight to gain the land in the first place?" asked another boy, Jarod, who was about 13 years old. "We had great armies then!"

"True, true," said Eli, shutting his eyes, and folding his hands in front of him. "Israel had a great army then."

The other shepherds began huddling close, bringing in more wood for the fire, settling in for the evening. They knew Eli was about to tell a story that would not only fill their hearts and minds, but also help to pass the long night.

"It was a glorious victory that brought us into this land," Eli began, as if seeing it all in his mind. "A great series of victories begun by Joshua." He looked at the little boy and winked at him. "Your namesake," he added.

The boy grinned proudly. So did his father.

"But Joshua himself realized that without the Lord there would be no victory at all. He depended on the Lord. After the great victory at Jericho, where the sound of trumpets brought down the proud walls, Joshua found himself defeated by Ai, a very little town that should have fallen very easily."

Eli sat up and shook his finger at the men. "And that was the beginning of a great lesson for our fathers of that day. They had begun to lose their way even as they were in the midst of great victories..."

As Eli recounted the great days of Israel, the two angels walked away from the shepherds. A voice came from behind them. It was Gabriel.

"Greetings my brothers," he said. "A glorious night for a glorious event!"

"Gabriel!" said Serus, who had been assigned to watch over the shepherds until the rest of the Host arrived. "Welcome, my brother."

Bakka also greeted Gabriel. "We were listening to this man Eli," he said. "He is speaking of the days of Joshua."

"You would do well to listen to this man and learn how the faith and minds of humans work," said Gabriel, looking at the very bright star that hung in the heavens over Bethlehem. He indicated

Daniel, who remained standoffish. "He also would do well to listen to Eli."

"He seems to listen to nobody," scoffed Bakka. "He'll hear
none of it. He's a very difficult man."

"Yes, Bakka, he is extremely troubled, " said Gabriel calmly.
"Tonight is a very important night for him. That is why I am giving you charge over him."

"What?" responded Bakka, obviously exasperated. "You are
assigning me to Daniel? But I thought perhaps I could be with one
of the Levites. Or perhaps that cantankerous Lippius—you know,
the one who is spoiling to fight the Romans?"

"Daniel is a troubled man who needs a compassionate
guardian," said Gabriel. "He also needs direction. You have been
assigned to see to both of those things. Tonight."

"Yes, my lord," said Bakka, still puzzled by his new assignment.

Gabriel led Bakka over toward the place where Daniel stood.
The man was quietly weeping, staring at the sky in the direction of
the bright star that had recently appeared over the land.

"Why is tonight so critical?" asked Bakka sheepishly. "I
mean, why must there be a resolution tonight?"

"This man matters," said Gabriel pointedly. "As all men do.
And tonight, all that Eli speaks about will speak to what shall happen in Bethlehem very soon. This will be a night that is very
important to both Daniel...and you."

Bakka started to respond, but Gabriel forbade him, motioning for him rather to listen to the words of the old man. Bakka
walked over next to Daniel. He did indeed have compassion for
the man. Since Daniel was now his charge, Bakka was determined
to do all that was allowed within his power to see this man back to
God.

Bakka sidled up next to Daniel and spoke gently into his
mind: "Why don't you listen to the old man?" He looked at

Gabriel and then Eli and muttered to himself, "Sounds as if we both need to hear him out."

At first Daniel didn't respond. But after a few more urgings, he glanced over at the other shepherds. He sat down, still staring into the little city of Bethlehem, but he cocked his head in such a way as to hear what was being discussed. Bakka grinned at Gabriel and Serus, who nodded in affirmation. Bakka then sat next to Daniel and listened to Eli.

The old man was quite a storyteller, eloquent and compelling. Even Gabriel caught himself listening with great interest as the story unfolded...from those days after the crossing of Jordan into Canaan...to the days when Israel was a new nation with a great vision...to the days when Joshua was leader over the people...days of a very different time with a very determined enemy...days that were all a part of the Most High's glorious plan to bring the Seed of the woman, the Messiah, to save the earth.

Chronicles of the Host

Nation's Eve

It was with much anticipation that the Host observed the passing of the mantle of leadership from Moses to Joshua. Now a man of 80, Joshua was to lead the people into the land for which they had waited over 400 years. Poised inside their walled cities on the other side of the Jordan, the Canaanite kings, steeped in idolatry and in agreement with every vile and detestable behavior possible, awaited the impending invasion.

Lucifer and his princes over Canaan had made sure that the people of the land were alert to the ambitions of the Hebrews. They had communicated through the forbidden arts of the Canaanite priests, in visions and dreams and ecstatic utterances, the darkness that was encroaching from the East. The cry went throughout the land that the people who had humbled Rameses were now closing in...and so the Canaanites prepared as best they could for the coming battle, never knowing that they were smaller pieces in a much larger game....

East of Jordan, 1225 B.C.

"They are behaving like maddened hornets on that side of Jordan," said Crillus, one of Michael's warrior scouts, as he reported on the movements of the enemy in Canaan. "They know that the Lord is about to move and they are in a panic." He smiled. "In fact, when they saw me coming in with a few other warriors for a closer look, they thought the attack had begun and began scattering like the wind!"

Michael nodded in acknowledgment of the report and looked across the great river to the other side where, unseen to the humans, a great cloud had gathered across the sky facing them.

"Make no mistake, my friend," said Michael. "True, some of the enemy are frightened. But there are untold thousands of the enemy in the land," he said. "And not all of them are given to fright."

"Yes, they have been entrenched there for quite a while," agreed Crillus. "They won't give up their territory easily."

"Nevertheless they shall give it up," said Michael, glancing at the holy angels who continued to pour into the area above the Israelites. "Our numbers are increasing as the people continue praying according to Joshua's recent command. Then you shall see that dark cloud scattered once and for all!"

The holy angels with Michael provided a covering of sorts, shielding the people from incursions that were frequently attempted by roving devils who penetrated the lines just enough to streak through the camp. Lucifer had assigned them to spread fear throughout the nation of Israel—fear of walled cities, and giants, and unimaginable evil. But they caused little real harm; they were powerless operating in proximity of a people so near to the Presence of the Lord.

Michael glanced at Joshua, who was himself at that very moment also peering across the Jordan. How strong he looked! At 80 years of age Joshua seemed stronger than ever. The Lord had certainly chosen well the man who would carry the people into the land of promise.

Michael remembered how, 40 years earlier, Joshua had entered the land with Caleb and the other spies; how ten spies had brought back a report to Moses and the people that the land was good, but that it would be impossible to conquer; how Joshua and Caleb had almost been stoned by the people for encouraging them that the Lord was with them to take the land; how God had judged that generation unworthy to enter the land; and how Joshua and Caleb had waited until this day to finally return to the land flowing with milk and honey. Now they were ready to enter the land of promise!

But were the people ready to fight? That had been the running debate among Joshua's leadership. The Lord had recently spoken to Joshua, encouraging him, and Joshua had resolved with his warriors that the attack would occur soon—and would include those men from the tribes whose land was already secured on this side of the river. And so it was that Joshua now gazed across the Jordan, readying his heart and mind for the coming conquest.

Two men approached Joshua. They were dressed in clothing more Canaanite in appearance than Hebrew. They listened and nodded as he instructed them and then they set off across the river, disappearing into the cool water. Joshua silently prayed God's favor upon the spies he was sending to scout out the strength of Jericho.

"Here they come again!" came a shout from somewhere down below.

As Joshua watched his spies make it safely to the other side, several very large demons—unseen by Joshua or any other human—battered their way into the camp, breaking through a line of holy angels, and entered a tent belonging to one of Joshua's generals. Try as they might, Michael's angels could not remove them.

A great row occurred as holy angels found themselves unable to make the demons budge. The demons merely laughed at Michael when he approached them. They stood over the figure of a general, who was clearly depressed. With his head resting on his hands, he stared blankly at the wall of the tent.

"Poor Michael," said one of the demons. "I'm afraid this one has given us permission to be here."

"You know the rules of this war," said another laughingly. "Once a human gives us permission there is nothing that can force us out—unless he does it himself!"

"You are taking advantage of this man's discouragement," said Michael angrily. "His wife and daughter just drowned and he is upset. But he will recover."

"He is more than upset," said the larger of the three demons. "He is angry at Joshua! And anger makes for good motivation." He began speaking soothingly into the distraught man's mind. "After all, if it weren't for Joshua dragging us to this place, your wife and daughter would still be alive…"

The man began weeping tears of bitterness and anger. The demon laughed.

"You see, Michael?" he said. "This man blames Joshua. And rightfully so!"

"And this is only one man," said another. "Sickness is beginning to break out. And more fear." He looked intently at the archangel. "I love how both sickness and fear are so contagious among humans—and so complementary. They both cause paralysis and death!"

Michael left the tent and ordered angels on sentry to watch the movements of the man. Crillus followed the archangel, wondering how he would handle the situation.

"He's correct about one thing," said Michael. "The longer we remain here the more opportunity these foul creatures will have to exert their influence."

"But why?" asked Crillus, walking with Michael as they neared where Joshua now conferred with some of the elders. "The Ark of the Testimony is here—God's very Presence. Joshua is firmly in control. The vast majority of the people are with him. In fact they took an oath to pay with their lives should they betray his leadership. Why would they give in to the enemy now?"

"Because humans have a knack for weakening," said Michael, looking at another enemy incursion into the camp—this time to harass a Levite who was having marital strife and was becoming increasingly bitter toward his wife.

"I have seen it all too often," Michael said resignedly. "Given time, men seem to follow the leading of their capricious natures. That is what prolongs this war."

Before Crillus could respond, Michael vanished. He had decided to call upon one of the wisest angels in Heaven for advice.

Chapter 2

"It will be difficult to fight them in their own land."

"The Council? In Jericho?"

"Yes, my prince," responded the aide. "They are convening here to discuss the coming invasion."

"Well," said Khasis. "It isn't often that we receive such splendid personages in our little part of the kingdom, is it?"

Khasis, formerly an angel of worship named Stepp, had been created prince over Jericho by Rugio on direct orders of Lucifer. Since the angel had been devoted to Lucifer from the beginning of the rebellion, Lucifer wanted not so much to honor Stepp as to purchase him. Stepp, who became Khasis, the local deity, saw in the appointment hope for greater things. If serving Lucifer in this rotten city furthered his own ambitions, then serve he would. Besides, Jericho was about to become the center of the war; and with the Council's impending visit, what better time to shine?

In the time that he had been prince over the region, Khasis had developed a following among the people. They worshiped him as the great wisdom who brought strength and commerce to

Jericho and were devoted to his cult. Khasis had an active priest-hood who helped keep the people in darkness; he had a city trea-sury filled with the commerce that comes from trafficking in the carnal pleasures of humans; and of course he had the walls. The walls of the city, which made his position unassailable by anything human, were the envy of most other cities in the region.

All in all he felt good....

And yet along with the building of the great walls, there had also been building in Khasis a slow burning jealousy against the other princes in Canaan, who ruled over larger and more presti-gious areas, such as Hazor or the five cities. Naturally, since Jeri-cho was a frontier city, it was out of the mix of much of the politics of the land. Still, Khasis intended to make a name for himself and become prince over all of Canaan. Perhaps this visit by the Coun-cil was truly fortuitous.

"The Council has arrived," came the announcement.

"Splendid," said Khasis. "Let's show them the hospitality of the prince of Jericho. We'll meet them in the king's theater behind his great house." He smiled. "What better place to map out this lit-tle drama?"

Crispin had just left the Academy of the Host when Michael caught up with him. Michael could always tell when his old teacher had just left a satisfying classroom situation. Crispin wore a look of extraordinary wisdom coupled with a rather rascally smirk—which usually meant that some angel or other had been caught in one of his famous logic traps. Michael hailed Crispin as he was about to enter the Academy courtyard toward the Great Temple.

"Ah, Michael," called Crispin. "Back from earth so soon?" He then added in mock seriousness, "Don't tell me the war is over already?"

Michael smiled at Crispin's humorous jab.

"Not by any means, teacher," said Michael. "Would that it were over soon."

"Yes," mused Crispin. "Every day that goes by on that planet without the great resolution means more souls lost to those for whom Sheol was created in the first place!"

They walked together down a beautiful pathway that led to a corner of the courtyard on the way to Crispin's offices. He knew that something was bothering Michael. He also knew that Michael would tell him at the proper moment.

"So how was your class today?" Michael asked casually.

"Splendid, splendid," answered Crispin. "Of course the nature of our instruction has changed considerably since the days when you attended the Academy—what with the war and all." He looked vacantly at Michael as if thinking about earlier times. "Those were the days when angels were more content learning about God rather than trying to become Him! And so we teach the sacred teachings—but one way or the other the talk always drifts to war. Perhaps it is for the best in these dark times…"

"The war," Michael muttered quietly.

"Yes. Just so," said Crispin. "I hear Joshua is doing splendidly with the people. They should be crossing over any day now, shouldn't they?"

Michael looked around to make sure they were quite alone.

"Joshua is doing well, Crispin," agreed Michael. "But these people…they are fearful in their hearts. Apart from a few of their leaders, and Caleb of course, the people seem on the verge of complete dissolution."

"I thought they were of one mind in this," said Crispin disappointedly. "That is alarming, I must say…although not exactly shocking."

"What do you mean, teacher?" asked Michael, happy to finally be getting into the matter that had led him to seek out this counsel.

"As you have said many times, Michael, these people are on the verge. They are always on the verge, it seems. Ever since they corrupted their natures, humans have been on the verge of catastrophic decisions. You know that."

"Yes, I know," said Michael. "But it's not just that. Most of the earth's people are completely deceived by Lucifer's angels—who have either set themselves up as gods to be worshiped, or as spirits to be feared, or both. But I'm talking about God's very own people. The people of covenant and promise…the people through whom will come the Seed who will eventually avenge the Lord and somehow rescue them…"

"Of course," said Crispin, who led Michael to a lovely spot in the garden. "Let's talk here among our Lord's wonderful creation." He indicated the surroundings. "Wonderfully beautiful, hmm? And to think that the Lord has created such beauty on earth as well—albeit of an inferior, material quality."

Michael was not about to let the conversation drift toward the flora and fauna of creation.

"What I am seeing are more and more incursions by the enemy," said Michael. "They have been held back until recently; now they seem to be coming in greater and greater numbers. They sweep in and begin speaking disparaging thoughts about Joshua, or whispering frightening scenarios of what lies on the other side of the Jordan, or…"

"But Michael, what do you expect of our enemy?" asked Crispin. "He is sworn to oppose us. In fact his very existence depends upon it. Oh, I know that in the end he cannot possibly win. We all know that, I think." Crispin looked at Michael intently. "Except for Lucifer himself. At one time I was convinced he knew in his heart that he could not possibly win this war. Now, I'm not so sure. Pride has a way of blinding one's ability to reason. In the end it becomes madness.

"And so the enemy throws at you what he can. But think of it, Michael. What weapons does the enemy possess? Only those that humans allow him to use against them really. God's people have learned that in prayer they can best the greatest of Lucifer's angels." He scoffed. "Of course getting humans to pray is another matter altogether. But when they do pray, they can hold off any devil."

Michael thought of the many times in the past when humans had prayed and God had dispatched him and a number of the Host just as Crispin had said. They always came with an extra sense of strength and anointing and they always overcame the enemy.

"Of course it is the Spirit of God who is really overcoming the enemy," said Crispin. "We are merely His instruments in the matter."

"So why the recent influx of Lucifer's angels?" asked Michael.

"I suspect that they—like we—realize that the crossing of the Jordan is a very significant undertaking," said Crispin, nodding to an angel who walked by. "And so they are increasing pressure. I also suspect that, for whatever reason, the people are not calling out to the Lord as they did—in prayer and in worship. This leaves us in the rather dubious position of becoming more and more the observer rather than the player."

"The people!" fumed Michael. "If only they realized the potential of a true and meaningful relationship with the Lord!"

"They did...once," said Crispin. "In Eden. At that time they had all the authority they needed. Lucifer could not touch them. And then of course they handed over to him what he could never have taken by force—their legitimate authority to rule on earth. And so the war goes on...a war fought to determine who is ultimately in authority in the hearts of men—the Most High, or a pitiful angel who proudly thought to usurp a position to which he was never called and for which he was never created."

"And so Joshua must somehow continue to rally these diffi-cult people to the cause," said Michael resignedly. "I hope they don't spend another forty years waiting to enter the land."

Crispin laughed.

"They'll make it over," he said. "In spite of all the frightful reports that Lucifer can muster, they'll get across. They are still fresh from Moses' death. I suspect they are more fearful of the Lord who devastated Egypt than they are of walled cities and giants." Crispin winked. "Besides, the memory of what a bad report caused forty years ago should be enough to get every one of them across that river!"

"So..."

"So return to earth encouraged, Michael," said Crispin, plac-ing a hand on the archangel's shoulder. "Go back and stand at your place beside Joshua. Fight the enemy as you can. Serve the Most High as you are commanded. But realize that not even the greatest angel in Heaven can violate the freedom of the human mind." As he spoke, Crispin cast a glance toward the Great Moun-tain of the North, the seat of God's Presence in Heaven shimmer-ing in the distance. "Even the Most High rarely places Himself between a man's will and his destiny," he added.

"So, whether the people respond to Joshua or not; or whether they pray or not; or whether they have faith in the Lord or not is not yours to resolve," Crispin concluded.

"Well, our enemies have the luxury of interfering with humans in any way they can," said Michael, grievously. "They do all they can to upset the human will and divert it to their end."

"Yes, that is the great paradox of the war, isn't it?" respond-ed Crispin. "Our enemy openly vies for control of the will of men, and we are bound to respect their will—even when it costs them everything." Crispin looked up at Michael, the slight suggestion of a tear in his eye. "Just as it did in Eden."

Khasis watched as the Council convened. He stayed in the background, honored that Lucifer would choose his city in which to confer with his leadership at so critical a time in the war. He also understood that Jericho was strategically situated and that it would play heavily in the upcoming invasion.

Watching the interaction among those present, Khasis witnessed a distinct hierarchy within the Council itself—a pecking order of sorts that revealed who was currently in favor with Lucifer and who was not. He had heard that such a situation existed within the Council structure, and he found it fascinating to witness it all firsthand.

Though nominally everyone had a voice within Lucifer's War Council, there were three main angels who dominated the deliberations and were also members of the Council of Seven. First was Kara, a very intuitive angel whose network of subtle spies made him dangerous both to angels and to men. He had information on everyone, it seemed, and thus made himself indispensable to Lucifer, even though Lucifer regarded him an ambitious buffoon. Then there was Pellecus, the academician who articulated Lucifer's personal philosophy and teachings in order to justify his actions. He acted as Lucifer's prophetic voice in order to instill a sense of sacred obligation to the cause in which they all found themselves. Finally there was Rugio, a brutal warrior whose cruel use of force among humans was well-known in the angelic world. He had a special hatred for Michael, and longed for the day when he could contest the archangel again.

They were cunning, cold, and motivated—three necessary attributes if one was to successfully navigate in the treacherous waters of Lucifer's hierarchy. All other members of the Council seemed like mere decorations in comparison with these three.

But regardless of the bullying and bluster and jockeying for position that was rampant in Lucifer's leadership, there was no question as to who was in charge. Lucifer had made it clear even before the war broke out that unless there was absolute unity behind his rule, all hope was lost. So whether through coercion or compromise, the Council continued taking their cues from Lucifer and disseminating his authority through their domains.

"Come to order!"

All the angels very quickly sobered up and looked in the direction of the familiar voice. Lucifer strolled in and nodded curtly to Khasis, who nodded back in effusive homage to the supreme angel who commanded him. Pellecus sneered at such toadiness, commenting to Kara that Khasis must be one of his disciples. Before Kara could respond, Lucifer took his place.

They sat around the small amphitheater in a semicircle, Lucifer addressing them from the front. He looked at Khasis.

"Come and join us, Khasis," said Lucifer, motioning the angel to join the group. "As prince over Jericho this will be of utmost urgency to you."

Khasis overlooked some of the sneering angels in the Council as he strolled over to them. He then turned to Lucifer.

"Thank you, my prince," he began. "And may I add that it is my honor to offer my kingdom for this august body. I am indeed most interested in the…"

"As well you should be," interrupted Lucifer. "For should Joshua prevail, you will no longer be hosting anything. You will have lost your kingdom and your place."

Khasis stepped back, totally taken by surprise at Lucifer's remark.

"And kingdoms are won by strength and cunning," added Kara. "Not by your pandering to the greater ones in this kingdom!"

"You would do well to remember that yourself, Kara," said Pellecus. "For when it comes to pandering, you are indeed without peer."

The Council began snickering.

"Enough!" snapped Lucifer. "Our enemies are on the other side of the Jordan. They are poised and prepared to enter the land that was promised to them. The Canaanites are in great fear for their very lives. We must do all we can do to blunt the effect of the preparations, for we cannot stop the invasion."

The Council looked around at each other, perplexed at Lucifer's admission that the Israelites would indeed enter the land.

"You mean to tell us that Joshua will prevail in taking the land?" asked Belron, with an incensed tone. "It was my belief that these people could be managed—especially after the disaster in Egypt!" He glanced a sharp look at Kara.

"Don't accuse me, Belron," retorted Kara. "You are so far removed from the war with your little peoples on your little islands that you know nothing of true conflict. You deceive with woodland gods and simple spirits. We are contesting the living God!"

"Puffs of smoke in great temples!" snapped back Belron. "In the end your deceit is just as crude as mine!"

"But that is the point," interrupted Pellecus, in a rare occasion when he agreed with Kara. "Our prince once said that religion is our greatest weapon. So whether we deceive through simple jungle spirits or complex cults, such as in Karnak or Babylon, makes no difference. The point is that Joshua is the responsibility of us all!"

"Precisely," agreed Lucifer. "The reason I never placed Canaan under any one authority was because I knew from the very beginning that the war would eventually center in Canaan. I wanted all of you to feel a collective responsibility for waging the war. And now the war has come home." He then added ominously, "And should any of you become out of touch with the true nature of the war, I will remove you from your place of authority and replace you with someone with more of an appetite!"

Belron looked slightly uncomfortable and sat back a bit.

"Naturally we are all pledged to fight this war with great energy," Belron said.

"Naturally," mocked Kara, grinning in delight at Belron's humbling.

"And so the war, as I said, has come home," continued Lucifer. "What began in Eden, continued with a promise made to Abraham, and was carried on through Moses, has now returned like a plague."

Lucifer began pacing in front of the group.

"Joshua *will* cross the Jordan," he began. "Make no mistake. We cannot stop him. Our attempts to demoralize the people have largely been ineffective. Oh, there have been a few encouraging signs from time to time. But for now the people are with him."

"I understand that even those tribes whose lands have already been established on that side of the Jordan will help their brothers win their own lands on this side," said Kara. "Such idiotic devotion! It says much about these people."

"It speaks volumes, Kara," said Pellecus, a bit alarmed. He then addressed the group. "The fact that three of the tribes will leave their women and children in Bashan and send their men over to fight for the land speaks of the enormous confidence they have—not to mention the trust they have in the Lord to protect their possessions while they are away. I tell you, my prince, these people are more than motivated…they are bewitched!"

Lucifer laughed.

"I thought it was *we* who were in the business of bewitching humans," he said.

The Council laughed.

"Nevertheless, my prince, the situation is critical," snorted Pellecus, looking around at the others who were still amused at Lucifer's remark.

"Pellecus is correct, my brothers," said Lucifer. "This is a critical moment. And a deadly one. We have known all along that the prophecy would work its way through these people like some sort of disease. So long as they were out of the land of promise we had a bit of comfort. While they were in Egypt we had a measure of control. Now they shall enter the land in which I believe the Seed shall be born."

"It will be difficult to fight them in their own land," mused Rugio. "I have seen how humans fight more bitterly when they have a personal stake in something."

"Of course," said Lucifer. "That is why we must always contest the legitimacy of their being in the land. The land is the key to defeating these people. All they have dreamt of is the land.They will hearken back to the rather dubious promises made to their ancestor, and we will oppose them outright. To desire the land is one thing; to occupy and be blessed in it is quite another!"

An angel who worked with Kara appeared, and Kara nodded for him to approach. Lucifer stood by to hear this latest bit of news. Put out as he was by interruptions, he always gave way to one of Kara's organization, since they usually brought the latest information.

"Well?" asked Lucifer.

"I am here to report that two spies have entered Jericho," he said, not knowing whether to look at Kara or Lucifer. "They were sent by Joshua to spy out the city."

Lucifer glanced at Khasis.

"Jericho is your domain," said Lucifer. "The enemy has now made an incursion. What shall you do?"

Khasis felt all eyes of Council upon him.

"I shall take measures to let the king of Jericho know that this has happened. Jericho is ripe for talk. It shall not be difficult."

"Excellent," said Lucifer.

"Do they know where to find these men?" asked Kara.

"We will find them," said Khasis. "And we shall destroy them. It would make quite an impression on Joshua to have his spies sent back to him in a basket—at least part of them!"

The Council nodded in affirmation.

"Quite a greeting from the king of Jericho that would be," said Lucifer, pondering the idea. "It would certainly cause some stir among the people. Very well, Khasis. We stand by your word. The war begins with the death of the two Hebrew spies."

Khasis nodded at Lucifer and, following a brief self-assured glance at Kara, vanished along with Kara's angel who had brought the news. Lucifer looked toward the direction of the Jordan where the Israelites awaited their crossing.

"Well now, Joshua," he said. "You are waiting for news on just what sort of resistance your forces shall meet in this land. I can assure you the wait will be as short as the news is grim."

He then turned to the Council.

"For generations the humans have spoken of returning to this place. They have presumed to call it their home. It has been told them by the Most High that it is a land flowing with milk and honey." He repeated with a sense of distaste, "Milk and honey!"

He walked over to a section of the great wall that surrounded the city and backed up to the king's house. He stood next to the cold stone and patted it. "Brothers, this land shall not yield milk and honey, but death and destruction. These walls will not flow with milk and honey, but with the blood of our enemies. Before Joshua takes Jericho, he will find it a very different land!"

He smirked at the Council. "If we have learned anything about these Hebrews, we have learned that they have no stomach for setbacks. Let's see how they feel about their land of milk and honey after we sour their milk and give them hornets in place of honey!"

Bethlehem, 4 B.C.

"Did the spies make it into Jericho?" asked Joshua, who like the other shepherds was hanging on every one of Eli's words. Of course he and every son of Israel already knew the answer to that one. Eli smiled.

"Yes, Joshua," the old man answered. "The Lord safely conducted the spies into Jericho. But the king got word of it and sent out his own spies to find them and bring them to him. They searched throughout the land and in every house in Jericho but the Hebrews were nowhere to be found…"

"Rahab," Joshua whispered a bit too loudly. His father smiled at his son's eager response. A couple of the shepherds laughed aloud.

"Yes, Rahab," said Eli. He then leaned toward Joshua as if telling him a great secret. She was a…she made a rather questionable living."

"Yes, she was a harlot," said Joshua casually, to the surprise of all and the delight of some.

"Well, er…yes," said Eli. With a quizzical look on his face and glancing at Joshua's father he followed with, "Do you know what a harlot is?"

"Of course," said Joshua. "A harlot runs an inn for men!"

Eli looked at a bemused Elron and some of the other shepherds, who were trying to conceal their laughter.

"A very questionable occupation indeed, Eli," said Jazzer, a middle-aged shepherd who was wiping his chin from a drink of water. "Very questionable those harlots…"

"Yes, well, at any rate, Joshua, as you know, Rahab took the spies in and hid them on her roof under some flax. She said she would help them if they helped her. They all agreed that she was to tie a red cord from her window, which would provide protection for anyone staying in the house. A bit like the lamb's red blood that protected our fathers in Egypt on the Passover night."

"Eli?" asked Joshua.

"Yes, young man?" responded Eli.

"It seems that whenever the Lord is saving His people He uses something red."

"Yes, He does," mused Eli. "It seems the color red and salvation go together quite well."

Chapter 3

"Are you for us? Or are you for our enemies?"

Gabriel watched as a few more angels came trickling in around Bethlehem. The opposition was sure to gather soon as well. Thus he had posted sentries all around the area, especially with a particular couple who would be making their way into the city to register for the census.

He looked across the meadow to where Bakka stood watching his charge, Daniel. Bakka glanced at Gabriel and motioned for him to come over. As Gabriel made his way to his friend he looked over at the group of shepherds still engaged in Eli's discussion.

"How is our friend doing?" asked Gabriel, looking at the sullen human.

"Still moping, I'm afraid," sighed Bakka.

"Looks like two moping spirits here," said Gabriel, eyeing Bakka.

Bakka was taken aback.

"Gabriel, I am not moping!" he said excitedly. "I simply wanted to be assigned elsewhere, that's all. Tonight is to be an incredible evening. Look at all the angels pouring in. And whatever is to happen, I wanted to be a part of it. Not guarding a contentious and shallow human!"

"You continue to encourage Daniel," said Gabriel. "That is your part."

They looked at the man whose head was resting on his knees. He seemed to be listening from time to time to the others, but never fully taking it in. Bakka looked back at Gabriel, who motioned for him not to say another word.

"Encourage his heart," continued Gabriel. "And never forget that every assignment by the Lord is an important one. Daniel has a great opportunity tonight to learn something of eternal importance."

He glanced sternly at Bakka. "As do you!"

Chronicles of the Host

Jordan Breached

True to her word, the harlot Rahab kept the location of the spies a secret. And despite all of Khasis's attempts to rouse the soldiers' suspicions through their clouded minds, the Lord, in answer to Joshua's fervent prayers, and in deference to Rahab's assistance, prevented the soldiers from finding the men hidden on Rahab's rooftop.

So it was that the children of Israel once more entered the land of their fathers, the land they had departed over four hundred years earlier. Having left before in search of security in Egypt, they reentered Canaan ready for war....

Jhara, a warrior under Khasis's command, and some of the angels in his troop watched from the opposite side of the Jordan as the trumpets were sounded. The people, who had been waiting 40 years for this moment, watched as the Levites lined up and carried the Ark of the Lord in solemn procession toward the banks of the Jordan. The other tribes watched and waited for their turn to cross.

Never mind that it was flood season, and that the Jordan was swollen in its annual deluge. Of course nothing was too difficult for the Lord, and from Joshua they had heard of the great crossing of the Red Sea. But the Levites were headed straight for the banks as if there was a bridge for them to casually stroll across. Joshua had given the order that as soon as the Levites began to move, the people were to follow—but not too closely to the Ark. They kept a distance of about one thousand yards between themselves and the sacred box.

All around the nation, and in great numbers, groups of holy angels created a whitish canopy that grew in intensity near the Ark. Following God's directions in the law, the Levites carefully carried the Ark, and set out in step, slowly moving to the water. Some of the people looked to Joshua, who stood on a slope watching the proceedings, and then back to the commotion of the Ark.

Devils had been moving in as well, hoping to throw confusion into the ranks of the people. But the Ark's proximity kept most of them at bay. Much as they would have liked to tear into the Ark and destroy it, the Presence of God—which they knew was resident within the golden container—was too much of a risk for even the strongest of the rebel angels to contend with. They would have to await another day to take the Ark as a trophy.

The Levites proceeded to the edge of the river and stopped, awaiting Joshua's final instructions. Joshua and his aides then came to the river to address the Levites and the rest of the people who could hear him.

"The Lord was with Moses and now He is with me. He has delivered us from Egypt and brought us to the land promised to us through our father Abraham. Therefore, we shall drive the enemies of our God from the land and claim it in His name. Only watch and be faithful!"

"But how are we to cross?" came a voice from somewhere in the area where the leaders of the tribe of Dan stood. A few other voices grunted in affirmation.

Joshua raised his hands to quell any further such questions.

"Hear me! When the priests reach the water with the Ark of the Testimony, the river will stop flowing and we shall cross over. This is the word of the Lord!" He glanced toward the Danites. "This will prove that our God will be with us both on this side of the Jordan and beyond!"

"What are they doing down there?" demanded Khasis. He began laughing. "He brings them to the river's edge and only then realizes that he cannot get across?"

The devils with him began laughing.

Khasis noted some spies sent from the king of Jericho were observing the movement of the Israelites from a bluff on their side of the river.

"Make sure that the king's men see this ridiculous display," he said. "I want all of Jericho to hear about this day!"

One of Khasis's aides vanished immediately and stood among the spies from Jericho. The men were puzzled by the commotion on the other side.

"What does this mean?" asked Jarez, one of the men from Jericho. He was peeking over the top of a red stone and looking down upon the river at the great cloud of people on the other side facing them. "Why have they stopped?"

"Perhaps the God of Israel cannot cross the gods of Canaan," came a voice—Khasis's devil whispering into the mind of the other spy, Zogor.

"Our priests have called upon the gods to stop the invaders," said Zogor. "Perhaps our gods are mightier than their gods!"

Jarez nodded back in nervous hope.

"We should report this to the king," continued the voice. *"Perhaps they will even turn on Joshua. Perhaps…"*

"Look there!" came the astonished voice of Jarez. He pointed to where the priests had begun moving toward the water. "What do they think they are doing?"

"Perhaps our gods are luring them to their deaths in our sacred river," offered Zogor, who felt for his weapon. "They carry the magic with them in that box. Let them and their sorcery drown in the Jordan!"

The devil with them looked up to where Khasis had stationed himself, indicating that he was completely puzzled by the Israelites. Khasis remained fixed on the movement of the humans. More urgently, he observed the great cloud of holy angels beginning to move along with them toward his domain.

The priests got closer and closer to the water's edge. Jarez and Zogor were now both watching from their perch in the rocks. This would be a great day for them! The king always awarded the bearer of good news with some bestowment or another. They would become great men in Jericho.

"I tell you our gods are the greatest in the universe!" boasted Zogor, who was now preparing his mount for the quick return to Jericho. "They have chosen to smile upon us this day."

"Then pray to them, Zogor," said Jarez, grimly surveying the scene. "For the river is opening up for the enemy to cross!"

Chronicles of the Host

First Conquest

What a delightful day when God's people set foot on God's holy land after such a long time! The Host sang praises of joyous celebration to the Lord, while the enemy scattered like frightened sheep as the Ark of God, carried by the Levites, was carried into Canaan. Khasis tried to rally the host that was with him, and they regrouped at Jericho where, like the humans, they waited behind the strong walls for the coming battle. As for Joshua, the burden of leadership drove him to his knees and he sought the Most High God's counsel in how best to besiege Jericho's proud defense.

It was a new day in Israel, a new strategy—a new deliverance, a new beginning. And nothing better illustrated this newness in all things than the cessation of the manna. After 40 years' provision of manna raining down every day from Heaven, it suddenly stopped. It seemed that God's provision in Canaan was to be something new...something different...something requiring a greater faith....

Joshua commanded his men to stay behind. They had been scouting the city of Jericho for the last hour, discussing the best point of attack, trying to pinpoint possible weaknesses. One even suggested they could use Rahab to help them gain entry. However it was to happen, the city had to be taken. Jericho, though small, was a strategic point of conquest and could not simply be bypassed. It had to be destroyed. To leave an entrenched enemy behind was only inviting trouble later on.

Joshua went on ahead of the men, and looked at the silhouette of the city against the sun setting in the western sky behind it. Proud and impregnable, its walls seemed to taunt Israel, daring the Hebrews to assail them and feel their sting. True, the reputation of Israel had preceded them in the land and cast a terror throughout the region. But Jericho was a formidable foe—and the first real test of Joshua's leadership in engaging the enemy on his own soil.

Joshua began to pray silently to the Lord. How was he to lead his untested people against this warlike, godless nation? How were they to breach the walls? He understood that God was with him, but how was he to orchestrate the attack? All of these thoughts exploded in Joshua's head as he looked upon Jericho in the twilight evening. Then something else caught his eye. Standing right in front of him was a large man—a warrior—with a sword drawn!

"How are we to conduct a war against humans if the Lord continues to step in and assist them?" asked Kara. "It is hardly fair!"

Rugio, who along with Kara and Pellecus had been given the task of keeping Jericho intact, growled at Kara. "You sniveling fool," he said. "The Lord has never been fair in this war. He always will side with the humans!"

"That's not entirely true," piped in Pellecus. "Yes, the Lord interferes from time to time. But for the most part He respects only men who cry out to Him...who seek Him earnestly...men of faith like Joshua."

"Joshua," muttered Rugio. "How I hate that man! First there was Moses, who humbled Kara's pharaoh, and now Joshua, who is on the brink of shattering Jericho." He added in great frustration, "When shall these Hebrews stop producing men of faith and become like the rest of the nations?"

"Soon, I suspect," said Pellecus. "When they have established themselves in the land, they will slip back into their old ways. It's the nature of humans to be motivated at the beginning of a great endeavor and then to lose interest over time. I'm sure that in a few generations they will have forgotten Joshua and become another mediocre nation of humans who are enslaved to their passions and forgetful of their gods."

Kara looked up scornfully.

"A wonderful summation, Pellecus," he said. "Provided we were in a classroom and you were lecturing. But we have been ordered by Lucifer to stave off the attack. Khasis is proving himself of little worth." He smirked at Khasis, who stood silently nearby. "So teacher, the question remains—how do we stop Joshua at Jericho?"

"Perhaps we don't," came the voice of Lucifer.

He motioned for everyone to remain seated at his appearance. They were meeting on the rooftop of the king's great house in Jericho.

"I sense fear in the king of Jericho," said Lucifer. "Which means he is defeated already. Fear is a great weapon—a weapon which we have become very adept at using. Unfortunately it cuts both ways."

"Are you saying we simply give up Jericho?" asked Kara.

"Not at all," said Lucifer. "But it occurs to me that Jericho is only the beginning of a very long campaign, to be followed with the task of creating a new nation with no king and only the memory of Moses to guide them. I quite agree with Pellecus. Given time these people will disintegrate into the madness of the rest of humanity."

Rugio stood up, a bit angry at what he was hearing.

"So we let them in?" he asked. "Surely we must resist!"

Lucifer looked at his chief warrior.

"Of course we must resist," he said, speaking in comforting tones. "Wars are won in the long term, Rugio. If we must give ground here and there to win the war, then so be it. It is who is standing in the end that matters."

"May I speak, my prince?" asked Khasis cautiously.

Kara snorted and was about to say something when Lucifer stopped him.

"Of course, Khasis," he said. "Jericho is, after all, your responsibility. I simply asked my three most important rulers to assist you in any way they might."

"I am of course grateful to you for their assistance," Khasis said, bowing slightly to the others in humble recognition. "But I must add that the talk here seems to be drifting from how to stop Joshua to whether or not he is to be stopped."

Pellecus smiled at Khasis's bold assertion.

"Excellent observation," said Pellecus. "But I believe what we are saying is that you should do all you can to stop the Hebrews— by all means!"

Kara snickered at Khasis's dilemma. Rugio grunted angrily under his breath and then exploded.

"Khasis is right," Rugio blustered. "We cannot simply give Jericho up without a fight. They must know we will resist them."

"Of course we shall oppose them," said Lucifer finally, looking upwards toward the heavens. "The Most High has shown what He intends to do in this war—He was quite clear at the Jordan when He stopped the river for them. He will fight for them so long as they remain faithful to Him."

Rugio responded, "Then our course is…"

"Our course, as always, is to defeat them at Jericho," said Lucifer resignedly. "It shall be a long war, my brothers. And there shall be many battles. And perhaps the Seed shall even find its way to fruition in this miserable land."

At the mention of the Seed a chill went through all the angels. Lucifer looked down over the little city of Jericho and glanced at the walls around it. "But ultimately the outcome of the war will not be decided by walled cities. It shall be decided in the hearts of men. And so long as the war is dependent upon men remaining faithful, we shall have hope."

Joshua knew that the enemy had scouts all around him and prepared himself to fight, reaching for his sword. But the man simply stood there. Puzzled, Joshua remained still and silent for a moment, returning his sword to its sheath. He scrutinized the magnificent soldier who stood before him. He didn't look like a Canaanite soldier. His appearance was very different.

Joshua walked over to the visitor, careful to keep one hand on his sword and to make sure that there were not others ready to spring upon him.

"Are you for us? Or are you for our enemies?" he resolutely asked.

"I represent nobody but the Lord God as commander of His Host. His Presence is quite near."

The voice was one of sharp authority that commanded immediate respect. Joshua's heart rallied and he fell to the ground before the angel. He cried out to him, "What does the Lord wish for His servant to know?"

"Joshua, the Lord Most High wants you to understand that you are on holy ground. Remove your sandals!"

Joshua immediately obeyed, taking off his sandals but remaining low to the ground and not daring to look up. After a moment or two of silence, he slowly looked up. The angel was gone!

Joshua started to get up when another Voice spoke to him. This one was unmistakable, penetrating the very core of Joshua's being. He fell low to the ground again, and this time answered unhesitatingly, "Yes, Lord?"

Michael stood at a distance as the Lord spoke with Joshua on the plain outside Jericho. He was still amazed at the relationship that a mere man could share with the greatest Person alive. The Most High wanted nothing to separate Himself from the one made in His image—even to the point of removing the man's sandals so that his feet would touch the ground of His Presence—and so Michael had instructed Joshua in preparation for this encounter with his God.

As Michael watched, Crispin sidled up next to him noticing Michael's keen interest in the dialogue between the Most High and Joshua. Of course not one of the enemy was present.

"Much like the Lord's meeting with Moses on Sinai, hmm?" inquired Crispin. "What with the sandals being removed and all."

"Very much so, teacher," said Michael. He then added with an unbelieving shake of his head, "The Most High and the humans who resist him. Such a paradox. Sometimes I wonder if Lucifer isn't correct."

He read Crispin's face and quickly moved to qualify the statement. "I'm not saying Lucifer and those who follow him are right in their position. They gambled and they have lost. But I mean the core of his opposition rests in the idea that, given the freedom to choose, humans will ultimately choose to oppose God. It is their nature."

"True, that image of God that rested in them so purely in Eden has been distorted beyond repair," said Crispin. "And yet our Lord finds men irresistible to the point of giving them a faint hope in a hopeless world."

"The prophecy," said Michael.

"Just so," said Crispin. "As we stand here, as the Lord speaks with Joshua, angels both holy and impure are contesting for the minds and hearts of men. All over this world, from east to west, humans are engaged in a war that most of them know absolutely nothing about. A small portion of these humans have been acquainted with our Lord, whose apparent plan through their father Abraham is to see the whole world ultimately blessed. We understand that to be somehow connected with the prophecy—the Seed of Eve."

Crispin looked at the archangel, captain of the Lord's Host. He understood Michael to be a passionate warrior whose one impulse was to serve the Lord with all his might. Naturally there were times when the war seemed so pointless—that ultimately humans would turn on their Creator.

"I understand your feelings in this, Michael," continued Crispin. "But ultimately we must trust in the Lord's wisdom despite human frivolity. Somehow this Seed of the woman promises something great."

He snickered a bit. "How Lucifer must tremble at the thought of what he unleashed in deceiving Eve!" He resumed his lecture to the archangel. "To be sure, Michael, our rebellious Lucifer's mission is not merely to disable humans. It is to destroy the possibility of the prophecy rising up one day and biting him just as he struck at Eve. He is not concerned with people who die apart from the knowledge of God. They are of little contest to him. But he realizes he is vulnerable to humans like Joshua, and others who believe the Lord and are committed to Him. Thus he opposes not a man, nor a family, nor even a nation. He opposes a prophecy."

Michael always enjoyed the words of Crispin. He had a way of making sense of situations. He nodded his head in agreement.

"And so Lucifer must contest such faith with fear," mused Michael.

"Exactly," said Crispin. "Because his greatest fear *is* faith!"

Chronicles of the Host

Peculiar Strategy

As one angel recalled, the lights coming from Jericho in the evening sky "danced above the imposing walls, creating a bizarre effect that made every shadow appear to be an enemy soldier, and every flicker a possible threat." So it was that

Joshua's men had surrounded the city and had been encamped about it for six days—and still Jericho remained safely in the hands of the enemy. We watched and waited for the coming battle. But apart from the unorthodox strategy of marching around the walls for the past six days, not much that smacked of real fighting had actually happened. This was not lost on the men...nor on the angels of both sides who watched and waited....

Gabriel and Michael stood on the low hill overlooking Jericho. They watched as the Hebrews lined up once more in procession, to march around the city. The Ark of the Testimony went before the armed men, borne by the priests, who were also carrying trumpets looted from Egypt years before.

"The city seems more still than usual," remarked Gabriel. "Even the enemy seems more subdued."

Michael agreed. Over the past six days the demon presence, which had played such a prominent part early on in cajoling and attempting to strike fear in the hearts of the men of Israel, had slowly ebbed. Now there were only those few devils who remained on in possession of particular people, or who remained loyal to Khasis—who had vowed to resist until it was over.

"I thought at first that Joshua's marching might only encourage the enemy to their usual mockery," said Michael. "Instead they seem to have vanished."

"There is more here than marching, Michael," said Gabriel. "They sense that the Lord is about to judge this place and they have abandoned it."

Just then an alarm went up in the city as a watchman observed the Israelites approaching in their usual procession. Soldiers began peeking up over the walls, watching with bemused looks the strange behavior of Joshua's men. Occasionally a man would curse the Hebrews, or dare them to come nearer the walls. But Joshua's troops resolutely began their trek around the city. One…two…three…and finally six times.

"Six times today," said Gabriel. "There is something different in this."

"I can sense a shift in Jericho," agreed Michael. "And the Host is moving in as well. They know it will soon be over too."

"They have been instructed in what to do?" asked Gabriel.

"Of course," said Michael. "On Joshua's signal they will move in."

Gabriel observed as thousands of shimmering angels descended upon the scene, preparing to do battle with an enemy that was largely vacating the battlefield. Every so often an enemy spirit would shriek and curse and fling himself through the angelic cordon, vowing that the fight was not yet over.

"Strange how the city seems so unaware…so ordinary," said Michael. "It's as if nothing has changed for them in these past six days. They seem totally unaware of what is about to befall them. Even their fear is beginning to subside in the face of no real war."

Gabriel pointed to a particular section of the wall.

"There is one in Jericho who is aware," he said.

High above the ground, dangling from a small window, was a red cord that cascaded down about 20 feet.

"Rahab," said Michael quietly.

Chapter 4

"How can a man sin against God on the heels of a great victory?"

"Shout! The Lord your God has given you this city!"

Upon Joshua's command, the men at arms who surrounded Jericho began shouting with all their might. The priests accompanying them blew on their trumpets—and a great noise filled the city.

Khasis and what was left of his demon attachment were filled with panic as they saw thousands of the Host descending upon the city. What was left of his troop scattered like dust and only he remained fixed—preferring to stay in Jericho in defiance.

The Host slammed into the walls, hitting them with their great swords. The men on the walls were still laughing at Joshua's men, making jokes about the concert they were enjoying. Some of them blew trumpets back in mockery.

Suddenly the walls began to shift and the men who stood upon them became silent. They looked about themselves in disbelief as first one, and then another section of the walls gave way with a great crash. Scores of men fell with the walls and were killed by the great stones.

As the walls continued collapsing, Joshua gave the command for the Israelites to attack. Joshua's men poured through the great cloud of dust that had engulfed the once proud city, and began killing the defenders. Panic had set in completely, as the people of Jericho fled in every direction, trying to escape the vengeance of the Lord.

Here and there, devils and angels were locked in battle, swords flashing and curses being uttered. Khasis knew he was defeated, but he and his few remaining defenders determined to face their former brethren from Heaven head-on. Khasis brought his sword down hard on Sangius, one of Michael's chief aides, who had led the Host into Jericho.

Sangius yelped in pain and swung back with his own sword, clipping Khasis on the shoulder. Khasis grinned and brought his sword down once more, narrowly missing Sangius's head. Then, over Sangius's shoulder he saw the red cord dangling from Rahab's window, and he growled and lunged in that direction. He swung at Sangius with his sword as he flew toward the harlot's home, narrowly missing him once more. Sangius could only watch him for a second before he was engulfed by several more of the enemy, including a captain of Jericho's evil host.

"I will at least see that traitor Rahab dead," said Khasis in a rage to his aides, his reddish aura manifesting in uncontrolled anger.

Several demon spirits accompanied him with enraged anticipation of what Khasis would do to Rahab. Inside her home, Rahab waited and prayed to the God of Joshua for herself and her family who had managed to find shelter with her.

Khasis and his devils burst into the room. There was only one holy angel guarding her, and Khasis immediately ordered his warriors to distract him. They immediately set upon the guardian, who fought them off valiantly. Even so, they forced him away from Rahab so Khasis might be able to approach her unhindered. He grinned and lifted his sword high. Her guardian watched, unable to get to her in time to help.

The crash of Michael's sword against the sword of Khasis was so loud that every angel in the region heard it. Khasis's sword spun out into the heavenlies, and he reeled and turned, cursing Michael, whose sword was lifted high for another blow. Khasis shrieked and vanished, as did every other enemy angel with him.

Rahab's guardian watched as Joshua's two spies, who had promised Rahab that she would be spared, entered the room and placed her under their protection. Outside, as Rahab and her family were escorted to Joshua, the last remnants of resistance were killed by the Israelites. Every man, woman, and child of Jericho was put to death as the Lord had ordered.

One of Joshua's generals, the one who had been fighting a demon-inspired depression, appeared before Joshua.

"A wonderful victory, sir!" he said jauntily. Joshua was glad to see his spirits up again. "A dreadful stronghold."

"The Lord is good," Joshua admitted, looking over the carnage. "I have pronounced a curse over this place. Should anyone ever attempt to rebuild this city it will be at the cost of his first-born."

Several of Joshua's officers walked about with gold cups and other valuables in their hands. They were enjoying the fruit of plunder. Joshua pointed to the men.

"Commander, remind the people that this unrighteous place is devoted to destruction. Everything in it is to be destroyed or left behind in honor of our Lord. No plunder!"

"As you wish," said the commander, who went to the men and spoke with them. The men looked at the commander and then over at Joshua. They dropped their goods where they stood and walked off, muttering a bit. The commander walked back to Joshua.

"I'll go throughout the ruined city and make sure that nothing is taken," he said to Joshua. "Although it will be difficult to explain to some of the men."

"You let me worry about the men, Achan," said Joshua. "You just carry out the order that nothing be taken."

"It shall be just as you have said," Achan responded, as he looked down at the small gold ring that he had let casually drop to the ground while talking with Joshua. After Joshua left, Achan looked at the ring that he had found and was going to give to his wife. For a few seconds he stood there as the sun hit the ring and made it shimmer. He shook himself to his duty.

"Such a pity," he said and ground it into the dust.

From within a ruined section of the wall Jhara and Khasis had been watching the whole scene.

"Interesting," said Jhara. "We might get a win out of this yet."

"Possibly," said Khasis carefully. "He is certainly unlike Joshua's other commanders. He broods. He is quite a thinker."

"And he is greedy," added Jhara hopefully.

They discreetly followed Achan as he went from house to house, ordering the clearing of the dead and making certain that Joshua's orders were being carried out. As he crossed over the courtyard to what had been the king of Jericho's great house, he saw the dead king, whose body had been crushed by one of the wall stones. In his hands he was clutching a small chest.

Achan looked at the chest for a moment and then continued on. As he walked Khasis scrambled up next to him, placed his hand upon his shoulder and began speaking into his mind.

"I wonder what a king would keep inside a chest," he said. *"What would be in that chest that his dying thought was to preserve it?"*

Achan turned and looked again at the chest that lay in the hands of the dead king. He looked about to make sure he was alone. He then stood there for a moment as if trying to decide what he should do.

"It certainly wouldn't hurt to see inside, would it?"

Achan reasoned within himself that just taking a look wouldn't be the same as violating Joshua's command. He slowly wandered over to where the box lay in the outstretched hands of the king.

"Open it."

Achan hesitated for a minute.

"Open it!"

Achan kicked the chest out of the dead man's hands, spilling its contents on the dusty pavement. He counted about two hundred shekels of silver, plus a gold wedge of about fifty shekels. He was about to bend down and touch it when someone came up behind him.

"Sir, look at this beautiful Babylonian robe I found in the king's house!" said Zara, one of his commanders. "It must be worth..."

"Leave it," said Achan, who led the man away from the spot where the chest had spilled open. "These things are not to be taken. Nothing is to be removed from Jericho. These are Joshua's orders."

Zara looked grimly at Achan and then with a great sigh started to take the robe back into the house. Achan called out to him.

"Leave that with me," he said. "I'll place it with the other things that are to be burned." He then shifted to a fatherly tone. "Besides, Zara, the Lord has promised us a land of milk and honey. We have no need of such pagan goods!"

Zara reluctantly handed the beautiful robe over to Achan.

"I must say these Babylonians certainly are luxurious people," Achan said, holding up the robe. "Decadent to be sure. But fine craftsmen!" He looked at Zara, who was watching him inspect the clothing like a tailor looking over a fine piece of merchandise. "Thank you, Zara. That will be all for now."

Zara nodded and walked off to join the other men, most of whom had already left Jericho to rejoin their families. Achan looked at the robe and the chest. He understood that these things were given over to the Lord as trophies to Him. Still it seemed such a waste to leave them for some scavenger who had not paid the price of battle. Besides, some of this would be given to the priests in honor of the Lord. What should he do?

"This land is your inheritance, is it not?" came a voice. *"Take what has been given to you. You have waited four hundred years for this day...take it..."*

"After all, it is my inheritance," he said to himself, as he gathered the things to put away until he could come back and reclaim them.

"Achan has taken something for himself from Jericho."

Michael stopped his address to his warrior commanders who were in charge of the conquest of Canaan. He looked at Gabriel in disbelief.

"What?" he responded. "Already the humans are degrading?" He hushed the stir among the other angels with him and then followed up with, "The things devoted to the Lord?"

"Yes," said Gabriel. "He has taken some gold and some other items and hidden them under his tent."

Michael could barely contain the rage he felt brewing inside him. How could this be? He was embarrassed for Gabriel. He felt compassion for the warriors who stood before him and were dedicated to helping this ungrateful people reclaim their land. Most of all he felt heartsick for the Most High, whose law seemed never to be respected by men.

"How am I to set up a strategy and support the humans when they are defeating themselves?" he asked in an exasperated tone. Gabriel looked at the other warriors and back at Michael. The archangel understood and dismissed his loyal angels, ordering them to scout out the enemy's movements outside of Jericho.

"Disappointment in humans should long be settled," said Gabriel. "Since Eden we have learned on numerous occasions of man's propensity to sin against the Lord."

"But on the occasion of such a great victory?" Michael asked. "How can a man sin against God on the heels of a great victory? What causes men to be so carnal?"

"That's easy," came a familiar voice. "The same thing that caused Lucifer to sin in the very presence of the Most High."

Michael turned to see Crispin landing on the hillside along the Jordan where Michael had been addressing his angels. Michael and Gabriel hailed their old teacher.

Crispin looked at Gabriel with an understanding demeanor.

"I heard the news already," said Crispin. "Heaven is abuzz with Achan's foolishness."

"But why?" asked Michael. "Why do they do these things? A magnificent victory at Jericho and now this?"

Crispin loved Michael's passionate loyalty for the Lord. He glanced at the archangel and responded.

"As I was saying, humans suffer from the same inclination that befell Lucifer," answered Crispin. "Pride."

Gabriel silently nodded in agreement while Michael continued stewing.

"Pride!" repeated Michael. "The stuff of sin."

"Just so," agreed Crispin. "Pride will bring down a man or an angel. In some cases it will bring down a nation."

Michael could only shake his head in utter disgust at the creatures into whom the Most High had placed His very image.

"So once more the creature turns on its Creator," he could only manage. "Incredible! Here I am planning with my commanders the coordination with Joshua's men to go before them and sweep out the enemy at Ai. And now this?"

Gabriel looked to Michael.

"There is more, my brother," he said sullenly.

Crispin didn't look at either one of the archangels. Michael glanced at both Crispin and Gabriel, trying to imagine what else might happen.

"I have a message for you from the Throne. You are not to accompany Joshua in the next battle," Gabriel announced. "Israel has defiled itself; the Presence of God, not any of the Host, is to be with these people in battle."

"Shall they lose this battle?" asked Michael.

"Yes," said Gabriel. "They will be defeated at Ai."

Michael nodded in agreement with the pronouncement. He could only picture in his mind the defeat that awaited even as Joshua and his commanders prayed for a victory. And one man in particular who prayed would be sinning in his prayer.

"Crispin, can the sin of this man Achan bring down the whole of Israel?" Michael asked. "Why not punish the man and not the community?"

"Crispin thought about his answer for a bit.

"Michael, do you recall the days before the rebellion? I mean, before Lucifer transgressed beyond his own ability to find his way back from the darkness he had entered?" asked Crispin.

"Yes," said Michael. "Of course."

"He was one angel—a powerful one, granted—but his pride brought with him one third of the angels. These creatures, once holy, defiled themselves and were caught up in his wickedness and swept away. In the same way, Michael, if the Lord does not deal severely with this sin—if all Israel does not realize the effect that one sin can have on an entire nation—then these people who are already given to failure are doomed to compromise themselves and become just as carnal as the nations they are now ejecting from Canaan."

"So the Lord must use Achan as an example to the people," said Michael. "And innocent men will die because of it."

"That is the nature of sin," Crispin said. "The lives of many are often caught up in the wake of sin. Humans believe that when they sin in secret, they are doing everyone else a favor. On the contrary, there is no sinning in secret. And unfortunately they do nobody a favor—rather they darken the entire community. That's why the whole of Israel is affected by Achan."

"So one man sins and all must suffer," said Gabriel.

"Yes," said Crispin. "If there was only another way…a better way. It would be much better if one man suffered for all sin."

Bethlehem, 4 B.C.

Jarod and Joshua were wide-eyed, enjoying the recounting of Joshua's invasion of Canaan. Some of the men around the fire had settled in for the night. When Eli stopped to get a drink of cold water, Jarod looked at his father, who gave him a knowing look, as if to say, "go ahead and ask him."

Daniel, in the meantime, had moved in closer to the fire, preferring the nonsense of Eli to the cold chill of the night. He still hadn't entered into the conversation, but brooded, mindlessly staring at the fire and trying with all his might to block out the old man's story.

When Eli finished his drink, Jarod spoke up.

"So Achan caused Israel to be defeated?" he asked.

Eli nodded.

"I'm sure that the Romans will be happy to hear that," chimed in Daniel, who could no longer hold back.

"The sin of Achan brought disgrace to the nation," Eli said, looking at Daniel. "The sin of one man can bring down a people."

"And who sinned that we are now in the hands of Rome?" asked Daniel. "As long as you are telling the boys about our glorious past, you might mention all the other nations who have conquered us—Alexander, the Ptolemies, Persia. And that's just a few of them!"

"Israel strayed from the covenant they made with God," responded Eli. "They forsook the words of the prophets. And the Lord judged us."

"And when does He stop judging us and bring us into our inheritance once more?" Daniel demanded. All of the men were looking at him now, ready to take action should he provoke any of them. He looked at all the angry eyes upon him. "When does your Messiah arrive and remove this Roman curse?" he continued, a bit more subdued in tone.

"Only the Lord knows when Messiah will come," Eli finally said. "You know this, Daniel. But come He shall!"

Daniel grumbled and buried his head back in the warmth of his knees. Eli continued talking to the boys, who didn't really understand the rough exchange with Daniel, but welcomed Eli's recaptured attention.

"And so, boys," Eli continued, "Achan's sin at Jericho turned what should have been a very easy victory at Ai into a defeat."

"But what did Joshua do?" asked Jarod eagerly.

Eli winked at one of the men and motioned his head toward Daniel, whose head was still buried in his knees in disgust.

"Well, poor Joshua was sort of like our friend Daniel here…"

Daniel looked up for just a second at Eli's pause.

"He was beside himself trying to figure out what was wrong."

Some of the men chuckled as Daniel grunted and dropped his head once more.

Jericho, 1225 B.C.

"You may not touch Joshua, Kara," said Michael. "Neither you, nor Berenius, nor even Lucifer himself can touch this man."

Outside the tent, where Joshua had thrown himself in front of the Ark of the Testimony, was a gathering of fallen angels led by Kara, Rugio, Khasis, and Berenius, plus a dozen or so lesser wicked spirits who were under their authority. They had come to discourage Joshua in his defeat and hopefully turn the tide of the war in their favor.

Also outside the tent were Michael, Serus, Sangius, and Crispin, along with several hundred holy angels who had been assigned to Joshua. They remained silent as Michael spoke with their enemy over Joshua's disposition.

"We are not here to touch Joshua," said Kara, looking at the commander of Israel scraping the earth before him with his hands. "We are here to help him after he makes his decision."

"What decision might that be?" asked Crispin, who had stepped up with Michael. "Joshua's mind is closed to you. He is a man filled with the Spirit of God."

"Just so," agreed Kara, looking down at the tent that they dared not enter for fear of the Ark. "I recall that Moses was also a man of faith. And yet he so failed the Lord that he was not even allowed to enter into the land for which he had given his life. Even the elders of Israel are in there with Joshua in this disgraceful display."

He pointed to Joshua.

"The same faithlessness will befall Joshua," he continued matter-of-factly. "Humans are destined to fail—even men of faith like Joshua! Dribbling over the Ark like some pitiful beast who has been cornered!"

"It is only the presence of the Ark that keeps me from tearing the man into pieces," boasted Rugio, glaring at Michael. "He would be dead already if I had my way."

"Yes," remarked Crispin casually. "The Presence of the Most High does rather foul up your plans, hmm?"

"And I will settle my score with you after this war is finished, dear teacher," growled Rugio. He pointed at the angel standing with Michael. "All of you will return to Heaven one day, humbled by the disobedience of the very humans you seek to protect!"

"If we ever return to Heaven it shall be on the Lord's terms," said Michael, "not on any humans'. And certainly not as a result of being humbled by rebel angels!"

"Nevertheless, Archangel, the man cries out to the Lord like a man who is losing his faith," said Berenius, whose hatred for Serus emboldened him. "A bit like Serus when he left Lucifer's service and went yelping to Michael."

The unholy angels laughed aloud.

"As I remember, it was an act of faith that brought Serus to Michael," chimed in Sangius, who also was once in Lucifer's circle. "He, like I, realized the shameful pride that was ensnaring Lucifer's mind and heart."

"Traitors come easily in Heaven," said Kara.

"You are quite the proof of that, Kara," said Crispin offhandedly.

Michael and Sangius laughed aloud.

"Just listen to Joshua," said Kara, ignoring Crispin's jibe. Imitating Joshua in contemptible tones, wringing his hands, Kara pleaded aloud, " 'O Lord, why have You deserted us? If only we had stayed on the other side of the Jordan!' How pitiful!" He looked at Michael with venom and added, "Such faith will never win a war that is determined by faith."

Before Michael could respond to Kara, the Tent of Meeting was suddenly visited by a rushing noise that roared through the land. Every angel recognized the approach of the Presence of God. Kara and his angels fell back, shielding their eyes from the brilliant light that began filling the area around the tent. Although unseen by any humans, the Presence of the Most High completely lit up the camp as He prepared to speak to Joshua from the Ark.

Kara quickly ordered his angels back, many of whom not only fell back but scattered like frightened animals. Rugio managed a low growl at Michael before he also pulled back with Kara and the others. The holy angels ignored their adversaries and bowed their heads to the Lord, all of them wondering what was going to happen.

"Joshua."

Joshua stopped in mid-sentence and became silent. The elders who were with him also were silent. Joshua looked back at them, and they immediately understood that the Lord had spoken to him, although they had heard nothing. They fell to their faces in great fear. Joshua looked back at the Ark.

"Joshua. Rise up! Why have you fallen on your face?"

Joshua realized that the Lord indeed was speaking to him and at first could not even move, much less speak. He slowly rose up, although the elders remained on the ground, prostrate.

"Israel has sinned. They have broken faith with Me by taking some things that were devoted to destruction. They have even hidden the things in their tent."

Joshua could sense a great shame rising up inside of his heart. He dared not look at the Ark. He thought back to the many times Moses had encountered the faithlessness of the people he was leading.

"Therefore, this is what you are to do..."

Chronicles of the Host

Judgment at Ai

Just as the Lord had spoken to Joshua, one man had committed a grievous sin against the Lord and against His own people.

The Most High would show Joshua through the lot the man who had defiled the nation and the covenant. All the eyes of Israel anxiously awaited the outcome as tent by tent, tribe by tribe, family by family, the verdict was rendered.

We angels wondered if, when confronted with his sin, the man Achan would try to hide as did A'dam, and as humans seem to want to do, or if he would admit his sin and confess before the camp. As it turned out, Achan, when confronted by Joshua, did in fact confess his greed. The evidence of his sin was brought before the assembly. We watched as the judgment of the Lord fell upon Achan and his family, and they were stoned to death outside the camp.

Chapter 5

"Even deliverers are corruptible."

Bethlehem, 4 B.C.

"Why is he so bitter?" asked Bakka, who stood near the group of shepherds outside Bethlehem. "Why won't he simply enter into fellowship with his brother shepherds?"

Gabriel, who was watching the growing number of holy angels gather on the hillside overlooking Bethlehem, shook his head.

"That is part of your mission," he said. "I told you that something momentous will happen here tonight. Your assignment with the man Daniel is a small part of that event."

"Yes, I have seen many angels arriving," admitted Bakka. "But what have they, or whatever is to happen here tonight, to do with Daniel?"

Gabriel looked at Bakka with compassion.

"Study the man," said Gabriel, ignoring Bakka's question. "Discover why he feels the way he does. Many destinies hang in the balance this evening, and as with all human destiny, it is a matter of his choosing."

The two walked to the crest of a hill overlooking the sleepy little town, leaving the shepherds at their fire. The area was beginning to light up from the many angels who were gathering. Bakka was puzzled.

"Gabriel?" asked Bakka. "What is to be decided tonight at Bethlehem?"

Gabriel looked at Bakka and then at the great star.

"Everything," he answered quietly. "Everything."

"And so, boys," Eli continued, "as to the remainder of the conquests...Refreshed with a new sense of holiness and mission, Joshua led his people through Canaan in victory after victory over the wicked nations that had made their stronghold in the land of promise." He cocked his head back and sighed aloud. "Those were glorious days for our fathers," he added, imagining the great clashes of armies.

He leaned in and said dramatically, "And many a devil lost his seat of worship, I can tell you! Places of detestable worship and religious wickedness were destroyed by Joshua's advancing armies. As for Joshua—he was to become one of the greatest generals we ever had!"

The shepherds all turned in the direction of some footsteps out in the darkness. It was Bezael, returning with a bit more wood for the little fire. He placed it on the embers and in a few moments, the fire crackled back to life.

"I like Joshua," said Jarod. "I wish we were in a war right now!"

"Oh we are, boy, we are," said Daniel, who was eating a bit of bread. "The enemy is right down there." He pointed toward Bethlehem. "Remember all the people we saw earlier today streaming into the town? They are proof of our enemy's control over us. The emperor ordered that all of Israel be taken up in the census so we can pay for the privilege of their occupation." He spat on the fire. "Roman census!"

"It's true our nation has fallen on hard times," agreed Eli. "Augustus' decree goes throughout the empire, though, and not simply our little part."

"Well it's our little part that concerns me," snapped Daniel. "The rest of the empire be hanged!"

"I'll bet Joshua could drive them out if he was here," chimed in little Joshua.

"You keep dreaming those things, boy," said Daniel sarcastically, staring vacantly at the new star that hung over Bethlehem. "Maybe someday a Joshua will return."

As he said this he looked at the boy, who wasn't sure of what to make of Daniel. All little Joshua knew was that the wonderful stories of old Israel and the rekindled fire had made it a very cozy night. And he desperately wanted to stay awake as Eli continued speaking. A few of the other shepherds had themselves fallen asleep, having switched off the night's watch.

Jarod, the older of the boys, also determined to stay awake the whole night with the other men, something he had never yet successfully done. This seemed the best night to do it—what with the great conversation, the talk of war with the Romans that was always bandied about, and the strange star that had been haunting the Bethlehem nights for a few weeks now.

Eli, refreshed with some food, was now ready to continue his storytelling. The other men implored him to continue, for they enjoyed his ability to cast the old days in such refreshing and lively terms. Only Daniel had objected to his speaking, but he was now asleep.

"So what happened after Joshua took Canaan?" asked Jarod, excited to get the conversation going once more.

"Well, Jarod," said Eli, "Joshua was never able to convince the people to conquer everything that God had promised them. So they took possession of most of the land, but left some of it unconquered. Such a shame."

But what did they do with it?" asked Jarod. "Is that when they got a king?"

"Jarod, you need to do a better job with your lessons," said Eli. "You should know this! It was not until much later that Israel begged for a king. No, this was the time of the judges over Israel."

"Judges?" asked Jarod.

"Yes," said Eli. "Holy men and women appointed by God to lead the land in times of trouble. And in the times of the judges there was much trouble, I'm afraid." Eli shook his head in shame. "Why we thought we needed a king—when we had as our ruler the King of the universe—will always baffle me!"

"What sort of trouble?" asked Jarod.

"The trouble brought on by sinful man," Eli answered. He looked at the boys and continued. "It seems that during this time our fathers were in a place of constant sin and defeat. Some judge or other would then lead them out of their difficulty until they sinned again. Deborah, Jepthah—these were some of the great judges of the time."

"But why were the people getting in trouble?" asked Joshua. "Weren't they happy to be in their new land?"

Eli looked down at the little boy whose innocent question held so significant an answer. "Because the people of God tend to stray, Joshua. Sort of like these sheep. That is why we must watch over them, keep them, take care of them—just as the Lord is our great Shepherd."

"But why should we stray if the Lord takes care of us?"

Several men averted their eyes from Eli, letting him know that he was entirely on his own in answering the boy's question.

"Because we humans are bent on idolatry," Eli said resignedly. "Truly it was a dreadful shame to see the people of God move into their land only to lose it to new enemies because of their choice to fail. And fail they did."

He said this with a pause and a bit of melancholy. "Turning from the true and living God, the people corrupted themselves, preferring the sensual, earthy, bewitching gods of Canaan—the Baals."

He spat with contempt after saying the name of Baal.

"And so, enemies like great storms would sweep in and defeat Israel—Moabites, Midianites, Amalekites and Philistines—and Israel would fall into dissolution and occupation."

"Like the Romans," mused Jarod quietly.

The eyes of the shepherds turned toward the boy and thoughts toward the Roman sentries in their town. Enemy occupation, it seemed, had become the rule rather than the exception. Many wondered if this boy might grow up in a free land, or if he too would spend his life under the heels of Rome.

"Yes, Jarod," said Eli. "Like the Romans. But in the days of the judges the Lord Most High, ever tender toward His people, would respond to the cries of Israel and send anointed men and women to disperse the enemy and establish the Lord's authority once more. And He shall do so again one day!"

"Who was the greatest judge of all?" asked Jarod.

Eli thought about it for a moment.

"I believe that the greatest judge of all was Samuel," he said. "He was devoted to the Lord and a great example of how the Lord uses an ordinary man who is faithful to Him. Of course all the judges were ordinary men and women who were willing to be used by the Lord."

Eli leaned back on his blanket.

"One of my favorite judges was a man who was quite afraid at first," the old man said. "Did you know that the Lord is especially good at using men who feel they cannot do what He is calling them to do?"

"Who was he?" asked the boys in unison.

"Gideon. He didn't want to lead the people and even tested the Lord's decision. But the Angel of the Lord would not take no for an answer and used him mightily!"

Jarod wrinkled his nose as Eli spoke to them about Gideon. Eli chuckled at the boy's obvious consternation.

"What's the matter, Jarod?" Eli asked. "Gideon not hero enough for you?"

"Well yes, sir," said Jarod somberly, as if caught in his thoughts. "But I thought the greatest judge was...well...Samson!"

Upon hearing the name *Samson*, Joshua, who had nearly nodded off, sprang to life. Eli smiled at the boys, as did the men sitting with them. Eli stroked his beard a bit.

"Ah yes," said Eli. "Samson is every child of Israel's hero."

He sat back to get his mind ready for the story he was about to relate.

"Now Samson was a judge who began with great hope for Israel...whose ministry was assigned him even before he was born...whose strength became renowned throughout the land..."

He glanced at Daniel and added, "And whose petulance and passions eventually destroyed him..."

Dan, 1126 B.C.

"Why should the Lord be interested in this woman?" asked Dheer, who was with another angel accompanying Michael through the streets of the little town of Zorah in the western foothills of Canaan. All that the archangel had told them was that they were to be witnesses to a very special grace of the Lord. They had stopped outside a modest little house that seemed identical to all the little homes on the street.

Through the window the angels could see a woman on bended knees, praying aloud to the Lord. It was always moving to an angel to see a human pray to the Most High in complete humility.

Dheer looked quizzically at Michael, wondering who she was and what their interest in her would be.

"This is yours, Dheer," said Michael. "This woman—and her family."

Dheer took a closer look at the woman to whom he had been assigned. She was an older woman, her hair tinged with gray and her hands leathery from years of hard work. She alternately cried aloud and spoke pleadingly, entreating the Lord on her behalf. She also had a deep compassion that was evident in her teary eyes.

Michael himself had escorted the two angels to this place, promising them that this was no ordinary assignment. But a woman crying alone in a room seemed fairly typical to Dheer. He continued studying the woman who was to become his charge. He watched her stand up slowly as if in just a bit of discomfort, and move over to the little cooking area, where a piece of meat was slowly roasting.

She picked up a small pitcher of water and brought it over to a table. She then put a piece of bread on the table along with some fruit, and sat down to await her husband. There was something about her eyes that struck Dheer—teary from anguish and yet with an air of determination—almost a defiant sort of faith that would not relent.

"Manoah?" she called out. "Is that you?"

The angels watched as the woman looked toward the doorway from where she thought she had heard something. Nobody was there.

"Now you will see that yours is no ordinary assignment, my brother," said Michael.

"Manoah?"

She stood to investigate the noise she was certain she had heard.

Suddenly a man stepped through the darkened doorway into the room. The woman was so shaken she could not even scream.

She fell to her knees and began to plead for her life. But the man only stood where he was.

"The Lord's Angel," said Dheer in astonishment. "Here!"

Michael indicated for him to stop talking and listen.

Overcoming her initial fright the woman looked up at the man who towered over her little frame. In an instant she knew—somehow knew—that the man intended her no harm. He was dressed in a white cloak that was strange to Zorah. His face was obscured by the darkness of the room, the only light of which was a small oil lamp in the corner. Finally the woman summoned the courage to look up, but could not ask the man who he was and what he wanted. Suddenly the man began to speak, saying:

"Do not be afraid, for the Lord Most High has heard your prayers. And though you are barren and can have no children, yet shall you soon bear a son! And he shall be a Nazarite from his birth and shall deliver his people from the Philistines."

And just as suddenly as he had appeared in the doorway, he disappeared. Recovering from the visit, she leapt up to pursue the man, and ran into her husband, Manoah, as he was coming into the house.

"Woman, are you out of your mind?" he demanded.

Dheer and Michael smiled at the comical event. Dheer then turned to Michael and asked him, "Am I assigned to the woman, or to her child?"

"You are assigned to both," said Michael. "The enemy will certainly want to destroy the child before he can fulfill the task of delivering his people."

The two angels watched as the woman explained to her husband all that had happened. Manoah was completely baffled; he wondered if perhaps the woman had gone mad or had been drinking some of the local wine.

"No, I am not drunk," she said. "I tell you the man came and said we were to have a son! And he shall be a Nazarite and…"

"Please!" he said. "Let me think this through."

He sat for a moment in silence and then, looking at his wife incredulously, got onto his knees and began pleading with the Lord to send the man to him so that he might understand what was going on. Dheer watched as the man prayed and prayed and...nothing happened. Frustrated, Manoah rose from his knees and sat silently at the table, gnawing on the bread that his wife set before him.

"It seems that the Angel of the Lord will not come again this evening," said Michael. He grinned. "Poor Manoah!"

"What a wonderful promise!" said Dheer excitedly.

"And an important assignment," said Michael. "I told you that something remarkable was happening in Zorah!"

Far above them, hanging silently over the little town, a dark angel named Shawa was watching the entire episode unfolding. As one of Kara's spies, he had been following Michael's movements ever since he had entered the area, and had witnessed the whole affair.

He smiled and said quietly to himself, "You are right, Archangel. Something remarkable is *indeed* happening in Zorah!"

"I should think that Michael would have sent a more important angel to Zorah if there was indeed something of importance happening there," said Kara, musing over the recent developments in Dan. He looked at Pellecus for a response.

Pellecus quelled the anger he felt rising in him toward Kara, who he thought was a posturing fool at times. For his part, Kara thoroughly enjoyed his role as interpreter of the information brought to him by his spies on the field. He believed that this made him not only powerful in his own right, but a valuable asset to Lucifer.

"The fact that Michael was in Zorah with Dheer is of little importance," said Pellecus, who had been given explicit instructions by Lucifer to work with Kara in keeping abreast of any movement by the Lord in Canaan. "However, the fact that the Angel of the Lord was involved is quite telling and therefore the promise of another deliverer must be taken seriously."

Kara looked at Pellecus and nodded in agreement with the angel in whom he had little trust but with whom he must now cooperate.

"I quite agree, Pellecus," he finally said. "We need more intelligence on this."

Kara smiled a knowing smile. "Have no fear, Pellecus," he said. "I have ordered Shawa to remain close to the family of Manoah and report on whatever transpires."

"I hope you have ordered him to stay clear of Dheer," said Pellecus. "He may not be competent but he is no fool!"

"Do you really believe that the deliverer is about to be born?" asked Kara.

Pellecus smirked at Kara.

"He must be born one day," he surmised. "If not this time, then some day. But the Angel of the Lord said he was to deliver his people from the Philistines. The Lord's Angel does not appear to humans without purpose. Remember Hagar? And Gideon?"

"Of course," said Kara. "And Gideon delivered his people from the Midianites. That cowering fool! It seems the Lord will use simply anyone—especially if they are incompetent or untrained!"

"That is part of His brilliance," came a voice. It was Lucifer.

"My lord, we were just discussing the situation at Zorah," stammered Kara. "I have ordered Shawa to keep an eye on the events there. We expect word at any moment."

Lucifer ignored Kara's usual pandering and walked up the ruined stone stairs of what had been a Canaanite noble's house, before it was destroyed in one of Joshua's campaigns years earlier.

"Joshua certainly made short work of this place, did he not?" said Lucifer, noting the charred stones that had tumbled upon one another. "Yes, Kara, I am aware of the Angel's visit to Zorah."

"It represents a disturbing pattern, my lord," said Pellecus. "This raising up of leaders who deliver the people from the snares that we encourage among them through their enemies. I see it as a rehearsal of sorts for the True Deliverer who will one day arrive in this land."

Lucifer looked sharply at Pellecus.

"A rehearsal?" asked Kara derisively. "For the Seed?" He began laughing. "Surely the Most High doesn't need to practice for His invasion."

"You miss the point, Kara," snapped Pellecus. "I am saying that the Lord is a God of order and system. I believe He is establishing such a pattern to demonstrate to His people that in the end He will come to their rescue."

"But only if they repent, Kara," said Lucifer. "There is always a price to pay for the Lord's favor." He indicated the ruined city around him. "Or disfavor."

"So what is He teaching them by coming to their rescue?" asked Kara.

"His price," said Lucifer. "The price of the Lord's favor is repentance. And that is why we shall win this war ultimately."

Lucifer led the two angels through the abandoned streets of the burned-out city. Little was left except ruined hulls of what had been homes facing the street and sections of wall that had not yet collapsed.

"Look at this city—or what is left of it," Lucifer began. "At one point it was a thriving community of humans. Then war came and their way of life was finished. For now, Israel enjoys the Lord's protection. But humans being what they are, I assure you that one day they will turn from the Lord completely, and He shall turn His back on them. Remember that He almost destroyed them in the desert? Had not Moses interceded for them, they would not have survived to this day. For now they resist the Baals. But one day they shall rejoice in them!"

An angel swept in from the north and came to stand in front of Kara. It was Shawa. He looked about and was surprised, as well as terrified, to see Lucifer standing nearby.

"Go on," said Kara casually. "Report."

Shawa looked once more in the direction of Lucifer and then, collecting his thoughts, began reporting that the Angel of the Lord had appeared again to the wife of Manoah—this time in a field near her house.

"He addressed the woman as before, my lords, and this time she ran and fetched her husband so that he might inquire of the visitor. He asked the Angel about the coming child, how they were to raise him. The Angel of the Lord repeated to the man that the child would be holy to the Lord—a Nazarite who could drink no strong drink and whose hair must not be cut."

"Interesting," said Lucifer, who strolled over to where Kara stood listening to Shawa. "A Nazarite vow to be taken by the child. He will be special indeed."

"The man Manoah asked the Angel his name, not knowing that he stood before the Angel of the Lord."

"Really," asked Pellecus, most interested. "And what answer did He give the man?"

"None. The Angel simply said that He would accept from the man an offering of meat. But when the fire began to consume the lamb, the Angel stood within its midst and disappeared up into the sky! At that point the man and wife knew they had been visited by the Lord and they fell to the ground and worshiped."

Shawa awaited a response or reaction from the three angels to whom he had reported. Lucifer contemplated in silence the report that Shawa had brought. Kara and Pellecus also awaited

Lucifer's response. Finally Lucifer spoke to the higher-ranking angels.

"How I envy the Lord's ability to make humans truly worship Him," he said.

"My lord, most of the world worships you," said Kara. "In one form or another people bow down to you through images and incantations and…"

"Snakes! Crude statues! Beasts of the field! Those are the objects of worship that we have managed to build into the minds of men," said Lucifer. "I enjoy the worship of minds twisted by sin. Only the Most High God truly enjoys worship in its purest sense."

Shawa stepped back as Lucifer's purplish aura began to manifest in his anger. As his rage subsided, so did the aura. He looked at the others and sighed…and then smiled a half smile.

"Ah, my brothers, we shall never be worshiped in purity," he said, much calmer now, even cordial. "But we can enjoy the fruits of corruption. We may not truly know what it is to capture the hearts of men—but we can have the satisfaction of capturing their minds. Thus we might prevent their worship of the Most High."

Shawa looked first to Lucifer and then to Kara as if to ask what his instructions were. Kara understood and then proposed that Shawa maintain a close watch on the family. Lucifer agreed.

"The child shall be born," said Lucifer. "Of that there can be no doubt. So we shall keep a close watch on him. In the meantime we continue pressing in from the Baals and that filthy god of the Philistines."

"Ah, Dagon," mused Pellecus snidely. "Very crude deity indeed."

"Sponsored by a very capable angel," said Kara defensively.

"Berenius runs Dagon, does he not?" asked Lucifer.

"Yes, my prince," answered Kara, looking at Pellecus with hate-filled eyes. "Berenius is one of our most devoted and capable angels. When he was given the principality over the Philistines, he began the cult of Dagon and has prospered with it."

"It seems there is about to be a revival in the land," said Lucifer sullenly. "For when this child has come of age he will wage war on us."

Kara and Pellecus nodded in agreement.

"Kara, I suggest that Dagon begin to impress himself on the Israelites—especially the Danites from whose tribe this child shall come."

"Yes, my prince," said Kara. "I will see to it."

"The Angel of the Lord is not the only prophet on earth," said Lucifer. "This planet is filled with prophets. I prophesy that the priests of Dagon will be inspired this year through all manner of signs and wonders and dreams. Make certain that Berenius begins this religious zeal immediately."

"It shall be done," said Kara.

"The Philisitine rulers shall thus become emboldened, and by the time this Danite deliverer is born, the oppression from the five cities shall be so great that the spirit of Israel shall be crushed!"

"And the deliverer?" asked Pellecus delicately. "Suppose he turns out to be another Moses?"

"Even deliverers are corruptible," said Lucifer. "Moses was a murderer and we used that to great effect." He thought about it a moment. "Shawa! You will make it your task to discover the weakness of this man—his peculiar passion—so that we might one day exploit it."

"I shall do so," said Shawa, proud of the important role he would now take on.

"And even should the child of Manoah manage to live to his maturity, and be greater than Moses, the fight shall already have been taken out of Israel. He shall be a deliverer of a stillborn people."

Chronicles of the Host

Samson

So it was that Manoah's wife gave birth to Samson—future scourge of the Philistines and deliverer to his people. The Spirit of the Lord was upon Samson. Unlike the other judges, Samson grew into a man possessing superhuman strength, with which he became a legend among both the Danites and the Philistines.

True to his dark heart, Lucifer and his angels pressed hard upon Israel, elevating Dagon among the people and oppressing the children of God with greater and greater hardship. Finally, the people of God began once more to call upon their Lord and repent of their wickedness, unaware that among them was one who had been born for such a time.

Shawa, ever desperate to please his master, did his dark work with great efficiency. He observed Samson closely, watching for an opening, waiting for a slip, hoping for a point of weakness. As long as Samson kept pure his Nazarite vow, the Spirit of God remained upon him. And though many holy angels were assigned to Samson to counter any movement by the enemy, not one could stop him from the foolishness that was starting to overtake him....

The warm air felt good on Samson's face. He had been traveling between Zorah and Eshtaol, lost in deep thought about his life. For some reason a brooding, almost melancholy spirit had been emerging. He knew that God had prepared something special for him. Many times his mother and father had related the story about the Angel of the Lord appearing to them. But when? And what?

He brushed back his long black hair as he thought about the Nazarite vow he had made—or rather that had been made for him by the circumstances of his birth. Truly it was a marvelous thing to be called of the Lord. But what did it mean? Of course he had heard of the great men and women before him—men like Ehud who, declaring that he had "a message from God," killed the king of Moab and rescued Israel from that nation's grip. He recalled Deborah, who stepped in with Barak to war against the Canaanites. But who was he? A Danite from a nothing little town called Zorah.

As he continued down the road near Mahaneh Dan, a small caravan of Philistines on donkeys came up from the distance— some of the local tax gatherers making their usual call. Samson hated how this godless nation made prey of his people. He watched the men approaching, escorted by several chariots, the pride of the Philistine army, which had swept much of Israel before them.

As they passed by, a couple of the Philistine charioteers cursed Samson for being in their way. They would have run right over him had he not jumped to the side. Behind the first chariots came the tax collectors, lolling about under a large umbrella, fat with gold and graft, and hardly batting an eye as they passed by Samson.

"How long, O Lord, must we endure these dogs?" he asked aloud after they had passed. "I have taken a vow to You. And my mother told me that one day I was to deliver the people. But what good is a vow kept that is not also paid?"

As he finished speaking the wind around him began to pick up, kicking some dust into the air. Turning once more toward the Philistines, he watched as they disappeared over the top of a hill. They seemed unaffected by the wind. In fact, the only place that the wind seemed to be gusting about was right around Samson!

A sudden realization overtook him. Stirred by the Spirit of God, and falling to his knees, Samson called out to the Lord, praising the Most High and singing the hymns of Israel to Him. He then fell face first onto the ground, crying out to God as the Spirit of the Lord stirred and spoke to him the things that he must do.

Dheer, who accompanied Samson everywhere he went, was overjoyed at this anointing of the Spirit of God upon him. He had followed Samson's life from childhood until now, longing for the day when God would confirm upon him the seal of His Presence. Now the man Samson had become Samson, judge of Israel!

Samson stood up, filled with a new sense of who he was. He felt so many things—as if he had been given a whole new life. His heart felt as if it were on fire, and his mind had never been sharper. But the greatest change of all in him was his strength. He suddenly felt that he could lift ten men.

Samson looked once more in the direction of the Philisitines who had passed him by. A crooked smile crossed his lips. He suddenly dashed up the road, from the direction he had just come. Dheer realized what he was about to do and stayed with him, wondering if perhaps he should call upon more angels.

In a superhuman burst of speed, Samson easily caught and passed the Philistine tax caravan, staying off the road so they could not see him. When he had gained a few hundred yards ahead of them, he awaited their turn around a small hill, standing in the middle of the road. Dheer remained alert to the situation, watching for any sign of the enemy, and curious as to the behavior of this very different man.

The lead chariot turned the corner and faced Samson. The horse stopped as if under instruction, refusing to go around Samson. Not able to see that Dheer was holding the horse back, the Philistine soldier picked up his whip.

"You there, get out of the way," he hollered.

Samson remained fixed, arms crossed and refusing to move.

"You heard me!" he said. As the other soldiers pulled up beside him, the one holding the whip looked at Samson completely confused.

"We just passed you on the road," he said. "What sort of sorcery is this?"

"The kind that needs a good whipping to discourage it," said one of the other soldiers, climbing out of the chariot. The rest of the caravan had by now caught up and was wondering what the disturbance was all about.

"Move, little man," said the Philistine, who stood in front of Samson. "We are on official business."

Samson looked at the fat collectors in their canopied seats.

"I'll move after you pay the tax," Samson said.

"What?" said the soldier, who was scarred above his right eye. He looked with amazement at the others in his group.

"What tax is that, Danite?" asked one of the tax collectors.

"Why, the taxes that I am charging for you to use this road," Samson said casually. "Now because you did not know about the tax, I will take only half of what you have taken from my people."

The Philistines began laughing. Dheer took his place next to Samson. He could sense the Spirit of God at work and wondered what Samson might do. He then looked up and saw Shawa for the first time, standing next to the soldier in the lead chariot.

"Well, well," said Shawa. "Heaven must be depleted these days. We must be doing better in this war than I thought!"

Dheer remained silent, fixing his gaze upon Shawa and readying himself for combat should it come to it. Shawa suddenly appeared next to the soldier who was now standing toe to toe with Samson. He began to speak into this soldier's mind, enflaming him with a hot anger.

"I said, 'Move,' " the soldier demanded, almost growling.

"Now you've done it," said Samson. "Now I shall have to take all the money you collected."

"Collect this, Danite!" said the soldier, raising his whip.

Samson grabbed the man's arm and broke it like a twig. The man yelped in pain and doubled over on the road. Shawa cursed and began enflaming the other men, who climbed out of their chariots with swords drawn.

"We'll teach you to attack a Philistine!" snarled one of the soldiers.

He lunged at Samson with his sword. Samson jumped out of the way, grabbed the man's sword hand, and squeezed hard. A loud snap told the story as the man's hand crumbled. Samson then picked up the whip that had been dropped by the first Philistine.

When the remaining two soldiers charged at him, he lashed them both across the face with the whip. They dropped to the ground in pain. The tax collectors began tossing out bags of coins, begging Samson to take the money and pleading that he not hurt them. Samson picked up the bags and tossed them into one of the chariots.

"Thank you for being so cooperative," he said, jumping into the chariot.

He then whipped the horse and sped off down the road, leaving the Philistines bruised and bewildered.

"Who was that?" asked one of the soldiers, bleeding from his face where the whip had cut into his cheek.

"That was Samson, the Danite," said one of the tax collectors, wiping the sweat from his face. "I have seen him in Timnah from time to time. He fancies a Philistine girl there."

"He is a devil," said the soldier with the broken hand, which he was now binding up with a piece of cloth. "And he shall die for this!"

"Yes, my friend," said another. "Not now, though. Next time...in Timnah!"

Shawa looked hatefully at Dheer, who had remained behind to make sure that Shawa maintained his distance. Shawa smirked at his one-time friend. The battle would have to be left unfinished. But that was just as well.

For now Shawa had the information that Kara had been waiting for all of Samson's life—proof that this long-haired Nazarite was in fact the deliverer and that the time for real war had come! Kara should be pleased. Shawa called out to Dheer in a rage as he vanished, "Just as the humans said, angel! Next time…in Timnah!"

Chapter 6

"Out of the eater came something to eat."

"Samson's father refuses to let him see this woman in Timnah," said Shawa. "They had quite an argument over it." He snickered. "I think he wants to marry the girl!"

Lucifer nodded in quiet contemplation. The Council of Seven had come together at Lucifer's order to sort out the coming conflict with Samson and his people. Though Lucifer had organized these critical leaders globally, and each was prince over large portions of the world, Israel represented a common threat that bound all of them together.

New at Council were Berenius, who had been Kara's willing assistant in the matter of Cain, and Tinius, whose recent profane acts in Canaan had earned him greater respect among Lucifer's inner circle. The prince of demons had requested their presence in accord with an important announcement he wanted to make.

"Before we discuss how to deal with Samson any further, I wish to announce my intentions to create a new governing body," Lucifer said.

A few angels squirmed uncomfortably at what that might mean for them personally. Berenius and Tinius stood at attention, waiting for Lucifer's declaration. He called them up and they stood next to him, on his left.

"I have created a new council that will be completely absorbed with our dealing in Canaan," he began. "Principalities and power work only insofar as they are efficiently administered. Brothers, since the days of Eden we have devastated the Lord's plan for humans. We have perverted their faith; we have polluted their minds; we have stolen their hearts. Everywhere on this planet where men live, we hold authority by fear and by fakery. From jungle tribes to the great cities in the East, we have created an earth dominated by men who believe in gods that we have made, laws that we have written, and passions that we have inflamed.

"Our legions have maintained a hold on the greatest civilizations that humans have engineered, from the Nile to the land between the two rivers, to the great Indus valley and on to the Yangtze of the Orient. Everywhere, men bow to images and creatures and ideas that are foreign to their Creator! Everywhere, we have great success!"

He picked up an image of a Canaanite deity and smashed it on the ground. "Except here...in Canaan. Only in Canaan do we have any real opposition—and any real threat. Only here is there any real resistance."

"Israel is too dangerous to leave alone," Lucifer continued. "As certain as Samson is the delivering judge, the Seed will one day spring from these people. That is why I have decided to form a Supreme Council—the Council of Liberation—to be attended by Kara, Pellecus, and Rugio. These three shall be my greatest resource in this war against the pretenders to Heaven."

Kara, who of course knew that this announcement should be made, looked around to see the responses in the room. If he was looking for great displays of enthusiasm, he was disappointed.

Capable as he was in many things, Kara was deemed unreliable in critical situations, and his vanity was insufferable. But his ability to gather intelligence and interpret and disseminate it was uncanny, and therefore very useful to Lucifer. Pellecus and Rugio nodded to one or two of their closest aides, who acknowledged their promotion with a nod in return.

"And so it shall be that Berenius will become prince over Egypt and Arabia in place of Kara, while Tinius shall take from Pellecus the matter of the eastern coastal lands of the Great Sea, the Greek and Macedonian worlds. Rugio will remain prince over Persia and the lands around until a capable replacement is appointed."

The group spent a few moments congratulating each other, stifling the undercurrent of rivalry and infighting that had plagued Lucifer's Council since they had vacated Heaven. After a moment of sizing up this new arrangement, they came back to order. Lucifer encouraged their efforts in their particular domains, then promptly dismissed the Council of Seven. After they had left he turned to the newly formed Council of Liberation comprised of himself, Kara, Pellecus, and Rugio.

"And now as to Samson..." Lucifer began.

"And now as to Samson," said Dheer.

Just outside the Academy of the Host in a garden built around a pristine pool, Michael, Serus, and Crispin had gathered to talk about Dheer's progress with Samson. Around them in groups of threes and fours, other angels were discussing their own earthly assignments.

Some spoke of encounters with mischievous devils; others told of saving this or that human from dangerous situations; and from time to time, an angel would proudly speak of having encountered Kara or some other higher-ranked enemy angel. That, it seemed, was many a warrior's dream: to give a good, sound thrashing to Kara or Rugio, whose reputations for obnoxious behavior and proud boasting had become legend in Heaven.

"Listen to them," Michael said, grinning. "I only wonder what they would do if they encountered one of those angels!"

"I'm sure they would find that Rugio is a bit more of a handful than they counted on," observed Crispin. "Still the Host is at war and organized marvelously, Michael."

"Thank you, teacher," said Michael. As commander of the Lord's Host, Michael had engineered the defensive coordination on behalf of the Kingdom. Though the people of God were generally under Heaven's watchful eye, the hope that the Coming One should emerge soon kept them vigilant. Only the Most High knew when, where, and through whom the Seed of Eve would finally be born. Both the Host of Heaven and Lucifer's angels knew that victory or defeat hung in the balance, and nobody could ever be certain when the prophecy would be fulfilled.

It was evident from Dheer's report that Samson had begun to walk in his authority as judge of Israel. Michael was amused at the encounter with the tax collectors that had been his first show of authority. And yet there were rumblings about Samson's rather reckless passion for Philistine women and his smug pride in his newly discovered strength.

"All men are susceptible to pride," warned Crispin, as the group of angels continued their discussion. "Pride is the root of all sin—and it is born in the hearts of men. Even those called of the Lord, like Samson."

"It is worse than that, dear Crispin," said Dheer. "His parents are entirely opposed to this marriage with a Philistine. Yet he persists!"

"These people will never change!" said Serus in disgust. "The Most High has repeatedly delivered them from their prideful folly—yet they continue to offend Him."

"And so they shall continue to do so, I fear," said Crispin. "Since Eden man's heart has been forever corrupted. He has lost his innocence and taken on the yoke of pride. He will never be able to shake it—at least not on his own."

Michael looked at Dheer and commended him for his service to the Most High in watching over Samson. He placed his hand on the angel's shoulder.

"Go back to Samson," Michael said. "Continue watching. You are learning what it means for us angels to not interfere with the will of men—no matter how much we would like to."

"Remember Eden?" asked Crispin. "Michael could barely contain himself from stepping between Eve and the serpent. And yet he could not violate Eve's decision."

"Not even the Lord will violate a human's choice to reject Him," said Michael.

"Then I'll return to Samson," said Dheer. "He is even now headed to Timnah to marry the Philistine woman, but perhaps along the road something will happen to change his mind."

"Yes," reasoned Crispin. "Perhaps something will happen on the road to Timnah."

Samson's mother followed along a few paces behind her husband and son as they made their way to Timnah. She was saddened in her heart that he liked the company of a Philistine woman, but she no longer wanted to contend with her son. She and her husband had tried reasoning with him to the point of outright arguments, but nothing could deter Samson from his intention to see this Philistine woman. Samson's father, however, still would have none of it, and continued the discussion vigorously, even as they neared Timnah.

"Can you find no woman among our own people?" he plead-ed. "This is an offense to our people...to our God! He will never bless such a thing!"

On and on he went. Samson remained silent, long numb to his father's opinion. He kept his eyes straight on the road, resolute in his decision. And then, kicking his donkey, he trotted along ahead of his parents, deciding to meet them at Timnah rather than remain with them along the way. Perhaps when they actually met the girl they would become more agreeable....

Dheer arrived as Samson neared the vineyards just outside Timnah. His conversation with Crispin had done little to encour-age him. Humans were prone to failure, it seemed—even those called of the Lord, such as Samson. But the Most High knew what He was doing in all of this; for that Dheer was grateful.

As they rounded a curve in the road, Dheer had just enough time to catch a glimpse of Shawa before that demon disappeared into a young lion. The lion, which had been lazily sunning himself on the side of the road, suddenly became enraged. Shawa goaded the animal, controlling him now, and making him jump out into the road. Shawa's plan was to kill Samson and his parents and fin-ish with this deliverer business once and for all.

As the lion snarled, Samson jumped off the donkey, having just enough time to catch his balance before the lion was on him. Samson's first thought was to look for a weapon, but before he knew it the lion had a lock on his throat. Shawa was laughing aloud, feeling the hate and fear of the animal that he was driving. He would kill Samson slowly, he had decided.

Dheer ordered Shawa out of the lion, but, of course, Shawa ignored the angel. Then, just as at Mahaneh Dan, the Spirit of God came upon Samson. He grabbed the lion's mouth and pulled the beast off himself. Samson felt strength coursing through his body, like a heat emerging from within and welling up through his heart, filling his whole being. Shawa, realizing what was happening, shrieked frightfully at the Lord's Presence, as he too felt the power of God working through Samson. He quickly abandoned the confused animal in Samson's hands. Samson killed the lion, choking it with his hands, and tossed the carcass on the side of the road.

Dheer looked at the lion and then back at Samson, amazed at what he had just seen. But he was reminded that this was a man called of the Lord by the Lord's own Angel. The incident only confirmed what Dheer had always believed about Samson—that he would one day avenge the people in God's mighty power!

He glanced at the dead lion on the side of the road. God was with Samson. Perhaps the marriage in Timnah would be alright after all!

Chronicles of the Host
War With the Philistines

Unknown to both the Host and the fallen angels, it was neither devil nor angel who had placed the Philistine woman upon Samson's heart—it was the Most High God. Seeking a provocation with the cruel and profane worshipers of Dagon, the Lord used the affection between pagan and judge to begin the deliverance of Israel.

So it was that when Samson came down again to Timnah, he planned to marry the girl and take her back to Dan with him. But the Philistine men, jealous of the girl and wanting nothing to do with Samson, came to the wedding party to provoke Samson and keep the girl with them.

Bethlehem, 4 B.C.

"The riddle! The riddle!" exclaimed Jarod, suddenly breaking into Eli's story. "Is this where he tells them the riddle?"

Eli grinned at the boy.

"Yes, Jarod," the old man said. "Samson knew that the Philistine men were only there to cause him trouble. So he told them a riddle."

Daniel looked up at Eli.

"You have been speaking in riddles all night long, Eli," he said. "Riddles are apparently not new among our people!"

"No, Daniel," Eli agreed. "As your attitude this evening indicates, we are a people filled with riddles."

Some of the shepherds laughed at this. Daniel smirked at Eli and casually tossed a small stick into the fire.

"Riddles don't deliver a people, boys," said Daniel, leaning back. "Cold steel and blood are all that will throw off that yoke!"

Jarod and Joshua glanced over at Daniel, a puzzled look on their faces. Some of the shepherd men also glanced his way. They were beginning to have enough of this man and his spiteful talk.

"Riddles do not deliver indeed," said Eli. "But God used a riddle that day to provoke the Philistines. Samson told the men that if they could guess the answer within the seven days of the marriage feast, he would give each of them a new cloak. Do you recall the riddle, Jarod?"

"I do!" Joshua said excitedly. Eli indicated that he should tell it. Joshua proudly stood among the men as if he were Samson, telling the riddle to the Philistine men: "Out of the eater, something to eat; out of the strong, something sweet!"

"Well done, Joshua!" said Eli, as the boy sat down. Joshua's dad winked at him proudly. "And indeed the men could not understand the riddle. For several days they tried to come up with the answer. Finally, they talked Samson's wife-to-be into getting the answer from him so they might not be taken in by this mere Danite. Do you recall the solution to the riddle?"

"Well," said Joshua, "when Samson had gone back home one time, he saw the body of the lion that he had killed. Some bees had made a hive in it, and he ate some honey they had made."

"Right!" said Eli. "Out of the eater came something to eat and out of the strong something sweet! It was a marvelous riddle. But when the men guessed it, Samson discovered that his wife had told them and he became furious. He went out and killed 30 men of the Philistines, taking their cloaks to give to the men at the party as he had promised. Samson then left for his father's house, and his new wife was given to another man. That began the deliverance of God's people as war broke out between Samson and the Philistines.

"Samson was killing many of the Philistines' best men and they didn't know how to stop him. Finally, they were able to force Samson's own people to turn him over, who bound Samson to take him to the Philistines. But as they approached Lehi, where the Philistines had come to collect him with over three thousand men, the Spirit of the Lord came upon Samson. There he killed over one thousand of his enemies that day."

Eli looked at the two boys.

"Do you know what weapon he used?" he asked them.

The boys tried to remember, looking at some of the other men, who made faces as if they could not remember either.

"God used a weapon to humble the pride of the Philistines—something that would show them and Samson that the Most High is not bound by the strategies or ways of men. He used the jawbone of a donkey! He killed a thousand men that day with the jawbone of a donkey!"

The men watched in amusement as the two boys jumped up pretending to be Samson, smashing in the skulls of invisible Philistine soldiers with a log that had become a makeshift jawbone. When they sat down again, Eli continued talking.

"Samson seemed unstoppable," he said. "And the lords of the Philistines were determined to discover the secret of his strength so they could destroy him..."

Gaza, 1074 B.C.

Since its occupation, Gaza had become one of the main centers of commerce and faith among the Philistines. It had always been a crossroad of the empire in the region; now it had developed into one of the chief centers for the manufacture of the weapons with which the Philistines had subdued their enemies. And with the newly completed temple of Dagon, Gaza had also taken its place among the other cities as a premier place of religious expression. Today, however, the streets seemed abandoned, as most of the people were either in the temple on the end of town, or standing outside its walls selling food and drink to the adherents who had gathered for a great celebration to Dagon.

Three figures, unseen by human eyes, strolled casually down the streets of Gaza. They too were in something of a celebrative mood, drinking in the success that they had enjoyed of late in keeping the people of God under the Philistine heel.

"I am something of an expert when it comes to the weakness of humans," said Lucifer. "All of them have their price—their point of compromise. Samson was no different."

He was strolling with Kara and Pellecus on a street near the edge of the city. From the temple went up a roar that could be heard throughout the city. They observed a drunken man stumbling his way toward the temple.

"Happy worship!" called out Lucifer, laughing at the man. The other two angels laughed as well. "The fool!"

"Look at these simple people," Kara said. "Happily content in their folly. That is the way of men."

"You know," said Lucifer, "of all the passions we stir among men, it is their need for religion which has proven most useful to us. What better way to get a human mind away from the Most High than to train it upon a god that we manufacture."

"Shawa was certainly grateful when you awarded him Dagon," said Pellecus. "He has done a fabulous job developing the cult around himself. Although I must admit Dagon is a bit crude."

"So are the Philistines," said Lucifer.

They walked down a street in front of a smaller temple that had been dedicated to Dagon years before the great temple had been built. Since assuming the deity, Shawa had seen to it that the priests of Dagon had heard from the god and constructed the temple in which the people were now worshiping.

"Of course Shawa deserved the honor," said Kara, who always felt it necessary to defend an angel who was under his authority. "It was, after all, his work through Delilah that delivered Samson into the hands of the Philistines."

"She had some help," said Pellecus. "Don't forget that it was Samson's own failures that placed himself in Delilah's hands."

"Agreed," said Kara. "Nevertheless, Shawa inspired Delilah to compel Samson to tell her the secret of his strength those 20 years ago."

"What a glorious triumph that was!" said Lucifer, clapping his hands together. "Remember the day after he had betrayed himself that he rose up to fight the Philistines in the Spirit of God— only to find that the Spirit of God was no longer with him!"

They all laughed.

"What a look of realization was upon him," said Kara, almost drooling at the thought. "The fool! The deliverer was undone by the deliverer. Delicious!"

It gives me heart, brothers," said Lucifer. "If the Lord will abandon the very instrument that He had promised to use in defense of His people, what will He do when the True Deliverer arrives? I predict that He shall turn His back on that one as well!"

Outside the grinding house, the noise of the grist mill continued. Dheer and Michael stood at the window through which they looked down upon Samson. He pushed the great stone as he had for the last 20 years, grinding wheat for the Philistines hour after hour, day after day. Blinded by the Philistines and bound with bronze shackles to the great millstone, Samson continued in an endless circle of darkness and despair.

Dheer had never left his vigil, watching Samson all this time. Michael had told him that he might move to another assignment, should he choose to do so. But Dheer determined to remain with Samson, and to see the man through to the end.

"I was there when the Angel of the Lord spoke to his mother," said Dheer, who noticed Michael standing behind him. "He was to be the deliverer of his people."

"He chose otherwise," said Michael. "He chose to follow his own path and to profane his vow to the Lord."

A great roar went up again from the temple. Michael felt an anger rising inside him as he thought of the proud Philistine people drinking to their god and making sport of the Most High in their unholy temple.

"Dagon is being celebrated," he said. "I should like to make some noise in that place." He smiled at Dheer. "One day the Lord will avenge Samson. Wait and see."

"Yes," came a voice. "Perhaps the Lord will have need for some freshly ground wheat! His deliverer will see to it."

Michael turned to see Lucifer, Kara, and Pellecus. They were now joined by Rugio, who had just returned from the temple.

"How is he doing?" Lucifer continued, in mock concern. "Do you suppose he is cold in there?"

"What do you want here, Lucifer?" asked Dheer.

"Well, well," said Lucifer, looking at Dheer. "I have come to pay my respects to this man. If it were not for him, we might not be celebrating Dagon's day."

"It is you that should not be here," said Kara. "You are the one who failed to help Samson. You are responsible for his imprisonment."

"You are wrong, Kara," said Michael. "Samson made his own choice."

"When will you ever learn that humans will always fail you?" Rugio growled. "Samson failed as will any future deliverer. So it seems, Archangel, that yours is a lost cause after all."

Michael resisted the temptation to thrash Rugio. Instead he looked down at Samson. "He is paying for his folly," he said.

"Not quite," said Rugio.

Michael turned to look at Rugio, whose smug look belied that he was about to say something he found very satisfying. Rugio turned to Lucifer.

"I have just returned from the temple of Dagon," he said. "The people are looking for a way to honor their god." He looked scornfully at Michael. "Shawa entered the mind of the high priest of Dagon and inspired him to bring Samson out and humble him before Dagon's image!"

"The deliverer bowing before an image," declared Kara. That's brilliant!"

"Be it ever thus to all of your deliverers, Archangel," said Lucifer.

Before Michael could answer Lucifer, some men arrived from the temple, dressed as priests of Dagon, along with some temple guards. They ordered the prison opened and entered Samson's grinding room.

Dori, the high priest's chief assistant, ordered that Samson be unshackled and led out of the prison. The men, still leery of

Samson's reputation, kept their weapons at the ready as they bound him in chains and led him outside.

"You always were a religious fellow, Samson," said Dori. "Today you will have the honor of bowing before the god in whose power you have fallen. Perhaps he shall have mercy on you!"

The men laughed as they led Samson up the street.

"I rarely set foot in a human temple," said Lucifer. "But today I am feeling particularly pious. Shall we?"

He then vanished, along with Kara and Pellecus. Only Rugio remained.

"You're finished, Archangel," he said. "You and your deliverers and your bloody Seed of a woman—it's all finished!"

He then vanished to join the others.

Dheer looked at Michael, who stood silent for a moment, looking at the grist mill that had been Samson's life for the last 20 years. Another loud burst of noise went up from the temple.

"I want to be with him," said Dheer. "Perhaps to encourage him in this difficult moment. I want to be there when they scourge him. I have such compassion for him—I saw such a melancholy spirit on his face."

Michael looked up from the millstone.

"Really?" he said, smiling. "I believe I saw quite another spirit."

Above the temple of Dagon, the sky was filled with boisterous, clamoring, vile, demon angels. There were so many that a dark haze canopied the temple in a blurry, crawling darkness. As several demons saw Michael and Dheer approach, they began to harangue them from above. Michael ignored their vitriolic harassment and kept his eyes on Samson, who was a few paces ahead of them.

As Samson was escorted into the common area in the temple, the crowd burst out in great cheers, as if their own champion had entered an arena. Just as the devils had opened up on Michael and Dheer with all manner of cursing, so did the people of Gaza begin to cajole Samson, throwing objects at him and daring their former enemy to break away and make a fight of it.

Lucifer had perched himself just above the 40-foot image of Dagon, enjoying the spectacle. Rugio kept an eye on Michael, and ordered his warriors to remain alert to any sudden moves that the archangel might make.

"Michael appears out of place here," mused Lucifer sarcastically. "I hope we have not been discourteous hosts."

"This is our territory," observed Pellecus. "He has no authority here."

"And he loves to be the one in authority," added Kara spitefully. "And Dheer simply looks ridiculous."

"Wait until Samson is made to bow," said Lucifer. "It shall be he that looks ridiculous—he and the Most High!"

A trumpet sounded long and low, and the crowd quieted down. The lord of Gaza, a slimly built man, nodded to the high priest, who stood at the base of Dagon's image where his priests were making oblation to their god. He held up his hands and made the pronouncement:

"Our great god, the god of the five cities, has for twenty years seen the God of Samson humbled! Today, we honor our god, Dagon, by bringing his enemy Samson into his house…"

The crowd began to murmur against Samson, cursing him again. The high priest held up his hands once more to quiet them.

"I know many of you lost friends and family because of this man! Your hatred for him is understood by Dagon and welcomed by him! And now Samson has been brought low and shall be scourged by the priests of Dagon!"

Upon those words three of the high priest's men knocked Samson to his knees, forcing him to bow to Dagon in mock worship. The crowd began chanting Dagon's name as the priests lashed at his back time and again with whips, slicing into his skin and making him wince in pain. Michael looked at the devils in the sky, swirling about like violent storm clouds. He then looked up at Lucifer, who nodded to him most charmingly.

Dheer looked at Samson, wishing there was something he could do to help. He then glanced at Michael, who continued looking about the temple. A few more holy angels had arrived, but there was still nothing that any of them could do. The priests finished their scourging and walked back to where the high priest stood.

"Wait!" said Michael. "Look there!"

Dheer looked at Samson, expecting at any moment that the man would die. But instead he was…praying. He had begun to cry out to the Most High!

Lucifer also saw what was happening.

"He is crying out in fear to the Lord," said Kara. "How pitiful."

"Not in fear, Kara," said Lucifer. "In faith."

"This cannot be!" screeched Kara, who immediately flew to the high priest. He stood in front of the man and screamed, "Shawa!"

Shawa, who had inhabited the mind of the high priest for this occasion, looked up at Kara through the eyes of the high priest. Using the man's voice he answered him.

"Yes, my lord?" he asked.

"Did you say something, my lord?" asked someone, who had heard the voice of the high priest. Shawa ignored him.

"Samson is praying," Kara said nervously. "Put an end to it now!"

"At once!" the high priest said, and turned to Dori.

"Go and get him," he ordered. "Bring him here. We shall bind him between the two pillars and scourge him until he dies. That will teach him to pray to his God in the house of Dagon!"

Dori led a group of men to where Samson knelt, still praying. They grabbed him by the shoulders and dragged him to the two pillars on which the house rested. The pillars were made of wood and sat on stone bases about six feet apart. Samson was led to them and allowed to rest there while binding was found to tie him to the pillars. The high priest approached him.

"What have you to say now, Samson?" he asked.

Samson knew the place where he stood, as he had been in this place several times before. Knowing what he must do, he began to pray.

"O Lord, remember me," he began. "Strengthen me once more that I might avenge myself on my enemies!"

Shawa realized what was happening and determined to put a stop to it. He raised the high priest's hands to strike him—but as Samson finished praying, the Spirit of God began to come upon Samson. Shawa was paralyzed with fear in the Presence of the Lord, and pulled out of the high priest.

Michael and Dheer watched as the Spirit of God caused a brilliant light to begin manifesting all around Samson. Lucifer and Kara were astonished at what they were seeing. Kara began shouting orders to the angels under his command to incite the people to rise up and kill Samson now. Lucifer and Pellecus simply watched incredulously. Rugio decided to attack the man himself and flew headlong into a group of angels, who by now had begun gathering around God's Presence.

Wrestling with them, he broke free and pulled out his sword, enraged and ready to cut into Samson once and for all. He flew to Samson and raised his sword. As he brought it down it was met with a loud crash that forced the sword out of his hands. Michael had knocked Rugio's sword away with his own sword. Rugio cursed Michael.

A loud grating noise filled the temple and caused everyone to become quiet. The high priest, recovered from Shawa's invasion, looked down in horror at the base of the pillars between which Samson was standing. He was pushing them apart!

"Kill him now!" he ordered.

Several soldiers began rushing Samson, only to be tripped up by angels who stood before him. Devils began diving at him like black birds diving at bits of food on the ground. Shawa was insanely crying out that his temple must be preserved and begging Lucifer to help him.

"What can I do?" Lucifer demanded. "The Spirit of God is upon the man!"

Just as he finished these words, the first pillar cracked and toppled over, spilling the roof section above it and crushing the high priest beneath its wreckage. Panic hit the temple, and the combination of Samson's destruction along with the maniacal devils, who now were inciting fear among the people, threw everyone into confusion. A fire then broke out near the first pillar that had fallen. On the rooftop, where some three thousand had gathered, the people were desperately looking for an escape route.

"And now, O Lord, let me die with the Philistines," Samson prayed.

Lucifer could not believe that the man would actually kill himself to destroy the temple. He ordered Rugio to regain order among his troops, who were chasing about enjoying the carnage that was happening. To them death was intoxicating, and once people started dying they lost all control of themselves.

Samson, bloody and dust-covered from the destruction, pushed against the second pillar. The lord of the five cities ordered him killed immediately, and several guardsmen jumped into the court to cut him down. Before they could reach him, the pillar snapped in two and brought the main house down on Samson.

Dheer said a silent farewell to the man whom he had watched grow up from his very first day.

As the temple collapsed in a great cloud of dust, smoke, and debris, the image of Dagon also fell from its place and broke into pieces, killing hundreds in its collapse. As the roof began giving way, the people who had been enjoying the spectacle now found themselves falling headlong into the jagged debris. The lord of the five cities found himself trapped by the falling temple stones, and was cut down by a huge cornice as he fled through an archway. Then all was still, apart from an occasional moan from a dying Philistine. Thus Samson died along with the Philistines, having killed more of the Lord's enemies in death than he had in his entire life.

Chapter 7

"Truly the Lord has occasioned something great here tonight."

Bethlehem, 4 B.C.

Bakka watched as the skies around Bethlehem filled with angels. He was amazed at the spectacle and often wondered what it must be like as a human to be unable to see such splendor. He smiled at Eli, who was still talking about the history of his people to the men and boys seated around the fire. Bakka himself had been a part of some of the very events Eli was retelling.

An angel hailed Bakka as he strolled to the crest of the hill overlooking the little town below. How strange that it was so quiet—and yet there was so much activity going on, at least for an angel! Even the stars seemed brighter tonight—one star in particular.

"Quite a display," remarked Gabriel, who had returned from a short watch around the area. "The Host are magnificent tonight. It seems the sheep are not the only things on these hills this evening!"

Bakka smiled at the archangel.

"Truly the Lord has occasioned something great here tonight," he agreed. "But where is Michael? I should think that with a gathering this great he would be in the midst of it."

"Michael has a very important assignment of his own," said Gabriel, looking to the eastern plains stretching away from Bethlehem. "Very important indeed."

Road to Bethlehem, 4 B.C.

The donkey lumbered along the evening road, carefully placing one foot in front of the other as it ambled down the dark path. On its back was a woman, bundled up in the night air, and looking uncomfortable with every jerk of the animal. A man led the donkey, holding its reins as steady as he could so as to make the ride as smooth as possible.

Ordinarily he wouldn't go to such precautions. But this was no ordinary passenger—this was his beloved whose time to give birth was at hand. The man, a gentle looking person whose hands showed the marks of a trade, winced every time the donkey lurched a bit, as if he were feeling the discomfort of his wife.

For her part, the woman, a girl really of about 14, had borne the journey very well and had not complained a bit—except that she was very tired. She had striking eyes and was very much in love with her husband. They had left Nazareth quietly, so that they might take part in the census ordered by Caesar and not cause Mary any trouble because of her condition.

"Only a bit further, my love," said Joseph. "A few more miles and we shall be in Bethlehem for the night."

Mary said nothing, but glanced down at Joseph, giving him a weak smile. He was dusty and dirty from the trip, and traveling at night was certainly not easy. She thanked the Lord for the very bright star that had provided so much light for them in the dark evening.

Above them, Michael and a large troop of warriors followed along. They kept a sharp eye out for any sign of the enemy. The angels with Michael knew that not since they protected Moses from the crocodiles of the Nile had there been such an urgency to watch over a coming baby. But then, this was no ordinary baby who was to be born this night.

"I see the enemy circling about," observed Serus, who had left Gabriel at Bethlehem to meet the party coming in.

"The enemy has been circling ever since we left Nazareth," said Michael. "They haven't a chance to get through."

Serus nodded.

"They haven't yet shown themselves at Bethlehem," he said. "All that is there are a multitude of the Host and a few shepherds watching their sheep."

"It's early yet, my friend," said Michael, watching Joseph give a sip of water to Mary. "When we arrive in Bethlehem, the enemy will be waiting."

Gabriel and Bakka completed their rounds of the area, and came back near the shepherd encampment. Eli had taken a break from his story while the men drank some fresh water and ate some bread. Bakka watched Daniel get up and take his turn at the flocks, relieving one of the shepherds.

"I still do not understand the man," said Bakka. "He is so very bitter."

"He is very frightened," said Gabriel casually.

"Frightened?" asked Bakka. "About what?"

"You need to discover that tonight, Bakka," said Gabriel, leaving it at that.

Bakka remained silent for a moment as Eli, back in full form, continued his story. Upon the mention of David, Bakka looked at Gabriel.

"Ah, David," said Bakka. "He was one of my favorite assignments."

"As I recall, you were not the only angel assigned to David," said Gabriel playfully.

"Of course not," said Bakka. "But it was a great mission. It too started here, in Bethlehem—David's city! Yes, it was a great mission." He sighed.

"No greater than the one you are currently assigned to," said Gabriel. "I assure you."

Bakka acknowledged Gabriel's words and then continued.

"But David. Now there was a man who was quite a task for any angel! Called as a child, killer of giants, conqueror, lover…"

"Murderer," said Gabriel.

"Writer of psalms," continued Bakka.

"Adulterer," Gabriel said, watching Bakka's reaction.

"A man after God's own heart," said Bakka, daring Gabriel to second-guess *that* one. "God's own heart!"

"Yes he was indeed," said Gabriel, smiling at Bakka's passionate defense of one of Israel's greatest kings. "He demonstrated as much as any human being that God can work through imperfection to realize His perfect will. David was indeed a paradox."

"True, Gabriel," admitted Bakka. "David was a paradox. But he was a magnificent paradox."

Chronicles of the Host

Dark Days

Following the years of the judges, the people of Israel took it upon themselves to ask the Lord Most High to give them a king—so that they might be like the other nations. As if they needed to be like the other nations! Coordinated through the efforts of Shawa and the other dark lords, the Philistines became Lucifer's most effective weapon with which he raged against Israel. But there was not only an attack from without, but a rottenness from within. It came to a humiliating climax when Israel, led by Eli, the compromised high priest, and his corrupt sons, fought the Philistines at Aphek, and were soundly beaten—for the Lord Most High was not with them....

Canaan, 1070 B.C.

"I am happy to report that the Philistine army was completely successful," said Rugio. "Israel was routed utterly!"

"Well done, Rugio," said Kara, inwardly ecstatic at the humbling of Israel. The corruption of the priesthood had become one of his main thrusts, and now it was apparent that the Lord Most High had abandoned his high priest.

"And the Ark?" asked Lucifer pointedly.

"Captured, my prince," said Rugio proudly. "Shawa saw to that. He is with the Philistines carting it back to Ashdod."

"Excellent!" said Lucifer. "Ashdod is where the new house of Dagon has been established. How fitting."

Kara stood to speak.

"In the interest of sound strategy, would the Ark not be better placed in a more prominent city?" Kara suggested.

Pellecus looked at him scornfully.

"Any particular city in mind, Kara?" he asked.

"I believe that one of the cities under my direct authority would be more appropriate," he answered. "After all, Shawa is not exactly one of us."

"I sometimes question how you came to be one of us," said Pellecus.

"The Ark shall go to Ashdod," said Lucifer with a tone of finality. "Shawa has earned the right. And as he has assumed and built up the cult of Dagon, it is his to humble the symbol of the Presence of the Most High God!"

Kara was perturbed but knew better than to contest the issue.

"Very well," he said. "Allow the Ark to remain at Ashdod. It is certainly encouraging, but we must remain resolute. They will of course want it back."

Lucifer clasped his hands together. The Council watched him pace about, knowing him well enough to realize that he was formulating something significant in his mind. Behind him, the foothills of eastern Canaan could be seen over the top of the small Baal temple in which they were meeting.

Pellecus stood to speak. He pointed to an Asherah pole nearby, where a recent celebration to one of the Baals had taken place.

"This sort of nonsense represents the future of the Lord's Presence on earth," Pellecus remarked. "I believe that with the capture of the Ark, the people of God will disintegrate into the same nonsense that the worshipers of Baal have become accustomed to. Men always tend to idolatry—it is fixed in them as the sun is in the heavens. Mark me, my brothers, the Ark will become a lost memory to Israel, and soon they too shall be dancing around poles and attributing to the Most High the trappings of Canaanite gods!"

"I view things a bit differently," offered Lucifer. "True, having the Ark is a great victory for us. And it represents a repudiation of God's people by the Lord Himself. But ultimately the Ark will be a liability. I suggest that we make use of it as a point of pride for the time being—a trophy of sorts with which to humiliate Israel—and then destroy it and the Testimony within it. Then perhaps, Pellecus, these people will lapse into idolatry and disappear as a threat altogether."

"Yes, my prince," said Pellecus. "And with their idolatrous demise they will take with them the possibility of the Seed ever emerging!"

Lucifer seemed encouraged for the first time in a while. He looked at his Council with a proud countenance.

"Not since the days that we mapped out the beginning of this war in Heaven have I felt more sure that we are going to win," he said confidently. "We must win! The alternative is unbearable."

"So what do you suggest is our next action?" asked Kara, who had recovered from what he considered to be a rebuff of his request to be custodian of the Ark.

"The people themselves are dictating the next move," said Lucifer. "They are now clamoring for a king. Idiots! They would throw off the rule of the Lord for a king who would come from among their own petty ranks."

"A king in Israel?" surmised Pellecus. "Men leading men. It would be the beginning of the end for the covenant people of God!"

"All kings are prideful and corruptible," agreed Kara.

"Their hearts can be turned in an instant," said Rugio.

"Let Israel find her king," said Lucifer. "And in proclaiming a royal leader, they shall become like the nations around them— proud, corrupt, idolatrous—and ultimately separated from the Lord."

"And the Seed?" asked Kara. "What becomes of the prophecy?"

"Lost to history," said Lucifer calmly. "After all, Kara, how could the Lord possibly bring forth Israel's salvation from so common a nation?"

Chronicles of the Host
Israel's Progress

How indeed? And yet as was often the case, the Lord confounded the wise with the simple, the lofty with the profane. As for the Ark, just as Lucifer suspected, it became a liability causing all manner of disease to break out among the Philistines. Even the great image of Dagon collapsed and broke into two pieces in its presence. So it was that the Philistines sent the Ark back to Israel, glad to be rid of it.

The Kingdom Begins

And so it was that the people asked for a king—a king who would lead them into battle; a king who would see the yoke of the Philistines overthrown; a king who would bring glory to Israel. Thus the Lord, ever gracious, had the prophet Samuel anoint Saul, of the tribe of Benjamin, king over Israel. And Saul led Israel on a path of glory...for awhile. But, as the enemy knew would happen among humans, Saul became plagued by his own prideful heart, and the Lord soon rejected him as king.

Lucifer thought the idea of a king a colossal mistake on the part of the Lord, knowing that human kings tend toward corruption, and was delighted with Saul's erratic behavior. He sent Rugio and all his warriors to plague Israel with all manner of death and disease and filthy corruption as a result of the king's perverse rule. In the end, they knew that Saul would only help in ferreting out and destroying the line of the Seed once and for all. Corrupt kings could bring a nation down, and Lucifer would bide his time until Israel was destroyed and the prophecy with it....

As it turned out, the Most High had already considered a new king, from the line of Judah. He was neither a great hero, nor warrior, nor man of experience. This again was a great surprise to the Host, as we sought out in our own minds a champion of the people; but the Lord had already seen a champion elsewhere...a most unlikely champion...and a most unlikely king....

Near Bethlehem, 1030 B.C.

Michael and Bakka watched as the last of Jesse's sons came before Samuel at Bethlehem. None of these men was to become king. And yet the Lord had instructed the prophet to anoint one of Jesse's sons. Samuel seemed a bit flustered, and the six boys who had been rejected were each disappointed.

"Have you no other child?" asked Samuel.

Jesse looked at his sons standing in the room of their house. They looked back at him, as if hoping he might not mention their little brother.

"Well, of course there is David," said Jesse finally. "But he is just a lad. In fact, I didn't call him in because he didn't seem to be what you were searching for..." Jesse's voice trailed off in unintelligible embarrassment.

"Go and fetch you brother!" he ordered Shammah.

Bakka looked at Michael with puzzlement. He indicated David's brothers who stood as if in a stupor ever since being passed over by the prophet. All of them seemed fine candidates for king: They were tall, with strong features, and the look of royal confidence that can command armies.

When David walked in with Shammah, he saw his brothers standing on one side of the room, a stranger seated on the other side of the room, and his father in the middle—and all of them were looking at him. He started to ask his father what was going on when Samuel stood up and announced that this boy was to be anointed king.

As Samuel poured the anointing oil over David, Jesse wept with pride to see his youngest son so honored. The brothers were astonished, but sensed the reverence of the moment and bowed their heads solemnly. As Samuel laid his hands on David, the Spirit of the Lord came upon the boy like waves crashing on the shore. Michael and Bakka knelt in the Lord's Presence, and when the ceremony was over, they were suddenly charged with a new mission that concerned this shepherd boy who would one day be king.

"Leave me alone!"

Saul's soldiers ran into the room where the king lay on the floor, his hands covering his ears. He was beside himself, half weeping, half sputtering nonsense. Saul's attendant helped him to a couch and gave him some wine. Saul grasped the goblet and drank deeply of it. He wiped his chin with his cloak and looked at the servant.

"The dream, Highness?" asked the servant.

"The nightmare," said Saul, his cloak drenched in sweat. "Only this time I was not asleep. I was seated over there looking at a map when I felt something staring at me. I thought that perhaps a messenger had arrived, or a servant had come into the room. When I turned, I saw a hideous creature—black and ugly. It was jumping about the room shrieking at me in some accursed tongue. Just like the dream except this time I was awake. You believe me, don't you?"

"Yes, Highness," said the servant. "It is undoubtedly an evil spirit!"

Saul cradled his head in his hands. The attendant looked up at the other servant and shook his head in pity. The men helped Saul to his bed. He ordered them to stay in the room with him until he fell asleep. In a short time he was sleeping.

"Is he losing his mind?" whispered one of the servants, as they exited the room.

"No," said the other. "This is the hand of God. The Lord is punishing Saul for his disobedience. We must find a way to help him."

"But how?"

"We must find something that will take the king's mind off this torment," the other answered. "And I believe I know what that is!"

"Well?" asked the servant.

"Music," said the attendant. "Played by the young man I saw the other day. I am convinced that this man is filled with the Spirit of God and that he will be able to bring peace to Saul's mind."

The other man thought about it for a bit. He then asked, "Who is he?"

"David," said the attendant. "Son of Jesse of Bethlehem."

"Saul..."

"Saul..."

Saul opened his eyes, awakening to the sound of his name being called. At first he was disoriented, having been sleeping soundly for the first time in many days. He answered, "Yes, who is it?"

Bizarre laughter began to fill the room. Saul bolted up in his bed, the fear rising inside of him. He tried to call out to his servants but began to choke, as if something had hold of his throat.

It was then that he saw two small black hands with long fingers and claw-like nails releasing him, and a grim visage with yellow teeth and red eyes looking straight at him. The horrible face began to grin and make ape-like noises, as if laughing. Saul jumped out of bed and ran out of the room, finally able to scream for his servants.

The demon laughed hysterically, enjoying Saul's fright. It was a wisdom angel named Aziel who had been allowed by the Most High to gain entrance to Saul's mind in order to torment him. Aziel watched as Saul came back in the room with his servants. The king broke down completely and began weeping aloud.

"Get David at once!" said the servant.

The spirit, which had attached itself to Saul's head and was clawing away at his mind as if it was a potter working clay, lurched when the name *David* was spoken. He growled a low growl and watched as the servant disappeared to fetch David. Within a few minutes David came into the room and sat next to the king.

The king reclined on the couch and kept his eyes on David the whole time that David played. The evil spirit began screaming into Saul's mind in a furious effort to resist David's music. But the Spirit of God began to fill the room, and as the Lord's Presence began to calm Saul's fragile mind, the evil spirit could bear the music no longer. He vanished with a string of curses.

Saul finished off another cup of wine and then sat up, closing his eyes as he listened to the music. He was feeling better. When he seemed to drift off to sleep, David stopped playing and started to get up.

"Keep playing, boy," Saul said, his eyes still closed.

The servant gave David a scornful look and motioned for him to start playing again. David played for almost two hours, until the king was finally and definitely asleep.

"Remain close by in case we need you," whispered the servant. "The king may have need of you."

"I need to return to my father," David responded. "But I shall always be available to serve my king. All you need do is send for me and I will come quickly."

The servants watched as David departed. It was amazing to them that the music of this insignificant shepherd boy could calm the fears of their king. David would be one to watch....

Shawa came into the room and strolled over to Aziel, who had returned upon David's departure. The strange arrangement with the Lord was working out splendidly, he thought. So long as the king of Israel was undermined, what matter if the Most High was involved.

"I would never have thought that the Lord would be so agreeable as to invite our torment of His anointed," said Aziel, when he saw Shawa.

Shawa nodded in agreement, looking at the now sleeping Saul.

"You certainly look the part of a horrid wretch," said Shawa. "Quite convincing."

"Saul is king," said Aziel. "If he were an ordinary human I would be less hideous. But since he is king of our greatest enemies, I wanted to be extraordinarily frightening—at least to a human mind. I must respect the Lord's tolerance of my torment, but I do not have to respect His anointing of this man!"

"You mean former anointing," said Shawa. "There is a new anointed. The Most High is finished with this one."

"A new anointed?" said Aziel, still alarmed by Shawa's revelation. "A new king over Israel? You mean David! Shall I begin tormenting him?"

"You forget that you are operating under the authority of the Most High God," said Shawa. "And you are assigned to Saul personally by Lucifer until you are relieved. I suspect the Lord wants to use you until He makes a point."

"King David," mused Aziel. "Incredible."

"But true. That foolish old judge Samuel has anointed David, the son of Jesse, to be Israel's new king," Shawa continued. "A mere boy of thirteen or fourteen."

"Again I ask you—is he to be destroyed?" asked Aziel.

"Not easily," admitted Shawa. "This one is a man who is after the Lord's very own heart. His is a very special anointing."

He smiled at Aziel and continued. "However, Lucifer and the Council of Liberation have been doing some anointing of their own."

"Really?" said Aziel. "A counter anointing of sorts?"

"Something like that," said Shawa. "We have had our eye on someone very special. Handpicked from the entire nation of the Philistines. Raised in a hostile family environment that was constantly under assault by Kara's angels. A brooding, angry child who grew into a brooding, angry man. A killer of brutal quality and a freak of nature who will strike terror into the heart of Israel. A murderous beast whose only thought is to bring down the Lord's anointed. And perhaps most importantly, a man personally groomed by Rugio for such a time as this."

"Who is this man?" asked Aziel.

"Goliath," said Shawa. "And he is even now on his way to challenge Israel!"

Chronicles of the Host

Goliath

Indeed, the Philistines were at that moment approaching Saul's position from their country in the south. When Saul got word of their encroachment, he rallied his army to oppose them. The two armies faced off on either side of the valley of Elah. The Philistines cursed Saul and dared him to come out and fight their champion, laughing at the people of God and blaspheming the name of the Most High.

We of the Host encamped ourselves around Saul's army, disposed in ranks as Michael ordered, and awaited the attack. The enemy angels, like their human allies, jeered at us from the other side of the valley, cursing the Lord and daring the holy angels to confront them. From time to time, the brute Goliath, a man nine feet tall, came out into the valley and called for a fight to the death between himself and Israel's champion. Rugio stood with him, proud of his creature, and mocked Michael as a commander of cowardly humans and angels.

For 40 days we endured the shame of this intrusion. The angels would have attacked immediately to avenge the name of our Lord, but Michael, honor bound not to interfere until released to do so, held back the Host. There was nobody in Saul's army who would dare face Goliath. We could only wait and hope for a champion to come out of Israel....

Rugio and Lucifer stood next to Goliath, who was putting his armor on once more. His dresser was by now used to the routine, and handed each piece of the heavy equipment to the man whom he was careful not to cross. Goliath took his helmet and strapped it on. Grabbing his javelin, he slung it onto his back. He pointed to the shield, an enormous disc, and his nervous shield bearer took it and went out ahead of him.

"This man is an absolute work of inspiration, Rugio," said Lucifer. "I have heard precious little else but how Goliath has stymied the whole nation of Israel."

"He is a fearful man—to humans," agreed Rugio.

"Fear is a great weapon, Rugio," said Lucifer, as they followed Goliath out of his tent and into the sunny day. "It is one of our greatest weapons. Fear can stop a man—or an army. It can put the plans of God in jeopardy and prevent the destiny of nations from being fulfilled. Fear can even stop a prophecy, Rugio."

Rugio looked at Lucifer, finally understanding the importance of his mission.

"Yes, my warrior," Lucifer purred. "If we can keep Israel in fear; if we can keep her armies confused; if we can keep her kings harassed, we can prevent the Seed of the woman from coming to fruit."

"I have so poisoned his mind and heart that his hatred for Israel will always drive him," said Rugio. "He shall not rest until he has destroyed Saul and all his sons. He will keep them in fear, my lord."

Lucifer pointed to the army of Saul. The glimmering numbers of angels shined in the distance over the whole side of the valley. Above them. Their own ranks of demons were seething and ready for battle, haranguing the other side as usual.

"All of those angels—a sea of them painting the sky white—cannot stop one man from being afraid, which prevents the will of God from happening. I tell you, Rugio, the Seed cannot be born in soil that is bloody with fear. It must have faith to root in. And where there is fear, there is no faith!"

Great cheers went up from among the Philistine soldiers as Goliath came out. He ignored the others and headed out of the camp. Standing at the crest of the gently sloping valley, he scanned the other side. In plain sight were the banners and tents of the army of Saul. He looked into the middle of the valley. Nobody. It would be another day without a challenge. Goliath was getting weary of the cowardice of Israel.

Today he would taunt them with a viciousness that he had not yet unleashed. He looked to his shield bearer and ordered him into the valley. The men cheered Goliath on as he headed down into Elah. Rugio bade Lucifer farewell and accompanied his monstrous charge for the day's challenge.

Chapter 8

"If we bring down the kings, we bring down the nation."

The angels on Saul's side of the valley were becoming more and more restless. When would the king make a move? How long would they have to endure this intrusion upon their honor and the honor of the Most High? They watched as Goliath and his shield bearer approached the center of the valley—again.

Michael ignored the complaints of the angels and focused instead upon the battle at hand. He ordered the Host to remain in their formations and be prepared for anything. He had warned that at some point the battle would begin and that they were to remain watchful until the actual conflict broke out.

The men of Saul were alerted to Goliath's approach and quickly took to their positions. Apart from a few officers barking orders the men remained disconcertingly quiet—none wanted to admit that the reason this had gone on for 40 days was that they were afraid. It remained the untold shame that hung over them all. Some thought it was Saul's duty to fight the monster. Others felt that they should simply yield this ground and go on. And so the men watched as Goliath stopped at his usual place in the valley to issue his usual challenge.

"There is Rugio," said an angel.

"That proud spirit," said another. "Lord Michael! Why don't you go down and talk a bit with Rugio? Send him back with a little humility."

"Quiet!" shouted Michael. "I want no nonsense in the ranks!"

"Michael! Michael!"

Michael looked down and saw Bakka coming toward him.

"What are you doing here!?" Michael demanded. "You are supposed to remain with David at all times!"

Bakka was taken aback at Michael's temper.

"But I am with David, my lord," said Bakka. "Jesse has sent David here with some food for his brothers and their officers."

Michael scanned the field until he saw David talking with his brothers. He pointed them out to Bakka.

"Very well," the archangel said. "Stay with him until he delivers the food. And then accompany him back to his father. He is the anointed one, Bakka. This war is meaningless if the enemy gets to him."

"Yes, my lord," said Bakka, who immediately turned to find David.

Bakka found David just as he had emptied his sack of its contents. The brothers greedily devoured the bread their brother had brought them and inquired about their father. As David spoke to them the air was suddenly filled with a booming voice coming from the valley. David turned and listened:

"Why will nobody come out and fight with me? Is there not a man in Israel? Choose a man! I am a Philistine and you are servants of Saul, your king. Send a man out to fight me. If your man kills me, then we will give way and you shall win the battle. If I win, then you will give ground to us."

David waited for someone from Israel to respond to the Philistine champion. He looked around at the men, whose eyes were locked upon the giant and whose hearts were sunken. Even his own brothers made no move to respond.

"Why is he getting away with this?" David asked innocently.

"Quiet," said Shammah, his brother. "You are a boy. This is man's work. Now be still and stop asking stupid questions."

Goliath was angry that nobody would take up the challenge. He spoke again, this time in a much louder tone: "I defy Israel today! I defy your worthless God! Give me a man to fight! I shall wait your answer!"

David again waited for someone from Israel to stand and oppose this man. He even heard among the ranks that the king would reward anyone who killed this menace with marriage to his daughter and no more taxes for his family. And yet nobody took up the challenge! Not yet, anyway.

"What are you all sitting around for?" said David anxiously. "Here is this uncircumcised dog defying our holy God! Will nobody fight this man?"

Eliab, the oldest brother of David, angrily denounced David in front of the others. "Listen to me, David," he said. "You are only here because you wanted to see the fight. These are warriors here. We will deal with this when the time comes. Now get back to your few sheep, little boy!"

David rose up, disgusted and amazed at the behavior of the army, and began walking toward the tent of Saul.

Where is he going? Bakka wondered.

Saul was seated on a small couch in his tent. From time to time Goliath's voice echoed through the air, causing many uncomfortable looks among the generals and officers with him.

"Perhaps one of our archers could get close enough to…"

"No!" said Saul, cutting off the officer. "That would be craven. I need a man who will oppose this man. I don't even care if he lives as long as he upholds our honor."

A guard entered the tent and whispered to one of the officers. Saul looked up as the officer glanced at Saul and then nodded his head to the man, telling him to wait outside.

"Well?" asked Saul, reaching for a cup of wine poured by his steward.

"It seems there is a man who seems willing to fight the Philistine," said the officer. "He is newly arrived at the camp and was quite offended by the giant's defiant challenge."

"We are all offended by him," said Saul. He then thought about it for a moment. "But of course we are not newly arrived. Perhaps there is something to be said for a fresh perspective. Send for him!"

The officer nodded and left the tent.

"At least we will field *somebody* and finish this miserable business," Saul said.

Bakka watched as Saul's officer walked over to where David stood near his brothers. The angel had suspected something like this might happen. Ever since fighting had broken out and his brothers had left, David had spoken of little else to Jesse than of joining his brothers in the war against the Philistines.

The officer approached David and took him aside. David's brothers all watched the scene, wondering what was happening. David looked at Eliab nervously. Eliab walked over to the officer and addressed him.

"May I ask, sir, what is going on with my brother?" Eliab asked.

"King's business," came the gruff reply. "Come on, boy!"

David walked off with the man and they headed toward the tent of Saul. Some of the men who had heard David boasting were now snickering among themselves.

"That will teach him to come up here and question our honor!" said one of the men. The other laughed and nodded his head in agreement.

Just as the man said this, Goliath railed once more, issuing his challenge. The two men looked at each other with the same frightened look that had been in so many eyes for the past 40 days.

"Anyway, that will teach him," the man said, his voice trailing off.

"Not you!" said Saul, as David walked into the tent.

"This is the lad who plays music for me," he continued. "David, what are you doing here?"

"I am here to fight the Philistine," said David.

The officers in the room smiled among themselves at this boy's audacity. Saul looked at them and shared in their humor. He then turned back to David.

"Go on back to your sheep, David," he said. "I need a man. A warrior. Someone who is skilled in war. You cannot go up against this beast." He stood up and brushed his hand against David's cheek. "Although I must say it is refreshing to see one among my ranks willing to fight." The men in the room all looked to the ground or in other embarrassed directions as he said this.

Bakka arrived and stood next to David, placing his hand on the boy's shoulder. He was proud of David but could only wonder if perhaps he would soon be assigned to someone else. Suddenly, the Spirit of the Lord came upon David. Bakka backed away and bowed low before the Lord's Presence in the room. David began to speak under the Lord's anointing:

"My king," he began, "you are right that I am a shepherd. I have tended my father's sheep. But when one of the sheep was in danger I acted. Majesty, when a lion or a bear attacked and took one of the sheep, I chased it down. One time I killed a lion after it turned on me."

He began acting out his duel with the lion.

"I grabbed the animal by his hair and I killed him and took the lamb from his mouth. I also killed a bear."

He looked up at Saul with a holy intensity.

"King Saul, the Lord Most High, who protected me from the lion and the bear, will now deliver me from the hand of this Philistine dog!"

Saul looked at the boy, tears in his eyes. He ordered his armor brought in so that David could be outfitted. But David grimaced at Saul's equipment.

"You expect me to wear these things?" he asked.

"This is the king's personal armor," said one of the men. "It would be an honor."

"Yes, and heavy," said David. "I don't need these things."

"The Lord be with you," said Saul as David exited the tent.

Abner, Saul's chief commander, added, "And the Lord be with all of us when this boy is laid out."

Bakka had never been so proud of a human as he was of David at that very moment. And he knew, like David, that the Lord was with him. Now he understood the significance of Samuel's anointing of David. He truly was destined to become king over Israel.

Bakka followed David down to a nearby stream, where the younger man carefully selected five stones from the bed. He placed them in his bag and then prayed for a few minutes.

"Now you will see the Lord's deliverance of Israel," came a voice.

It was Michael.

"He will kill the giant then?" said Bakka hopefully.

Michael looked at David praying.

"The Lord is with him, Bakka," he said. "What more does he need? If only humans realized that their faith in God's ability makes all the difference!"

"Shall I go with him on the field of battle?" Bakka asked.

"We shall both accompany David," said Michael, smiling. "Goliath is not the only one out there needing humbling."

Rugio was aware that the Spirit of God was visiting the camp of Saul. He had seen the Host give way to the visitation and had become immediately suspicious. Lucifer, too, had seen the Lord's Presence in the camp and had joined Rugio in the center of the valley where Goliath now rested.

"What is going on now?" asked Rugio angrily, as he saw Lucifer approach. "Why is He here?"

"Don't mind Him," said Lucifer. "He never stays long. Perhaps one of the men is actually praying!"

"Has it come to that?" said Rugio in a mocking tone.

"The people of God have lost their nerve," said Lucifer. "We need not worry about them sending anyone to fight your man."

"Really?" asked Rugio, looking toward the Israelite camp. "Then who is that?"

Goliath's shield bearer stood and ran to the giant. The man pointed to a figure approaching him from the enemy side.

The Philistine soldiers cheered loudly, gathering their weapons, as Goliath stood to meet the challenger. He was relieved that someone was going to end this incessant delay in the war. The shield bearer was astonished as the challenger came into view—it was a boy!

Goliath looked around to see if someone was coming behind David. Surely the Israelites were not expecting this boy to do their fighting. He scratched his head, confused and expecting that this was some sort of trick.

"Give me my shield," he said.

"Well, well," said Lucifer. "I see that Israel finally found a champion. A boy champion. Even I never would have guessed *that* one!"

Michael and Bakka ignored the taunts and stayed close to David.

"You know the rules, Archangel," said Rugio. "You may not interfere with this battle. This is between humans!"

"Poor King Saul," added Lucifer. "Reduced to sending a boy to be slaughtered because he could not find a man in Israel!"

"This is the boy whom Samuel anointed king, is it not?" asked Rugio. "He shall be killed before his reign even begins!"

"His blood shall run on this field just as Samuel's oil ran over his head," said Lucifer. "Such a wasted anointing!"

"There shall indeed be blood on this field, Lucifer," said Michael finally. "But it will be the blood of a dog, not a boy."

The closer Goliath got to David, the angrier he became. Perhaps Saul was mocking him, sending this boy out to fight him. Was this what Saul's army was made of?

"Hey boy!" shouted Goliath loudly enough for the Philistines to hear him. "Go back and fetch your father!"

Rugio and Lucifer enjoyed Goliath's comment, as did the men on the Philistine line, who howled with laughter. Michael noticed that the swirling, dark cloud of devils were also enjoying the spectacle.

"Is that your weapon?" Goliath continued, pointing to the staff that David held. "What am I? Some sort of dog that you are coming at me with sticks? By Dagon I will feed your body to the wild animals!"

David studied his adversary—a nine-foot killing machine covered with armor from head to toe, and holding a javelin with a head that weighed some 15 pounds. He wore a bronze helmet and a coat of scale armor. He stood proud and towering, with yellow teeth and eyes as black as his heart.

The Philistines burst out in laughter again.

Lucifer sensed that something was happening as David stopped a few meters from Goliath. He could see an aura shimmering around David, the anointing of the Most High beginning to create a wavy light all around him.

"Better get this over with quickly," he said to Rugio.

"Right," said Rugio, who also saw the Spirit resting upon David. Rugio quickly entered into Goliath. The giant felt a surge of strength building inside him. He looked down at David and continued to mock him.

Michael placed his hand on David's shoulders as the boy began to speak:

"You come at me with sword and spear and javelin? You think those things will overcome the Lord Most High? I come at you in the name of the Lord Almighty—the living God of the armies of Israel! What's more, it is you who shall be cut down and fed to the wild beasts. It is your head that shall be removed from your evil body!"

David took a step forward. "The battle belongs to the Lord of Hosts, and He will deliver you into our hands!"

Upon that declaration Rugio was thrown from Goliath by a mighty force. Lucifer, too, was knocked over as the faith of David met with the word of God. Lucifer and Rugio looked at each other, worried for the first time about what was happening. Michael continued to stand behind David, and Bakka watched from a distance, making sure no other enemy angels tried to interfere.

"Get back into Goliath and kill David now!" Lucifer ordered.

Rugio flung himself back into the giant just as he was raising his javelin to kill David. Goliath once more felt a surge of power as Rugio inflamed his mind to kill the boy! Goliath stepped up, his javelin at the ready. It should be an easy mark; the boy was without armor and close enough for a quick kill.

Bakka looked at Michael, wondering what he would do. But Michael simply remained behind David in quiet confidence. David reached into his bag and pulled out one of the stones he had picked up a few minutes before.

"Watch him," said Lucifer. "Kill him now!"

David took the stone and placed it in the pouch of his sling and began swinging it in a wide, circular arc around and around. It was so quiet on the battlelines that both the men of Israel and Philistia could hear the whirring sound of the sling.

Suddenly Lucifer saw the Lord's Presence manifest itself around David. He cautioned Rugio, who had already seen what was happening. Goliath raised his javelin and took aim at David. *This should pin him neatly to the ground*, he thought to himself.

It was his last thought.

David let go the rock that was in his sling; a hand of brilliant light took hold of the stone and sent it soaring toward Goliath. The giant never knew what had hit him. The stone cracked open his forehead and entered his brain.

Goliath simply stood there for a moment, dazed. His shield bearer wondered what Goliath was waiting for—then he noticed a small trickle of blood coming down the front of the giant's face from underneath the bronze helmet. Goliath began to swoon a bit.

Rugio abandoned the giant as he felt Goliath's life ebbing. He looked at Lucifer, who was aghast that the man they had raised to kill was himself dying. Suddenly Goliath fell down and hit the ground face first. He was dead.

Lucifer glared at Michael and vanished, vowing that David would never know peace. Rugio also vanished, but not before he witnessed David grab Goliath's sword and cut off the giant's head. A great roar went up from Saul's camp as the army of Israel swept into the valley, charging the Philistines. With their champion dead, the Philistines lost heart and fled the battlefield.

Michael and Bakka watched David being congratulated by the men of Israel. Even his brothers were proud of him and hoisted him upon their shoulders. Saul came out to meet David. Looking at the severed head of the dead giant, some of his officers showed him Goliath's enormous weaponry.

But Saul was not looking at the weapons. He watched the men crowding around David, patting him on the back and offering to serve under him should he decide to join the army.

"A great victory for Israel," said Abner to Saul. "And for you!"

"A great victory indeed," said Saul, watching the men carry David off toward the camp. "But for me? Perhaps I have traded one giant for another."

"Sir?" asked Abner.

"Never mind, commander," said Saul. "For now."

Bethlehem, 4 B.C.

"Those were such glorious days for Israel," said Eli, as he relived the moment when David became a hero. "David became one of the greatest kings in Israel's history."

"Did he really kill the giant with one stone?" asked Jarod excitedly.

"One stone is all it took to bring down the giant," said Eli. "But David knew that it was not his sling or stone that brought Goliath down—it was the power of the Lord!"

"And David became a great hero!" chimed in Joshua. "David, the giant killer!"

Jarod rolled his eyes at Joshua.

"David, the giant killer," repeated Bakka. "Those were certainly marvelous days of service to the Most High, weren't they, Gabriel?"

"Every day is marvelous in service to the Lord," said Gabriel. "Even now, tonight, you are assigned to a marvelous situation."

"Yes, so you have told me," said Bakka, looking back at Daniel, who was just returning from his watch. "But Daniel is certainly no David."

"No indeed," said Gabriel. "But David had his challenges as well."

Bakka nodded. He recalled how, after killing Goliath, David had become a national hero; how Saul became violently jealous of David and sought to kill him; how David fled Saul's presence and was on the run for many years; how Saul and his son Jonathan died fighting the Philistines; how David became king in Jerusalem and brought the Ark back to the holy city; how David committed a great sin against the Lord by having an adulterous affair with Bathsheba and having her husband murdered; how his own sons rebelled against him. It was certainly a life that was both glorious and shameful.

"And yet, the Lord loved David and faithfully brought him through the many obstacles he faced," remarked Bakka.

"Yes, but remember, Bakka, the Lord never excuses sin," said Gabriel. "There is always a consequence to disobedience. Somebody must pay when a sin is committed. Sin never occurs without a price—sometimes a very great price!"

Near Jerusalem, 988 B.C.

Somewhere near Jerusalem, in an olive grove of a great estate, Pellecus was reporting to the Council on his findings about the state of David's kingdom. He had been assigned to discover a weakness, a point of attack that could be used to bring David down as he approached the end of his reign.

"Thus far," Pellecus continued, "we have had varying degrees of success. The incident with Bathsheba, the revolt of Absalom, various other indiscretions—all of these have been modestly successful in challenging David's authority. Yet the man manages to come back—to remain true to the Most High…"

"And why is that?" asked Kara. "What is so special about this man that he is able to withstand our plans against him?"

"Faith," interjected Lucifer. "He may be imperfect. And surely he has had his defeats. But in the end he is a man of faith. Ever since I saw him kill Goliath, I knew that he would be a problem for us."

Rugio growled a low growl at the thought of Michael standing behind David that day in the valley of Elah.

"I vowed that day that I would find some way to trip him up—to destroy him and make him lose face before the Lord. Not merely to avenge that day at Elah. But because David is a critical part of the prophecy which is pointed against us."

"The Seed," said Kara. "Always the Seed!"

"Yes, Kara," said Lucifer. "The Seed. The Lord has decreed that the Seed shall come through the house of David—that a king shall one day rise in Israel through the line of David! The Lord has made an everlasting covenant with David. We must do whatever we can to discourage him and his children after him until this accursed line is destroyed once and for all. We bloodied his life enough that the Lord will not permit him to build the great temple in Jerusalem. That shall be left to one of the other sons of Judah."

"The Lord has done us a favor really," observed Pellecus. "Until recently we had lost sight of the Seed. Now we know that it shall come through the tribe of Judah. The rest can do as they please—but Judah will remain our focus from this point forward."

"Precisely," agreed Lucifer. "If we can bring down the kings we can bring down the nation—and once the nation is destroyed, the Seed will have no place to root."

"We have been over this time and again," complained Kara. "And yet we have never been able to sufficiently bring down this man!"

"It is not a single blow that brings down a great man," said Lucifer. "It is a constant chipping away that destroys even the mightiest of men. Remember that! Persistent and unrelenting attack is what will cause the godly ones to stumble."

"I have been working on some of his generals," said Rugio. "There are several who are ripe for revolt. Perhaps…"

Lucifer cut him off.

"Until now our attacks have been from the outside," he said. "At this point in his life, David has much to be proud about. I suggest therefore that we hit him at the point of pride. There is nothing more susceptible to defeat than a proud heart."

"Shall we take something from him?" asked Kara. "Something in which he places great pride?"

"No, Kara," said Lucifer. "Rather than take from his pride, we shall inflame it. I suggest we create something that will be born in David's heart, but will bring shame on the nation." He looked over the others. "And to make certain that it is done well, it will be something in which I am personally involved…"

Chronicles of the Host
Satan's Fury

True to his word, Lucifer the adversary rose up against Israel. Appealing to David's pride, he tempted David to number his army! Joab, David's great commander, warned him against this foolishness, for even he saw it as a prideful move that could also expose the nation's power to the enemy. But Lucifer had set the hook deeply, and David sinned against the Lord by conducting a military census.

So the Lord sent His Angel to ravage the land, causing great calamity. If not for the Lord's great mercy upon Israel, and His compassion for David, the nation might have been utterly devastated. Thus did Satan tempt David into a grievous sin at the end of his reign. Nevertheless, David was recorded in the chronicles as one of the greatest kings in Israel—a man who saw by faith the day when the Seed of the woman would arrive and a greater King in Israel would reign forever.

The Great Temple

Upon the death of King David, his son Solomon became king in Israel. Solomon ordered the building of a glorious temple in Jerusalem. It was to be a holy place that honored God's Presence on earth, and would be a wonder to behold throughout the world. Artisans and craftsmen skilled in their labor created a magnificent house of praise, and on the day of its dedication, the Glory of the Lord so filled the place that the priests could no longer remain in the building. Such times those were for the Host when God manifested His Glory among mere men!

But...as ever with humans, the tendency to rebellion remained alive and well, and it was not long before Lucifer would take advantage of the proud hearts of men to lead the nation astray....

Chapter 9

"The dream ended at Eden."

Jerusalem, 940 B.C.

"Solomon is dead!"

Lucifer looked up at Kara, who had made the announcement in his usual dramatic fashion. "We can now proceed one more step removed from David."

Kara entered the garden area of a ruined Canaanite temple at the base of Mount Carmel where Lucifer and Pellecus were meeting to discuss the latest developments in Israel.

"Yes, Kara," said Lucifer. "Your news is welcome but also late. We have known since he took his last wretched breath."

Kara glared at Pellecus, who returned the glare with a "yes, I am the one who told him" smirk. Kara fought the desire to lash out at Pellecus, preferring to deal with him when he was not with Lucifer.

"Solomon was quite an opponent," said Lucifer. "He will not be missed. Although I must say that at the end of his life he realized how much of it he threw away in useless, human pursuits."

"Nevertheless the temple was built because of him," said Kara. "Just one more step toward the fulfillment of the prophecy against us."

He looked about the area with an annoyed expression.

"Where is Rugio?" he demanded. "He is supposed to be with us in developing our long-range strategy against Israel."

"Rugio is assigned to another nation," said Lucifer. "He is in Nineveh."

"Assyria? Why is he there?" asked Kara with a mixture of suspicion and jealousy that Rugio was assigned a new task.

"The Assyrians are a crude and warlike people," said Pellecus, assuming a lecturing posture. "They are also a nation that is on the rise and by our estimation will become a threat to Israel within the next century."

"Rugio shall help to encourage those cruel tendencies that are a part of these people," said Lucifer. "Therefore the three of us shall determine our course for Israel."

Kara sat down on a broken wall overgrown with wild grapevines. Lucifer had decided that the best way to crack the nation was to divide it from within. He pulled on one of the vines near Kara.

"This vine was once trained and pruned and fruitful," Lucifer began. "But over time it became wild and unrestrained and as a result the fruit it bears is not good." He plucked a tiny cluster of grapes. "Like this vine, Israel is ripe for barrenness."

He began to pace in the garden as he spoke.

"As Kara said, with David and Solomon now removed, their reigns will become a distant memory—phantoms of a glory that once was Israel. The nation will become unrestrained, untrained, slothful in the things of God. The temple will become a place of empty religion rather than true worship. And as the nation disintegrates from within, we shall present new adversaries from abroad! Nations like Assyria, Egypt, and Babylon shall rise up and bring the people into bondage—because they will have forsaken the Most High God for the gods of this world!"

"Wonderful plan," said Kara. "But where to start?"

"Actually Kara, you shall spearhead the latest thrust," said Lucifer casually.

"I'm honored, of course," said Kara. "And I shall not let you down!"

"Yes," remarked Pellecus. "Just as you did not let us down in Egypt."

"You are completely suited to this task, Kara," Lucifer interjected before Kara could respond to Pellecus's offensive remark. "The new king in Israel..."

"Rehoboam," offered Pellecus. "The son of Solomon."

"Yes, Rehoboam," continued Lucifer. "He is the son of Solomon but without the wisdom or the diplomatic sharpness." He looked at Kara. "In short, Kara, he is vain, ambitious, and a complete fool."

"Which is why you are so perfectly suited to this task," said Pellecus dryly.

"As I said before, this kingdom is ripe for division from within," said Lucifer. "The people are already groaning from the burdensome taxes placed upon them by Solomon so he could complete his building projects. They are weary and are looking for relief. I suggest that Rehoboam's arrogance might be used to give them something quite different. Influence him, Kara, to drive the people into the ground!"

"An oppressed people will cry out for liberation," Pellecus threw in. "Possibly even revolution. Political chaos will result and within a few generations Israel shall disappear as a nation and as a threat to us."

"By then the Assyrians shall have taken prominence in the region and, with a bit of guidance from Rugio, will greedily devour whatever crumbs of Israel are left!"

Kara nodded in agreement. He liked the plan. If men could be destroyed from within, why not an entire nation? Corruption begets corruption—whether for an individual or a state. Yes, this would do quite nicely!

"It will be an honor to serve in this matter," said Kara dutifully.

"Go to Shechem at once," said Pellecus. "Rehoboam has just been anointed there and is gathering with his council to discuss his first action as king. And with Jeroboam back from exile in Egypt, things will get very interesting."

"Jeroboam?" asked Kara. "Ah yes. He rebelled against Solomon, and the Lord promised him that he should be king over a divided Israel one day!"

"Exactly, Kara," said Lucifer. "So all we are really doing is helping the Lord along in one of His own prophesies. The kingdom will be divided. The Lord has decreed it. But we can use what the Lord has decreed and turn it to our advantage."

"I shall have the people under Rehoboam's heels in a week!" boasted Kara.

"He is already headstrong, Kara," cautioned Lucifer. "All he needs is a little encouragement. Nothing more."

"Have no worry, my prince," said Kara, smiling. "I have become quite adept at encouraging humans!" Kara then vanished.

Lucifer looked toward the heavens.

"Once again the Lord must bow to the free will of men," he said. "That is the critical fact with which He must contend. He set up the rules and now He must abide by them!" He indicated the wildly growing grapevine again. "Humans are lost to Him. Unruly and unfruitful like this vine. They will never adequately find their way to Him—not on their own, anyway."

The assembly at Shechem was hopeful. A new king might mean a new manner of ruling. Elders representing the various tribes, administrators appointed by Solomon, Jeroboam and his faction—political opponents normally—found themselves bound together in an uneasy alliance as they met at Shechem. The binding issue? Reform. They hoped that the new king, Rehoboam, would lead Israel into a new, reformed kingdom.

Kara was not at all impressed with the human way of doing things. He sneered at the silly pride of the king and his young aides as they came out to greet the others in the governor's palace at Shechem.

He walked over near Rehoboam and studied him. Rehoboam was everything that had been described to him—arrogant, confident, and tactless—a sure recipe for rebellion! Kara noticed that the men who advised him were not much better. Rehoboam had surrounded himself with younger men who had not been in the service of his father. It was fresh voices he was interested in hearing—not the same old droning of his father's court.

Rehoboam seated himself in the room and his aides stood behind him. Kara positioned himself to the right of the king to watch the proceedings. After the preliminary introductions of the assembly, Rehoboam invited the various representatives to speak. He had come to receive their homage and oaths of loyalty. They had come to extract a promise of reform. Kara could hardly wait to see how this would play out.

"It is fitting, my lord, that we meet together in Shechem on the occasion of your new reign," began one of the elders of Israel. "As you know, it was in Shechem that Joshua renewed our covenant with the Lord our God. It is our hope that with your reign a renewal of sorts might occur, concerning your manner of governance over us, who are your loyal subjects..."

As the elder spoke, Keriah, Rehoboam's chief counselor, whispered something in his ear. Rehoboam's eyes shot a glance to the back of the room, scanning the faces until he saw a particular man. He looked at Keriah, who nodded in affirmation.

"I would hear from Jeroboam straight away," said Rehoboam, interrupting the elder, "—our former brother in exile now returned to our kingdom."

The crowd made a low murmur as Jeroboam slowly made his way to the front of the assembly hall. Some of the ministers who had served Solomon and had been a part of Jeroboam's exile were clearly ill at ease at seeing him once more in a royal court of Israel. Jeroboam ignored the tension in the room and bowed his head low before the king, standing silently before him.

Rehoboam studied the man for a few moments. He drank in the moment of seeing his father's former enemy now humbly standing before him. If only Solomon could see this! The room awaited the words that might mean the difference between peace and civil war.

"You are most welcome to our court," said Rehoboam, "after such an extended leave from our service."

"It is indeed wonderful to be back in the nation I love, majesty," said Jeroboam. "Although I fear that not everyone in this room shares the sentiment!" He smiled.

Rehoboam laughed aloud, as did a few of the courtiers. The king looked at his new, young group of ministers with which he had surrounded himself.

"I have no idea what he is talking about, do you?" he said humorously. After a few seconds the king turned his attention back to Jeroboam.

"We sent for you because we have heard that you are wanting to present some...shall I say...grievances to the court," the king began. He motioned for his cup, which a steward immediately brought to him. He sipped the wine and continued. "I also understand that, much as some of these among you would rather not have you here at all, they need your voice in court. This is your moment, Jeroboam, to speak frankly."

The room became quiet as Jeroboam began to speak.

"It is no secret, majesty, that in the time of your father, the great Solomon, he and I had a falling out…"

"Falling out?" said the king in a mocking tone. "I thought it more a running out." The room exploded in nervous laughter.

"Yes, majesty," continued Jeroboam. "Truly I was run out of Israel because of certain disagreements in policy that I had with your father. But even while I remained in Egypt, I hoped for the day that my king would call me back into his service."

"And what would you say to the king of Israel now?" asked Rehoboam.

"Majesty, if I may be bold…"

"Of course," said Rehoboam. "Be bold."

"Solomon the king led us into greatness," he began. "There is no question of that. Israel is the better for his glorious reign."

"But…?" asked the king, leaning in.

"But, in doing so he laid upon the people unbearable taxes and levies that have broken the backs, and consequently the spirit, of the people. I wish to serve you with all of my heart, as do we all."

Everyone present affirmed in hearty agreement.

"Majesty, we respectfully request that you undo the harsh taxes and burdens that your father pronounced upon the nation. We ask that you slow down the work and give our laborers rest. We ask that you reform the nation. Do these things, mighty king, and we shall serve you with all of our heart!"

Rehoboam nodded that he quite understood Jeroboam's position. He looked at his aides who surrounded him and then thought about it for a few minutes. He then pronounced his decision:

"Leave me for three days to pray and consider these motions," he said. "Let me think about what you have said and seek out wise counsel in the matter."

After the room emptied, Rehoboam adjourned to a private chamber with his counselors. They followed the king into the room and watched as he stood looking over Shechem from a window. He turned to the men who were his closest advisors.

"Most of you never really knew my father," he began. "Apart from occasionally attending a royal function with me as a guest, you never understood his depth and vision. The old man had his faults, to be sure—women primarily were his ruin. But he was a magnificent king. And he left me some wonderful advice.

" 'My son,' he said, 'incline your ear to wisdom. Do not rush into agreement with men whose feet rush into sin and whose hearts are not pure.' I have never forgotten those words. These men ask us to change the course of the kingdom to buy their loyalty. Is it fitting that we change royal policy to placate those whose feet would rush to sin and rebellion if we do not comply with their demands? What sort of loyalty is that? I suspect that our answer given to them will be quite different than the one for which they hope!"

The king ordered wine into the room and the young men drank to the future of the kingdom and Rehoboam's future glorious reign. During the festivities a messenger entered the room and whispered to Keriah, who nodded and walked over to the king.

"Majesty, a number of your father's ex-ministers wish a word with you," he said. "They are waiting outside."

"Very well," said Rehoboam, strengthened by the wine. "Show them in. We'll settle this now."

The old men came into the room, ignoring the sneers of the young ministers who had replaced them. The eldest among them, Zabud, who had been with Solomon from the beginning, approached Rehoboam.

"Majesty, bid that we speak with you over the matter concerning Jeroboam?" he asked.

"Of course," said Rehoboam. "But I think the matter does not concern him as much as it concerns me."

The young advisors snickered.

"Be that as it may, majesty, it behooves us to move rather delicately upon this matter. These men represent a strong and growing contingent of people who wish to preserve the peace of this kingdom and to serve you. But, it requires a decision on your part to serve them as well. A king who serves is a great king indeed. If you will serve the people today, by making the reforms which they have requested, then they shall serve you all the days of their lives and you shall be a great king."

"A great king," came Kara's voice. *"Is whether or not you are a great king dependent upon a rabble of troublemakers? Is the peace of this kingdom riding on the backs of men who were exiled by your father?"*

"Are you saying that the greatness of my kingdom depends upon the decisions of people my father had condemned?" asked Rehoboam.

"No, majesty," said Zabud. "Greatness is bestowed upon men by God. But in ruling wisely, one invites such greatness."

"Will you throw away the authority of the king that your father worked so hard to secure, because you have a group of lazy ministers and complaining people? Who is king in Israel—you or Jeroboam?!"

Rehoboam was becoming angry now, though he managed to control his speech. He thanked the delegation of elders and dismissed them, promising an answer in due course. Turning to the young men who had grown up with him in Solomon's court, he asked for their opinion.

Keriah, pouring the king some more wine, began to speak.

"You know how I feel about it, majesty," he began. "If I were king and this group of old tricksters came to me, I would look beyond them and see Jeroboam. This delegation may be led by Zabud, but it is driven by an ambitious ex-fugitive."

The others in the room grunted their approval of what Keriah had said.

"They think your father was overbearing?" said another. "I would tell them, 'My little finger is larger than my father's waist!' "

" 'My father's yoke was heavy?' " chimed in a young officer. " 'Wait until you see the yoke that I lay upon you!' "

" 'My father scourged you with whips,' " threw in still another. " 'But I will scourge your worthless bodies with scorpions!' "

The room broke out in raucous laughter and more wine was ordered in. Rehoboam loved the fellowship of these men—the only truly loyal men in the kingdom. He could hardly wait for three days hence to deliver his answer to the elders in Shechem.

Three days later, when the king entered the room, he was greeted with the customary oblations from the hopeful crowd. Jeroboam tried to read the king's face to discern a glimmer of hope. Zabud also tried to glean intuitively what he could. So much depended upon a peaceful resolution in this matter. They awaited his decision.

Rehoboam waited until all of his chief advisors and military commanders were around him. He then stood to address the assembly.

"You have asked me something and I have considered with great deliberation and prayer the answer for which you are all waiting. I must tell you directly that what you ask is impossible..."

A low murmur of shock coursed through the room. Jeroboam glanced at Zabud, who shook his head in shame.

"You are asking the king to abdicate the power given to him by the Lord Almighty. I am anointed king over Israel. I am not to be dictated to by groups who have unreasonable grievances born out of their own petty frustrations. Therefore I shall not grant your request."

He stood up and held out his hand. Keriah handed him a scroll bearing his seal.

"In fact, I have signed this decree ordering new levies and taxes in conjunction with a great project that I wish to begin." He pointed the scroll at the assembly. "You would have me live forever in the shadow of my father. But I shall cast a greater shadow than Solomon."

Rehoboam sat down before the stunned assembly. A detachment of palace guards came into the room as Keriah stood and dismissed the assembly, thanking them for coming to Shechem for the coronation. As he left, Jeroboam now understood that what the Lord had spoken to him was being fulfilled—that the kingdom was splitting and that he also should reign in Israel.

"Lucifer was quite right," Kara sneered. "Rehoboam's ridiculous headstrong manner will drive this with little effort on my part."

"Poor Israel! The dream ends," said Shawa. "And the rot begins."

"You are wrong, Shawa," Kara corrected. "The rot may begin now, but the dream ended at Eden!"

CHAPTER 10

"Humans seek such gods as suit them."

Chronicles of the Host
Israel Divided

Unknown to either Kara or Lucifer, the nation divided not because of the headstrong action of Rehoboam, but because the Lord had brought judgment upon the land because of Solomon's compromise. Two lands emerged from one; Judah remained the kingdom in the south, with Jerusalem as its center, and Israel with ten tribes occupied the northern portion, with its capital at Samaria.

Divided hearts and a divided kingdom brought great strife in the land as brother fought brother in sporadic periods of war between the two nations. Lucifer was prompt to infect the northern kingdom with Baalist worship, and the things of the Lord quickly fell into disgrace. King followed king in a succession of scandals and assassinations as Israel plunged deeper and deeper into the abyss.

And the Seed?

Lost in the bloody and murky waters that had become Israel, the hope for the Seed became more and more dim. Every angel, both holy and unholy, knew that somewhere in the blackness of Israel and Judah the promise remained. But so long as the nation continued to disintegrate from within, Lucifer felt that he had the advantage and possibly the key to winning the war. With the ascension of Ahab—a vile Baal worshiper who openly promoted wicked high places of worship on behalf of his wife, Jezebel—to the throne of Israel, Lucifer was particularly hopeful.

Then out of the morass arose a man sent from the Lord who was a beacon of prophetic hope; a man who spoke boldly the words of the Most High; a man calling upon the nation to repent; the first of many such prophets whom the Lord in His mercy would send to abate the coming destruction and judgment. He was a man whose anointing was powerful and who openly contested the darkness that had overtaken the land with a zeal unseen since the days of Moses. His name was Elijah....

Samaria, 879 B.C.

The demons watched as the Baalists concluded their worship, dancing a lewd and sensual processional around the Asherah pole in the center. Next to it was the altar to Baal, still smoldering from a sacrificed animal that had been dedicated to the god of the Canaanites. The priest blew a horn signaling that the rite was completed, and the worshipers gathered their things and left.

"AWAY FROM HERE!" came a fierce voice.

Michael the archangel landed in the center of the high place, and the demons scattered with loud shrieks as if they were a nest of hornets disturbed by a rock. The demons left, cursing Michael and complaining about their right to be there.

Crispin landed beside Michael, as did Serus and Dheer. Crispin examined the scene where only moments before the men had engaged in all manner of carnality with the high place prostitutes, both male and female, as acts of worship.

"Shawa, I believe, is the angel who is running Baal for Lucifer," observed Crispin, as the last of the humans disappeared down the stone path. "He is doing a splendid job, I must say."

"Why must humans always degrade in matters of worship?" asked Serus, disgusted by what he saw. "Dheer—when you were assigned to Samson, you saw that even he who was called of God slipped into this...this trap of idolatry."

Dheer could only nod in assent.

"Humans will always degrade if they are not properly aligned with the truth of the Most High," said Crispin. "You know that. These poor lost Baalists are products of the sensual world that their forebears created by their disobedience in Eden."

"Crispin, I have no doubt that this is the case with ordinary humans," said Serus. "But I speak of the people of God—the covenant people of Israel. They are even now led by a king and queen who allow and even encourage such behavior!"

Crispin surveyed the carnage of the worship—the smoldering evidence of sacrifice, the spirit and odor of human lust that still hung in the air. Michael turned to hear Crispin's answer as well, so the teacher sat next to the altar of Baal and began to speak.

"Why do humans do such things?" asked Crispin. "I cannot answer that any more than I can answer why angels do such things. Don't forget that before Eden there was the rebellion in Heaven. The first sin did not begin with humans but with angels. The issue is not one of human or angel but of free will to do as one wishes."

"But what does Baal offer these humans that they cannot find in the Most High?" asked Dheer.

"You were in Ashdod, Dheer," said Crispin. "You saw the worship of Dagon. You witnessed the manipulation by the priests of Dagon to work the people up into a ritualistic frenzy. I tell you—humans need to be led and they desire to be led from something or somebody greater than themselves. So they seek out such gods as suit them and, inevitably, deceive them in the bargain."

"But what does Baal give them in return for their worship?" insisted Serus.

"Peace of mind," said Crispin. "Short-lived to be sure, and in the end destructive. You must not forget that the people of Canaan—and this includes the Lord's own people—are very much tied to the land. This land must produce. Milk and honey does not simply happen. It is seen as a blessing of the Most High, or in this case, of the gods of Canaan. Baal is a god of the earth and he must be satisfied in these carnal charades so that the fertility of the ground is assured. Baalism is security for a very insecure people."

Michael shook his head in disgust.

"Then Lucifer has won, good teacher," he said. "For the kings of Israel have given themselves over to this god of the earth."

"You mean they have given themselves over to the manipulations of fallen angels," reminded Crispin. "Remember, Michael, that there are no gods of this world apart from the fallen and dark angels who supply such gods through their mystical representations in the minds of men. Deluding men into thinking they are sorcerers and diviners while secretly creating the illusions themselves. It's a rotten business, Michael, but far from over."

"You mean the Seed can still emerge from this wreckage?" asked Serus. "God would still send the one to crush the head of the serpent after all this?"

"Our Lord is not a fool, but He is longsuffering. And He is honorable. He has made a promise and He will keep it—even to His disadvantage. The time might come when it will cost Him a great deal more than even we can understand to keep His promise."

As the group pondered these things, Gabriel landed with some news. Michael greeted his brother angel, whom he had not seen in some time.

"The Lord has sent a man filled with His power and Spirit to contest the idolatry in Israel," he said. "He is a Tishbite from Gilead by the name of Elijah."

"Elijah," said Crispin smiling. "The name means 'the Lord is my God.' I like him already." The others laughed.

"Where is he now? What is he to do?" came the questions.

"He is on his way to Ahab," said Gabriel. "And Serus—you and I shall accompany him on his mission."

"Thank you, my lord," said Serus.

"As he is a prophet—a messenger to the people—the Lord ordered that I should watch over his ministry. And I believe you have earned the privilege by having overcome a bit of idolatry in your own past," Gabriel finished, winking at the angel.

"It's true," said Serus. "To my shame I almost threw in with Lucifer."

"Ah, but at the last you made the right choice," said Michael.

"Yes indeed," said Crispin, "and now you can go and see if Ahab will make the right choice!"

"We will leave immediately," said Gabriel. "He has just been presented at court."

The two angels bid their friends farewell and disappeared. Michael sighed as he looked over the unholy place of worship in which he, Dheer, and Crispin stood.

"Perhaps one day we shall have a king in Israel who will destroy these places rather than build them," he said.

"Perhaps," said Crispin. "But just to let them know how the wind has changed with Elijah here…"

He touched the Asherah pole, snapping it in two with a brilliant pulse of light. The top half fell to the ground with a thud.

"May it ever be with all such places," he said, as they all vanished.

Ahab's palace at Samaria was a luxurious and magnificent complex. The walls in the main reception area as well as the king's chambers were inlaid with ivory. On the walls were glorious reliefs and inlays of flowers and animals, many of which showed a definite Egyptian influence. In deference to his wife, Jezebel, Ahab also made sure that there were Phoenician elements throughout the palace as well.

Apart from the physical beauty of the place, there was a definite sense of kingly authority. For all of his personal flaws, Ahab was a capable ruler who used his power to keep Israel's external enemies at bay. Unfortunately, the subtle enemies that were gnawing at him from within were the greater threat.

Gabriel and Serus walked alongside Elijah as he climbed the few stairs that led to the entry of Ahab's palace. The prophet drew strange looks from the guards as he approached the main protocol. Serus and Gabriel also drew strange looks—unwelcome looks—and howling jeers from the many demons who hung about the palace.

"There is a very strong spirit of control in this place," said Gabriel, sensing the spiritual condition of Ahab's home. "Control and religious idolatry. Such shameful strongholds to be at the king's residence!"

"Away from here, Gabriel," came a voice from the throng. "You are not welcome here. And take the traitor Serus with you!"

The howl increased as they proceeded through a hallway where Elijah was greeted by an aide to the king. The aide said that he would announce the prophet and that Elijah was to wait in the hallway until he returned.

"Welcome to Samaria," came the familiar voice of Shawa.

"Ah, Shawa," said Serus. "Or is it Dagon? No, that was before Dagon was humbled. I believe it is Baal that you are assuming now?"

"Careful, traitor," said Shawa sharply. "You are on unholy ground now."

"Where is Kara?" asked Gabriel. "Surely his ambition does not give you free reign in Samaria."

"I have authority in Samaria," said Shawa defensively. "I am the true power behind the king. I have Ahab's mind and Jezebel's heart. And your prophet is finished before he even begins here. We have prophets—hundreds of them!"

"Ah yes," said Gabriel, looking at the Baalist inlays in the ivory. "I have heard of your school of prophets for Baal. They are centered at Mount Carmel, are they not?"

"Carmel is only one of the sacred sites," sniffed Shawa. "And they are a particular favorite of the queen." He smiled an angry smile. "It won't be long, Archangel, until the prophets of Baal are the only voice heard in Israel. And then you can find another nation to plant your accursed Seed!"

"The Seed is planted, Shawa," said Gabriel. "Far too deeply for you to ever be able to get to it!"

Before Shawa could answer, the steward returned and asked Elijah to follow him in to see Ahab. Shawa raced ahead to stand by the king. By the time Gabriel and Serus arrived with Elijah in Ahab's elaborate reception room, Shawa was standing next to the king. Kara was there as well.

"Ah Gabriel," said Kara. "What a pleasant surprise. And you brought along a prophet and a traitor—neither of which will do you any good."

Gabriel ignored Kara's jibe and listened as Ahab spoke.

Ahab was a man of about 40, slender and regal in appearance. He carried kingly authority well on the outside, though he was ruled by his wife, Jezebel, from within. He stood to greet Elijah and offered him food or drink. Elijah declined the offer and began to speak.

"Ahab, the Lord made you king over Israel so that you might be a keeper of His covenant, not a destroyer of it," he began. "Yet you have tempted the Lord through your allowance of high places and abominable places of worship for the Baals. You have married an idolatrous woman who, out of her own purse, has created a school of such false prophets."

At that point Jezebel came in and took her seat next to her husband. She had clearly heard what the prophet had said. She was an attractive woman, dressed in the royal garb of Tyre, and decked out in much jewelry. Around her neck was an amulet with Baal markings engraved upon it.

"You would deprive me of my school of prophets?" asked Jezebel in a mock voice of desperation. "Whatever would I do?"

"Madam, you are inviting the judgment of God upon your head," Elijah answered.

Gabriel liked this man. He had not heard a human speak with such authority since Moses confronted Rameses. This would be interesting. Jezebel looked at her husband, waiting for some response from him to silent this insolent holy man. But Ahab remained silent, much to her dismay.

"And so to prove to you that the Lord is God, and that He cannot be mocked by the Baals, or by earthly kings, there shall be neither rain nor dew for the next few years unless I decree otherwise."

Ahab began to smirk. Jezebel laughed out loud, almost spilling her wine out of its golden cup. The others in the court began to laugh aloud as well.

"You shall stop the rain," said Ahab as the laughter subsided. "Interesting."

"When the animals are dying; when the crops have failed; when your people cry out for relief—you will send for me, Ahab. And then you will know that the Lord God Almighty is God."

Elijah left the palace and headed into the streets of Samaria. A crowd gathered around him as he lifted his voice to the Lord:

"Here now, O Israel. You have forsaken the living God, the God of your fathers, and have run after other gods. Therefore this is the word of the Lord: There shall be no rain nor dew upon the land for the next few years!"

The crowd began to laugh at the man, who was obviously deranged. One man asked if he wanted some more wine. Elijah merely looked up to the sky and ended his declaration with the words, "So be it done!"

From a window in the palace, Jezebel watched the entire scene. It was bad enough that this man had intruded upon the king and queen. But now he was spewing his poison on the streets. She summoned her chief aide.

"Yes, my queen," said Dobri.

"I want that man who calls himself a prophet followed. See where he goes and with whom he speaks. Send me regular reports. And if he discovers you...kill him." She tossed him a small bag with several precious stones in it.

"As you command, my queen," he said.

"Gabriel!"

"Gabriel, what is the matter?" asked Serus.

Gabriel ignored Serus, indicating for him to be quiet and follow him. The two angels walked with Elijah until he came to a place just outside the city where nobody else was around. Elijah was filling his skin with fresh water.

"The Lord will speak to him," said Gabriel solemnly. The words were hardly out of Gabriel's mouth when the silence was broken:

"*Elijah!*"

Elijah looked about.

"*Elijah!*"

Gabriel and Serus bowed their heads as the Lord spoke.

"Lord?" said Elijah.

"*Hear the word of the Lord, Elijah!*"

Elijah fell to his knees. "What is it, Lord?" he asked.

"*You are to leave here and turn to the east. Go to the Kerith ravine east of Jordan and hide there, for your enemies are seeking you out. There you shall drink from the brook and you shall be fed by the ravens that I have ordered there!*"

Elijah stood up and hurriedly gathered his things to begin the journey east. As he got back on the road leaving town, Serus turned and saw several demons accompanying Dobri, who had just passed the gate, riding a chariot and accompanied by another man. They were obviously looking for Elijah.

"Look there," said Serus, pointing to the man.

"It is Jezebel's servant," said Gabriel. "You remain with Elijah. I'll see to these."

"Elijah, you must hurry," Serus said.

Elijah considered the idea in his heart and picked up the pace, heading eastward from Samaria onto the road that led to Kerith. Gabriel stood in front of the demons who were with Dobri.

"We would pass, Archangel," they said. "We are on assignment with this man."

Gabriel began to unsheathe his sword. Seeing this, the devils abandoned Dobri, preferring to meet up with Gabriel when they had a greater advantage of numbers.

"Go ahead, Archangel," said one of them. "We shall yet have our vengeance upon both you and the man of God!"

He then vanished.

Dobri continued his hunt, asking people if they had seen Elijah. Gabriel determined to deal with the man. Assuming the form of a human, a merchant entering Samaria on a donkey, he rode near Dobri.

"Did I hear you inquire about a certain man?" the stranger asked.

"Yes," said Dobri. He then began to tell the merchant, who was really Gabriel, about Elijah in great detail.

"Ah yes," said the man. " I ran into him a mile from here. He said he was headed west toward Carmel. I believe that he was picked up by a man on horseback!"

"Thank you," said Dobri, tossing him a coin. Dobri and his companion took off on the road leading west. Gabriel looked at the coin, which bore Ahab's inscription. Tossing it away, he vanished so that he could catch up with Serus and Elijah.

Bethlehem, 4 B.C.

Eli stirred the embers, bringing life to the fire. It responded to his coaxing with a lively pop. The Bethlehem night seemed colder than usual. Most of the shepherds were now settled around the fire in half-sitting, half-reclining positions. The boys, however, still involved in the evening's story, remained vigilant in their attention.

"Wouldn't you boys like to rest for a while?" asked Eli.

"Now?" asked Jarod. "Just when Elijah has the bad king after him?"

"Bad queen," corrected Eli. "Jezebel hated Elijah with all that was in her."

"But why?" Jarod asked. "I thought prophets were good to have around."

Eli chuckled at the boy's response.

"They are, lad," said Eli. "Most of the time. But Elijah's message was a hard one. It was a message that people did not want to hear because they had turned their backs on the Lord. Jezebel hated Elijah because he was a threat to her hold over the Baal worship in the land. That worship made her lots of money and gave her a great measure of control.

"The rain had stopped for several years—just as Elijah had decreed. So Ahab and Jezebel hated the man—but they also needed him if the rain was ever going to return."

"So what did he do during that time?" asked Jarod. "Where did he live?"

"Oh, the Lord took care of him—as He does all His prophets. For a time Elijah lived near a brook in Kerith where the ravens fed him. Then he went to Zarephath, where a widow woman took care of him. While he was with her, Elijah raised her son from the dead! In the meantime Jezebel was on a bloody rampage, killing the Lord's prophets wherever she could find them. Of course, Elijah was the one she really wanted.

"Finally, the Lord told Elijah to present himself once again to Ahab. The Most High God was going to finally send rain. He wanted Ahab to know that it was the Lord, and nobody else, who had commanded the rain. So Elijah met with Ahab at Samaria."

"Did he bring the rain with him?" asked Joshua.

"No, Joshua," said Eli. "He didn't bring the rain. He brought a challenge...."

Samaria, 876 B.C.

Elijah approached Ahab in the same assembly hall as before, although this time it was empty except for several guards. Most of the administrators and officials were out in the country dealing with the famine and drought that had become the focus of Ahab's reign. Kara and Shawa stood behind Ahab as before, though this time they seemed in a very different humor.

"How long will the cruelty of the Most High continue?" asked Shawa. "His people are suffering throughout the land!"

Gabriel, who had come in with Elijah, was incredulous.

"You are concerned with the suffering of the people?" he said mockingly. "Shawa, all that concerns you is the fact that the Baals are losing face. And with that your power is diminished."

"Nevertheless people are dying," interjected Kara. "It is a cruel God who plays games with the lives of people. He shall never win them back!"

"This is no game, Kara," said Gabriel. "And the Lord need not win anyone back. The people will one day return to Him on their own!"

"If there are any left alive," Kara sneered.

Elijah stopped in front of the king's chair.

"Is that you, troubler of Israel?" Ahab asked.

"I have not made trouble for Israel, majesty," said Elijah. "It is your following of the Baals that has brought on this disaster. And your murder of the Lord's prophets."

"I see that you are in good health," said Jezebel, who had rushed to the hall when she was informed that her hated enemy had dared present himself.

"Yes, madam," said Elijah. "I am in the best of health. But in your zeal for Baal many of the Lord's prophets have been murdered."

"Can I help it if the people seek out heretics?" asked Jezebel. "I am not responsible for the actions of others who are incited by religious fanatics."

"The power of Baal is not real, madam," said Elijah. "It is dark and devilish and forbidden by the Lord."

"Did you come here to provoke me?" she asked, visibly angry.

Ahab gave her a look that told her to calm down and be quiet.

"I have come that you might see that the Lord God of Heaven is Lord over all gods," Elijah said. "I have come to bring you a challenge."

Jezebel looked at her husband. She was immediately on guard for a trick from this crafty old prophet who had been so much trouble to her. Ahab, however, was interested in Elijah's mention of a challenge.

"What sort of challenge?" Ahab asked.

Elijah spoke as if he were repeating words being spoken by somebody else; a sort of faraway look was in his eyes: "Summon witnesses from throughout Israel. And gather together the four hundred fifty prophets of Baal and the four hundred prophets of Asherah. Have all these meet me at Mount Carmel, one of the holiest places for the Baals. Then we shall see whose god is greater."

Ahab looked at Jezebel. She liked the idea. This would be her chance to demonstrate the power of Baal once and for all—and to be rid of Elijah at the same time. She shook her head enthusiastically.

"We accept," said Ahab. "It shall be done. Now leave this place! We shall not see you again until we meet at Mount Carmel."

Elijah bowed slightly and left the room. Only the angels remained. Gabriel grinned at Kara and Shawa, who were in deep conference with one another.

"Well, Kara," said Gabriel. "It looks as if there will be another contest. If it goes anything like it did for you in Egypt, your next assignment will be Sheol."

Kara gave Gabriel an icy stare.

"The gods of Egypt were divided," said Kara. "Each of the angels running those gods was too concerned with his own territory and prestige. Baal is under one angel, Shawa, and each of the prophets are assigned an angel as well. You will see, Archangel, that when we are united we are unstoppable."

"In that case, may I suggest you ask Lucifer to attend this little exhibition of Baal's power?" said Gabriel. "This is your crowning moment, Shawa. The defeat of one of the Most High's greatest prophets."

"Lucifer will be there," said Shawa proudly. "As will the rest of the Council. Isn't that so, Kara?"

"Yes, of course," said Kara. "I have every confidence in the outcome."

"You don't look too sure of yourself, Kara," Gabriel said, half smiling....

Kara looked at Gabriel haughtily. "I'm quite confident, Archangel. We are the gods of this world. We have the authority!"

"And we have the Most High God," said Gabriel, "who *is* the authority."

Chronicles of the Host
Contest at Carmel

What was it about the Baals? This was a question that became a matter of great interest in the Academy of the Host during the ministry of Elijah. The simple answer among the angels was that men are prone to idolatry—and of course they are. But Baalism had an appeal for the people of God that we always found puzzling.

Baal means "lord"—and as a result of efforts by Shawa and those fallen angels assigned to Canaan, Baal became the chief god in Canaan. His was a sensual religion, steeped in fertility rituals and tied closely to the seasons. In fact, these deceived humans believed that with each winter and spring the god died and rose again! How perverse the notion of devils whose twisted black art often mimics sacred life!

Through the activity of cultic temple prostitutes, the Asherah, or female counterpart of Baal, was honored in the high places with the vilest acts ever committed in the name of worship. For Israelites, who depended upon the land for their survival, Baal held an attraction—especially if they felt that the Lord had forsaken them in times of famine or drought. In these times they turned to Baal for relief. Such is the fickle nature of humans!

So it was, on Mount Carmel, that Elijah faced off with the prophets of Baal to demonstrate that God was indeed Lord not only of the desert, but of all the earth....

The atmosphere around Carmel was more reminiscent of a festival than of a religious contest. From all over Israel people came: the curious, the faithful, the seeking, hard-core Baalists, and servants of the Most High—all wanting to see which god would show himself that day.

The prophets of Baal also assembled, proud and confident, carrying the many emblems of their worship. Several erected Asherah poles in anticipation of the great celebrations that would certainly follow Elijah's humbling. As for Elijah, he kept to himself, awaiting the proper time to address the people.

Finally, the angels—both good and bad—assembled. Not since that fateful day in Eden, when so many angels watched the contest between the serpent and Eve, were so many holy and unholy angels gathered in one place.

As Elijah requested, Ahab had summoned people from throughout the land to witness the spectacle. Only Jezebel had remained behind in Jezreel to await the outcome. Unknown to her husband, she had given orders that once the demonstration was over, Elijah was to be killed on the spot. Thus she waited for news of Elijah's death.

"Look at all the fallen angels!" said Bakka. "I haven't seen many of these since they lost their place in Heaven!"

"It is a rather dark reunion," noted Crispin, who had arrived from Heaven with several of his students. He wanted them to observe the contest, for academic as well as for historical reasons. "Grim lot, these unholy creatures."

"Teacher, why have they become so...so out of control?" asked one of the student angels who was with him. He was pointing to some of his former brothers who were chasing about like mad dogs, shrieking hysterically.

"Result of pride," said Crispin, matter-of-factly. "Pride erases the boundaries set up by the Lord so that once they are violated, one moves farther and farther from the ability to rationalize and behave in a controlled manner. The end result is complete insanity. It happens with humans and with angels. Of course, not all of those who fell have given themselves over to complete madness...not yet anyway."

"Still lecturing, I see."

It was Pellecus, Crispin's former colleague at the Academy, who had become his chief opponent in matters of doctrine. "How will these poor students ever be able to discern truth from fantasy as long as you continue to fill their heads with such nonsense?"

"All of you remember Pellecus, I am sure," said Crispin. "He was one of the most brilliant wisdom angels ever created by the Most High. Why, even I sat under his teaching on occasion. But he allowed the pride of wanting to be right to overcome the need to be truthful—and as a result he is neither right nor truthful!"

The angels laughed.

"We shall see after today, dear Crispin, who is right and who shares in the truth," said Pellecus. "Confidentially, I say that whoever wins this war will ultimately dictate what is truth and what is right."

Crispin turned to the angels with him.

"As I said, dear students, pride erases boundaries of reason— so that any desired outcome justifies the method of achieving that outcome."

"Pride will erase you one day, Crispin," said Pellecus. "Mark me!"

He then vanished to return to his vantage point for the contest.

"Pride is also a poor loser," Crispin said, winking.

Pellecus found Lucifer near the prophets of Baal. Many demons were encouraging the Baalists by speaking into their minds or performing small manipulations of religious trickery with amulets or charms. Observing their antics, Lucifer shook his head in disgust at the foolishness of men to be so easily deceived. He saw Pellecus coming toward him.

"These humans amaze me," Lucifer said. "A spark of fire here, a bit of smoke there; a voice in the night or an appearance of one of their stupid gods—and they are completely given in. Incredible!"

"I see that Crispin is here as well," said Pellecus, fuming a bit from his earlier encounter. "I only hope that we are successful so that his foul mouth will be silenced."

"Well, well," said Kara, who had just arrived. "Another academic brawl? I certainly hope that you were more successful this time than when you debated him in Heaven…"

"I only want to see him silenced," said Pellecus.

"This is not an academic excursion," said Lucifer sharply. "This is war. See that you keep it in its proper perspective. At any rate, these Baal prophets are very motivated, and they have the force of Jezebel behind them. She is quite a tool—completely deceived but useful."

"So many of the enemy here," said Kara, looking around him. "It reminds me of when we would all come together in the Kingdom for one of the assemblies. I remember being in the Council of Elders when Michael…"

He noticed Lucifer's annoyed look and stopped talking.

"You long for those days of imprisonment?" asked Lucifer suspiciously.

"No, my lord," Kara responded quickly. "I was simply remarking that it had been a long time since so many angels were together. I much prefer our current predicament...er... I mean our current situation."

"I wouldn't reminisce too much about the old times, Kara," said Pellecus. "You might find that what others remember about your leadership might not be exactly the way you remember it."

Kara began to respond, but Rugio interrupted with the announcement that Elijah had arrived. Lucifer looked down in the direction of a large crowd following the prophet up the hill. With him were Gabriel, Serus, Michael, and a number of other angels.

"This shall be quite a day," said Lucifer. "I only hope Shawa is ready to perform."

"Of course he is," said Kara. "The prophets of Baal are completely entranced and ready to call upon their gods. Shawa's angels are ready to perform whatever signs and wonders are called for here."

"Excellent," Lucifer responded. "But nothing too wild. Just a demonstration or two to show the people that Baal is their benefactor in this land."

"Shawa is ready, my prince," said Kara proudly.

"Yes, my prince," agreed Shawa. "I count it an honor to serve you in this. And I pledge not to fail."

Lucifer looked hard at Shawa.

"Very well, I accept the pledge," he said ominously.

CHAPTER 11

"From a traitor to a commander of traitors in such a short time."

Elijah stood to address the assembly. To his left stood the prophets of Baal, quiet and confident, waiting their turn to please their god and king. Next to him were the materials brought up to build an altar. Ahab had brought in extra material so that both Elijah and the prophets of Baal could call upon their gods equally. A couple of oxen brought up for the sacrifice could be heard lowing above the murmuring crowd, completely unaware of what awaited them in the next few hours. Then Elijah began:

"I am the last remaining prophet of the Lord who has not been hunted down and killed and who is not in hiding. But look around, and you will see four hundred fifty prophets of Baal. Therefore this is what we shall do. Bring the two bulls for us and we shall cut them into pieces and place them on the two altars. But do not set fire to them! You shall call upon your god and I shall call upon my God, and the god who responds with fire from Heaven will be the true and living God!"

All seemed agreeable to this, so Ahab gave the order for the oxen bulls to be killed and cut into pieces. The prophets of Baal tended their altar and with great ceremony placed the pieces of the bull upon it. Elijah also placed his pieces of the animal upon the altar that he had fashioned. He then indicated to the Baalists that they could begin at any time to call upon their god.

The angels on both sides watched as the drama began to play out. Shawa and his angels immediately stood with the prophets of Baal, speaking into their minds, and in some cases entering them and bringing them to bizarre ecstatic behavior.

Shawa had decided that after the prophets had called upon Baal for a few moments, he and some of the others would dazzle the spectators with a very powerful flame from above—something they could very easily produce. The contest should be over after that.

Rugio kept an eye on Michael.

"He will try to intervene," he said to his aide. "Have our warriors encircle the Baal prophets. Not one of Michael's angels should get through."

"Yes, my lord," said the warrior, who disappeared to give the order.

The prophets had reached a frenzied crescendo in their efforts to conjure up Baal. The chief prophet now began to call upon Baal to accept their offer and show the world that he truly was the greatest god. Shawa gave the order to his angels to begin creating the flaming illusion that would consume the offering.

As they began to manipulate the elements and create the fire, they suddenly became powerless. Several of the angels fell to the earth, completely blocked in their ability to move, much less conjure up the pseudo-flame. Shawa watched in complete stupification and ordered his angels to return to their task.

"I cannot move," said one of his warriors, who lay on the ground next to the altar. "It is the Spirit of God!"

To his horror Shawa looked up and saw a great hand in the sky, the arm of which reached up into the heavens. The hand rested above the Baal altar and would let nothing through! Every angel who tried to penetrate the hand found himself immobilized and dazed. The hand of God was interfering with the contest!

Lucifer saw what was happening and ordered Shawa to make something happen! Shawa, now panicked, told his angels to whip the prophets up into a further frenzy. Many of the men began dancing around the altar—but there was no answer from Baal.

Crispin and Michael stood next to Elijah, watching the contest stretch into the middle of the day.

"Why don't you shout louder?" Elijah asked. "Perhaps your god cannot hear well. Or maybe he is asleep."

Crispin laughed at Elijah's comments.

"I like this man," he said. "He is something of a great wit—a bit like me!"

"Yes, well Lucifer has a bit of wit himself," said Michael, not yet ready to let his guard down. "We should be ready for any tricks the enemy might decide to play."

The prophets had actually begun to cut themselves and offer their own blood to coax Baal into action. "I rather think the enemy has just run out of tricks," Crispin said.

Elijah then announced that it was his turn to call upon the Lord. He took twelve stones, one for each of the tribes of Israel, and began rebuilding his own altar that had been wrecked in the frenzied attempts of Baal's prophets. Next, he gathered the prophets around to speak with them. They looked up at him— angry, bleeding, and exhausted.

Elijah then did something that puzzled every human and angel present: He ordered jars of water to be poured over the wooden altar that he had built! The prophets gladly obliged and eagerly filled the jars with what they hoped contained the death sentence of this pesky prophet.

"What is he up to?" asked Gabriel.

"Making it more interesting, I suspect," said Crispin.

Elijah's actions were not lost on Lucifer either. He glanced in the direction of Gabriel and motioned for Kara to investigate.

"What is your prophet doing?" demanded Kara, who had come over to where the archangels were standing. "He is not following the rules!"

"Since when do you respect rules, Kara?" asked Gabriel.

"Nevertheless this shall not stand! If he wins the contest it shall be dishonorably!"

"Our side must be doing well, Gabriel," said Crispin. "When Kara speaks of respecting rules and of honor, something devastating must be going on."

"This is not over yet," said Kara. "Our prophets are merely resting."

"Yes," said Crispin. "And so apparently is their god."

Three times Elijah had the prophets of Baal pour water on his altar. Even the trough in which the altar rested was filled with water. When the last jar had been emptied, Elijah announced that he was ready to call upon the Most High.

Shawa saw this as his last opportunity. Rallying his angels for one final thrust, he sent them swirling around the altar of Baal and in and around the prophets. Some of the men uttered guttural sounds as demons entered them. Shawa, remembering his pledge to Lucifer, hoped if nothing else to distract and possibly frighten Elijah and make his prayer ineffective.

"O Lord God of Abraham, Isaac, and Israel," Elijah began. "Let it be known today that You are God in Israel and that I am Your servant. Answer me now, O Lord, that these men might see and know that the God of Israel lives!"

He looked at the people watching him—even the prophets of Baal had become quiet as he prayed. He turned his head upward once more. The holy angels, sensing God's presence beginning to fall upon the place, bowed their heads and knelt in holy reverence. The demons along with their commanders stopped as if frozen, as they too anticipated the Lord's Presence.

"And now, O Lord, answer me that these people will know that You are the true and living God, and that You have turned their hearts back again!"

The brilliant flash of white light caused everyone to flinch. The prophets of Baal threw themselves backwards from the intense heat falling all over them. The people watching gasped and became frightened, and many of them fell on their knees in the Presence of the God they had forsaken.

Shawa, reasoning that it was better that Lucifer see him resist to the last, ordered his angels back into action—but even he knew it was pointless. Lucifer watched as the demon, in one final show of defiance, thrust himself into the river of light that had set the altar ablaze. Sword swinging, Shawa shrieked and disappeared into the brilliant holy light. In an instant he disintegrated in a bright, bluish flash—never to be seen again.

In spite of the water that had been poured on it, the altar disappeared as the Lord consumed not only the wood, but also the stones, the meat, the dust, and the water. Then, just as quickly as it had come, the light vanished.

When the devils who had been under Shawa's authority saw what had happened to their commander, they immediately began to abandon the prophets of Baal. The people began shouting, "Elijah's god is God! Elijah's god is God!" They seized the prophets and brought them before Elijah, who ordered them taken to Kishon to be killed.

Kara was dumbfounded. He looked to Lucifer, who could barely contain his rage. Glancing at Michael, Lucifer demanded to know whether all the Lord's prophets were such bloody murderers.

"Those Baal prophets followed you, Lucifer," said Michael, adding these chilling words: "The sentence of death was already upon them—as on anyone who follows you, be they man or angel."

"Watch your prophet well, Archangel," sneered Lucifer. "I assure you that the Most High is not the only one handing out death sentences."

Chronicles of the Host

Fugitive Prophet

True to his word, Lucifer raged against Elijah for the humiliation of Baal at Mount Carmel. Inflaming the hatred of Jezebel, he found a willing accomplice to carry out his wrathful vengeance. Jezebel ordered that Elijah be found and killed at any cost. Thus Elijah could did not savor his victory at Carmel for very long before he became a fugitive from Jezebel's fury.

Making his way down to Beersheba, Elijah despaired of his life. So sullen was he, and so disappointed with his plight, that he begged the Most High to let him die. Now this is a wish that no angel has ever understood, coming from a creature made in the image of God. Yet Elijah prayed such a prayer and lay down under a juniper tree to await his death....

"Elijah. Get up and eat!"

Elijah lifted his head and saw a figure towering over him. It was Serus, dressed in a flowing white cloak. Serus touched the prophet on the shoulder to encourage him to rise up. Elijah jumped up, startled, and Serus indicated food and water that he had provided.

Elijah kept an eye on the angel as he ate, relaxing more and more as he understood that this was a messenger from the Lord. When he had finished, he lay back down and waited for this angel to fulfill his prayer. Instead Serus awakened him again with the words: "You must eat once more, because the journey you are about to take will be too great for you."

"Journey?" Elijah said disappointedly. "I thought you were here to take me with you to be with the Lord!"

Serus restrained a smile and only repeated his words: "You must eat again so you will have strength for the journey."

Elijah got up reluctantly and ate and drank. Then, scanning the horizon around Beersheba, he took off for the south.

"Whether I die here in Beersheba or someplace else is of no consequence," he muttered to Serus, as he began his journey once more.

Bethlehem, 4 B.C.

Michael was touching Mary, trying to comfort her as the donkey walked the last couple of miles to the city. Joseph could now see the light of lamps and watchmen's torches in Bethlehem, and he pointed this out to his wife.

"It won't be much longer, love," he told her, gripping her hand.

Mary said nothing, but she smiled down at her husband of whom she was so proud. He had trusted the Lord's angel in a very delicate matter, and she would always treasure that in her heart.

Michael also could see the lights of Bethlehem—but not from the torches. Above the city were thousands of angels, gathered for the momentous event for which they had been waiting. He smiled proudly at the warriors encircling the city, and thought of the long and bloody trail that had brought God's people to this point. Preserving the prophecy had not been without great cost to Israel—in fact it had cost them their nation.

"Now Ahab was a cruel and indifferent ruler," Eli said. "And to be sure he married a wicked wife in Jezebel. But he was a great commander in the field and very successful in his wars against the Arameans."

The shepherds were enjoying their second evening meal— some fruit and goat milk cheese—and the fire roared cheerily. Some of the men had gone home for the evening, their time of watch having been completed.

"Daniel!" Eli called out. "Come join us!"

Daniel, who had been sullen for most of the night, came over.

"Thank you," he said. "I think I shall."

He sat down among the men, who were puzzled by his change in attitude. Jarod handed Daniel a piece of bread, which he took gratefully. As he chewed he looked at the old man whose storytelling had dominated the evening.

"My father wanted to be a priest," he said.

All the men looked at him.

"Really, Daniel," said Eli. "Is that so? You are a Levite?"

"Yes," he said. "But many generations back my people became shepherds rather than priests. Now of course we are not acceptable. And with Herod as king, the priesthood is far less pure."

The other men were still in shock that Daniel had so suddenly opened up to them. The boys, too, did not understand the change that had overtaken him.

"Daniel?" asked Joshua.

"Yes," he responded.

"Why were you so cross earlier?"

Elron, Joshua's father, shook his head vigorously, indicating that the boy should be quiet. But Daniel smiled a half smile.

"It's alright, Elron," he said. "The boy was not asking anything that the rest of you were not thinking."

He turned to Eli.

"You have been speaking of our nation, our heritage," Daniel began. "As I was looking over Bethlehem, I began thinking of my fathers and their commitment to the priesthood. How God had selected my family to serve Him and how my family broke away from that service."

He leaned back from the fire and continued.

"Eli, I must know…is the promise still alive? Because if it is, I wish to rejoin my brothers in the temple and fulfill my family duty."

"Yes," said Eli. "I would not believe otherwise. Someday the Messiah will arrive and save His people. But your question is understandable, Daniel. For even after Elijah's ministry passed to Elisha, the kingdom of Israel was in great peril."

"Yes," Daniel said. "You mentioned the series of wars with the Arameans."

"Not just war with nations, Daniel," Eli said somberly. "War within Israel itself. Elijah's ministry came to a close shortly after Ahab was killed in battle. Elisha, his disciple, took the old prophet's mantle when Israel's enemies were pressing in both from without and within…and he continued the work of the Lord in Israel's last days…"

Jordan River near Jericho, 868 B.C.

Elisha, who had been with Elijah for some 11 years, watched as his mentor took his mantle and beat the surface of the Jordan

River with it. He had seen many bizarre things over the years, so nothing much really surprised him—not even the splitting of the river that allowed them to cross over! As they crossed the river bed together to the other side, Elisha thought back over his life with the greatest living prophet in Israel.

Elisha had been Elijah's loyal attendant. Together they had faced hostile foreign kings, attempts upon Elijah's life, and the tricky intrigue of the Aramean wars, in which Ahab had finally been killed. Elisha had also been with the old prophet when an angel appeared and told him to speak against Ahaziah, the king who succeeded Ahab, for consulting with Baal diviners. Twice, Elisha had witnessed Elijah call down fire from Heaven that consumed two companies of Ahaziah's men and their officers! It had been quite an adventure so far.

Now the end of Elijah's ministry was near. Prophet and disciple arrived on the other side of the Jordan, neither one speaking a word. Elisha looked with deep feelings at his mentor, dressed in his shaggy mantle and the leather belt around his waist. The old holy man turned to Elisha and spoke.

"What can I do for you before I am taken away from you?" he asked.

"I have seen the Lord work through your life," said Elisha. "And I know that if I am to succeed, it must be by the Lord's anointing. Therefore give me a double portion of your spirit."

Elijah considered this request for a moment or two, the sun beating down upon his wrinkled face. He then looked at Elisha.

"You are asking something very hard," he finally said. "But if when I am taken away, you see me depart, then the anointing is yours. Otherwise, it is not."

Elisha continued walking with the prophet, chatting with him and recalling some of their experiences together. He wanted to glean whatever wisdom he could from Elijah before he was taken away.

Suddenly they both stopped. In front of them a strange apparition appeared—horses and a chariot that appeared to be made of flames! There was nobody in the chariot, and Elijah walked toward it. Suddenly the wind picked up around them. A great whirlwind swirled in from the north and enveloped Elijah, picking him up and disappearing into the sky.

"Master! Master!" Elisha screamed. "I see the chariots! I see the horsemen!"

Elisha watched until his teacher disappeared completely. He knew that he would not see his mentor again until he saw him one day before the Lord. He also knew something else: that the mantle left behind was now his and that the double portion he had asked for was also his. He picked up the old coat and put it on. It was heavy indeed.

From a distance, several demons who had been assigned to Elisha watched as the new prophet of Israel made his way back toward the Jordan. They had not dared come near the men while Elijah was still around—especially when the chariot of fire had arrived to escort Elijah to Heaven.

One of the demons, a particularly hateful assistant to Rugio by the name of Grolius, had a particular vendetta against Elisha. Having lost a great companion and mentor in Shawa at Mount Carmel, he had sworn vengeance upon Elijah and Elisha. Rugio determined to give Grolius a chance and dispatched him with several warriors to find an opportune time to kill the prophet.

"Elisha is never without escort, is he?" said Sar, whose last important task was during the fight against Moses in Goshen. "Always an angel around."

"And not just an angel," said Grolius. "Several warriors—and usually an archangel somewhere about. They always seem to accompany the humans who have the greatest anointing."

"He took the mantle, my lord," said Corell. "It is his now."

Grolius watched as the prophet, now wearing Elijah's mantle, disappeared down the bank of the Jordan. He smirked and said,

"The prophet told him that it was a burdensome mantle. Let us therefore oblige him!"

Chronicles of the Host

Elisha

The Spirit of the Lord was indeed upon Elisha, and with the company of some prophets who also served the Lord, he traveled throughout the land. These were hopeful days for the Host. Elisha conducted himself with such faith—subduing his enemies; doing great miracles, including the raising of a boy from the dead at Shunem; and perhaps of greatest satisfaction for the holy angels, frustrating Lucifer's plans to stop the word of the Lord by leading a reform against the Baal prophets.

Thus it was that a new king arose in Aram, the sworn enemy of Israel. He found that the very words he spoke in his bedroom were being repeated by Elisha the prophet to the king of Israel! Such was his rage, that he sent an army to surround Elisha and his servant in the little city of Dothan, there to capture him....

Grolius was riding in the chariot with the Aramean commander. The night before they had come upon Dothan and surrounded it. Their last word was that the prophet Elisha was there. Now they had an opportunity to end the career of the man of God who had been so troublesome to them.

Along with Grolius were hundreds of unholy angels, all of whom wanted to witness the final chapter in Elisha's life. Many of them had been at Mount Carmel, and like Grolius, sought revenge for their humiliation there. The angels moved in and out of the Aramean position, fanning the Arameans' hate and preparing them for possible resistance by the other prophets and some of the townspeople.

Over the city, in a large and organized concentration, were holy angels under the command of Serus. He had called in a legion of warriors after he had heard of the approaching Aramean army. He knew that Grolius had been with the king of Aram and expected a great fight. Michael had left, promising to return in due course with more angels, but as yet had not returned.

Serus positioned himself directly over the house in which Elisha slept. He saw Grolius approaching and went to meet him at the city's edge.

"Well, Serus," said Grolius. "From a traitor to a commander of traitors in such a short time. Congratulations!"

Serus ignored the comment and watched as the Arameans drew in closer and closer to the city. He called to one of his aides, an angel who stood nearby, to awaken Elisha's servant. Within moments, the servant of the prophet stepped out and saw the Aramean army surrounding the city.

"Master!" he cried out, running back into the room where Elisha was sleeping. "An army has surrounded us with horses and chariots!"

Elisha woke up, looked outside the door, and saw the army that was awaiting the signal to attack. Elisha stretched and looked at his servant. Some of the others began to awaken as well, and within a few minutes there was a low drone of concern. All eyes were on Elisha, who seemed quite calm about it all.

"I suppose it's me they are after," he said casually. "Shall we go and talk with them? Or do you think they want to fight?"

"Master!" said the servant. "They will kill you!"

Elisha smiled and indicated for his servant to follow him outside.

Grolius saw Elisha step outside and pointed him out to his warriors.

"There is the prophet!" he screamed. "Make sure to clear the guardians around him so that he can be captured by the soldiers!" Several of Grolius's angels closed in around Elisha. Serus responded by moving in with his warriors, who now were tightly around the prophet with their swords drawn.

But Elisha told his servant not to be afraid. "Those who are with us are more than those who are with them!"

The servant looked about and did not understand. He knew that they could not count on a handful of prophets and a few of the locals for help—against a trained veteran army.

"How can that be, master?" he asked nervously.

Elisha shook his head as if it were all so easy. He looked up toward the still dark morning sky and began to pray: "Lord, open his eyes so that he might see!"

Suddenly, dots of light began appearing all over the hills around the little city. At first Elisha's servant could not make them out. Maybe they were fires from a relieving army! Perhaps Elisha was going to pull a trick like Gideon had done with his torches. But then the servant saw that they were not torches but horses and chariots of fire! It was the Host of the Lord all about them!

The angels under Grolius began to back off the city when they saw that it was they, not Elisha, who were surrounded. Many of Grolius's commanders tried to rally the fleeing spirits and were able to restore some order among them, although all were unnerved by the appearance of the large army that had enveloped them. Enraged, Grolius saw that the commander of this newly arrived host was Michael!

"I told you I would return," said Michael to Serus. "And I brought a few friends along for company!"

"Perfect," said Serus. "The enemy was just about to move on Dothan."

"Now it seems they are moving out of it!" observed Michael as the last of the demons backed away, leaving the Aramean army to its own devices.

Grolius, however, would have none of it and moved upon the commander of the enemy army to begin the attack. The roar of charging horses and chariots filled the dust-filled morning air as the Arameans moved in to take Elisha.

Michael watched as Elisha looked toward the heavens and declared boldly, "Lord, strike this army with blindness."

Michael, compelled by the Spirit of God, ordered his angels to attack the Arameans, striking the men with their swords. Grolius's demons moved to block as many of Michael's angels as they could, but the strength of the heavenly host overwhelmed them, pushing them aside. Each Aramean, as he was struck by an angel, suddenly became blind, wrecking his chariot or slowing his horse to a walk. The Aramean army was frozen where it stood—blind and helpless because of the Lord's angels and Elisha's great faith.

Chronicles of the Host

Israel in Decline

Grolius was powerless to stop the demoralization of the humans who, when confronted with their sudden blindness, dropped their weapons and cried out in surrender. The Aramean commander awaited his disposition and asked to speak with the prophet. Elisha, pretending to be another man, offered to guide the army to a place where they might indeed find the prophet. They consented and he delivered them into the hands of the king of Israel—the ruler of their enemies!

Throughout the remainder of his life, Elisha, led by the Lord and kept by His angels, continued in service to the kings of Israel. These were perilous times for both kings and prophets, as war and assassination were ever present, and the prophets brought unwelcome messages of impending destruction.

Hard-hearted as always, and fed by the lies of demon-inspired prophets, Israel refused to repent and in the end was destroyed. The nation that had been stirred up by Rugio, the cruel Assyrians, came in and destroyed Israel and Samaria, taking many people into captivity into their dark and dismal land.

Having thus seen the northern kingdom of Israel destroyed, Lucifer looked forward to the destruction of Judah. He met in council with those wicked angels who were the princes over Assyria, determined to bring a quick and bloody finish to Jerusalem, and to put to rest forever the threat of the Seed that hung over all of them....

CHAPTER 12

"I will make myself like the Most High!"

Samaria, 710 B.C.

"Well done, Rugio," said Lucifer, pacing in front of the hulking warrior who was seated in a place of honor in front of the Council. "If all my leaders had the resourcefulness and ability that you have demonstrated over the kings of Assyria, we should have destroyed these people long ago."

Rugio nodded in humble agreement, stealing a glance at Kara, who was quietly stewing in moody contemplation. The Council was meeting in the occupied city of Samaria, former capital of Israel, now the capital of the newly annexed province of the Assyrian empire that Israel had become. Ahab's former palace, the proud heritage of the house of Omri, gave evidence of the recent hardships. Much of the marvelous ivory inlaid walls and panels had been stripped and sent back to the Assyrian king in Nineveh as a trophy of war. Other parts had been burned out by fleeing nobles.

"Of course Rugio never really had a difficult task of it," snorted Kara. "When I was prince over Egypt I had to face much greater opposition."

Pellecus could only roll his eyes in disgust at Kara's posturing.

"Yes," agreed Rugio. "And as a result of your indecisive leadership we not only lost Egypt's greatness but also allowed Moses to escape with the people."

"Enough!" shouted Lucifer. "We are gathered to enjoy the fruits of a great victory and discuss our next move against the Lord's people."

Lucifer moved about the former throne room, now shabby and abandoned, with charred beams littering the once magnificently polished stone floors. He stood where the throne of Israel's kings was once positioned.

"Israel is finished," he began. "The kingdom of ten tribes is liquidated and will vanish into the bloody history of humanity. The kings who sat in this room are forever removed. It has been a magnificent time."

He looked intently at the group.

"I must however caution you all on something," he continued. "It is of course a sweet victory to have dealt this blow to Israel. But unfortunately, many of your commanders in the field have speculated, foolishly, that with the obliteration of Israel the threat of the Seed has diminished. However, the war is far from over and talk of this sort will only prove disappointing later on."

"Why so, my lord?" asked Rugio. "With Israel finished it demonstrates that God's people are not only vulnerable but conquerable."

"Because, my dear warrior, there is always a remnant—a loyal contingent bent upon serving God. Recall the number of occasions when we believed that the Seed was abandoned to this murky brood. Up would rise a Moses or a Joshua to further the prophecy just a bit closer to its fulfillment—always a hope rising out of depression, always a light out of the darkness. This is why the war is far from over."

He looked about the room as if some unseen person or thing were stalking him—as if the shadows in the room plagued his mind. He looked at the others and almost whispered, "Even now the prophecy closes in."

Lucifer looked at Pellecus, who nodded and unrolled a scroll from which he read:

"These are some more words of one of the Lord's prophets: 'Behold—a virgin will be with child and bear a son, and she shall call Him Immanuel...

" 'To us a child is born...to us a Son is given...and the government shall be upon His shoulders...and He will be called Wonderful, Counselor, Mighty God, Everlasting Father, Prince of Peace...

" 'A shoot shall spring from the stem of Jesse, and a branch from his roots will bear fruit...the Spirit of the Lord will be upon Him...the spirit of wisdom and understanding...the spirit of counsel and strength...the spirit of knowledge and the fear of the Lord....' "

Kara groaned in the light of yet another prophecy. Rugio listened intently, trying to interpret the meaning of the words. Lucifer simply listened in quiet contemplation.

"And," continued Pellecus, 'He shall reign on David's throne and over his kingdom, establishing and upholding it with justice and righteousness from that time on and forever.' There is more, but I believe that these are some of the more critical passages. Not very hopeful words, hmm?"

"Deadly," said Lucifer grimly.

"The Seed," whispered Kara. "Again."

"Yes, Kara, again and always," said Lucifer. "As I said it is closing in. The prophets speak more and more to its arrival. They give us more and more detail as to the nature of this Coming One—this Immanuel."

"Immanuel means 'God with us,' " said Pellecus. "It is obviously the Lord Himself of whom the prophet speaks. This Messiah—this Anointed One—is not an ordinary man. It will be the Lord Himself!"

The room became still as the angels suddenly realized that the Seed of the woman would be the Lord Himself! The chilling words unnerved the angels.

"The prophecy is quite clear," continued Pellecus. "Should this Child—this Coming King—be born of Jesse's seed—which is to say the house of David—it will be difficult to contest Him."

"However," continued Lucifer, "the prophecy is equally clear that it should happen during the kingdom of David."

"But David died long ago," pleaded Kara. "How can this be?"

"Recall that the Seed shall come through the tribe of Judah," answered Pellecus. "The house of David. It does not mean David must be alive when the Seed arrives."

"What it means," added Lucifer, "is that the final battle of the war must be centered in Judah and Jerusalem."

"So you see, Rugio, that your victory is not quite as complete as you believed," Kara said bitingly. "Whose words are these latest outrages?"

"Another prophet, of course," said Lucifer. "This one is called Isaiah."

"Isaiah?" responded Rugio. "He has been prophesying since Uzziah's time. Nobody has taken him seriously."

"These prophets!" fumed Kara. "Always stirring the people up to some such nonsense. When will they learn that the people never listen?"

"Perhaps they will listen one day," said Lucifer, with a faraway look in his eyes. He was imagining the Lord Himself, speaking to the nation, talking to them as one human might speak with another. "Many prophets of the Lord have come and gone," he continued. "And we have managed to surround the kings with prophets who speak what their deceived ears wish to hear. Perhaps it shall be the same with this one. These people are hardhearted and stiff-necked..."

"How can we possibly contest this?" complained Kara. "If Immanuel is God Himself, how can we intervene?"

Lucifer smiled at Kara's typically panicked response.

"While it is true that the prophetic voices pose a real threat, it is also true that they give us a vital clue to Immanuel's arrival," reasoned Lucifer. "In short, the Most High has given it all away."

"Another lapse of judgment on the part of the Lord," said Pellecus proudly.

"How does this help us?" asked Kara.

"By sending these swaggering, browbeating prophets to Israel and Judah, the Lord has also given information about this Immanuel," said Lucifer. "As always the Lord has left Himself open. I believe that what we have learned from the Lord's prophets will help us to prevent the Seed from ever being safely delivered."

Kara and Rugio both looked at Lucifer incredulously. Could it be that there was still a way to win this never-ending war? Lucifer smiled and indicated to Pellecus that he should continue the briefing.

"As our prince Lucifer said, the Lord has sent many prophets to His people," said Pellecus, in a lecture stance. "Many of them have been sent away, murdered, or otherwise ignored. However, what we cannot ignore is that thus far they have proven accurate—whether or not the people listened. The prophets said Israel would be destroyed if the people refused to repent. Well, they refused...and were destroyed."

"Neither did Ahaz listen to Isaiah when this very prophecy was given. Rather than trust the Lord he made a deal with the

Assyrians—and Judah became a tributary of theirs." He grinned at the others. "We are destroying Judah by inches!"

"So Rugio's stirring up of Assyria was actually working in complement with the Lord's prophecy of destruction," reasoned Kara. "Now that is interesting." He glared at Rugio. "You are the Lord's executioner, Rugio."

Rugio began moving forward as if he were about to lunge at Kara, but, looking at Lucifer, relented and settled back in his position.

"Whether or not we are instruments of the Lord's justice is no matter," said Lucifer sharply. "The point is that Israel was destroyed." He picked up a piece of a broken candlestick. "The Most High is a prisoner to His own ethic. He must destroy the nation that He threatened to destroy, or be called a liar. If He dispossesses Himself of both Israel and Judah, then He will become a forgotten light—like this ruined candlestick!" He tossed it aside. "What matter that He orchestrates the destruction so long as our enemy is destroyed?"

"Nevertheless, we must look ahead," said Kara.

"We must also look behind," Pellecus interrupted. "We must be mindful of what the prophets have spoken. Hosea is telling the people that this Messiah—this Anointed One—shall be a person of great love, desirous of mercy, which is His choice—but punishing sin, which is His character.

"And Micah? He has even given us the place of this Child's eventual birth—Bethlehem—the city of David."

Pellecus stroked his chin as if in great puzzlement. "I must admit that the idea of childbirth threw me until Isaiah cleared it up. Isaiah speaks of a virgin giving birth to this Child who shall be called Wonderful, Counselor, and all that other nonsense. So you see, the prophets are giving it all away whether or not the people are understanding it."

"This is wonderful intelligence," said Kara. "But what are we to do with it?"

"We will use it against the remaining nation," said Lucifer. "If this Child shall one day be born in Bethlehem, which fits in nicely with the prophecy of the house of Judah—David's tribe, David's city—then it is reasonable to assume that should Judah cease to exist there will be no kingdom of David for the Seed to enter."

"Excellent!" cried out Kara. "So how do we defeat him? It is impossible to stop the Lord Himself."

"True," said Lucifer," we may not be able to stop the Lord—defeat the Seed, as it were. But perhaps we can rob the Seed of the soil it must have."

Kara and Rugio looked at each other.

"Once more the Lord has given away His plan," said Lucifer. "The prophets speak not only to God's people—they speak to us as well. Hear me: The child must arrive during a period of time when a kingdom ruled by a stem of Jesse is in place. For now, Judah, the kingdom founded by David, son of Jesse, thrives and waits for the introduction of the Seed into its national womb..."

"But," said Pellecus, picking up the thought, "should the kingdom cease, the threat is removed—because there is no kingdom of David in which to introduce the Seed!"

"Exactly," said Lucifer. "How can this Coming One reign on David's throne and over David's kingdom if neither of them exists? How can he be born in Bethlehem of a virgin womb if Bethlehem is occupied by an idolatrous empire?"

Lucifer relished the effect of his words upon the Council. A sense of hope was building among his leaders as he had not seen in some time. Perhaps the war was shifting in their favor after all.

"And with Assyrian proximity to Judah at this very moment," Lucifer continued, "it seems advisable to mobilize them against Hezekiah and destroy Judah immediately. I feel another war coming on!"

Rugio grinned at the prospect of the Assyrians—the nation under his authority—being involved in the final destruction of their enemy. His would be the greatest name in the new order—second only to Lucifer should he successfully bring the same destruction upon Judah. Lucifer looked intently at Rugio.

"Sennacherib is a king with an appetite, Rugio," said Lucifer. "His army is well trained and tested. I suggest that you fan his desire for glory a bit more to the south to subdue the rebellious tributaries that are seeking to break away from his grip. Judah is leaning toward joining this pack of rebels."

Rugio nodded in understanding.

"As for Hezekiah, he is no Ahaz," commented Pellecus. "Hezekiah has a heart for the Lord that is disturbing. His reforms under Isaiah's guidance have proven disastrous for us. He has abolished the worship of other gods that we labored for so vigorously. He has repaired the temple, which had begun to fall into ruin. He has abolished the shrines, smashed the high places, and cut down the Asherah poles."

"If only we could cut *him* down," muttered Rugio.

Lucifer smiled at the thought of Rugio tearing the poor king into pieces.

"Indeed he has a different spirit than his fathers," Lucifer continued. He turned to Kara. "Therefore we must work to separate his heart from his head. I am particularly concerned with these prophets of the Lord who currently haunt the Judean court."

The three angels looked at Lucifer with hope for the first time in a very long time. Lucifer looked at the three angels who were his chief princes on earth.

"We must see to Judah's destruction," he said. "We must go at once to Jerusalem and begin a rampage of fear of the Assyrians among the people in anticipation of Rugio's inducement of Sennacherib to invade. Part of Rugio's work is already done. Hezekiah has crossed Sennacherib by agreeing to join this ridiculous coalition of kingdoms in rebellion to Sennacherib's authority in the region. Kindle that pride."

"Yes, my prince," said Rugio.

"Kara, you and Pellecus shall begin the fear among the people while Rugio inflames Sennacherib. And I shall work to persuade Hezekiah. Perhaps together we can introduce a seed of a different sort in the kingdom of David—a seed of destruction!"

Chronicles of the Host

Assyrian Threat

Flushed with his destruction of Israel, Sennacherib and his generals met to discuss the disposition of the nation of Judah, which had recently sought help from Egypt. Why must humans always seek to provide for their own safety, when their Creator longs to do just that? As the Host watched Lucifer's continued efforts to incite Assyria to war, the prophet Isaiah sought to assure Hezekiah that the Lord would indeed be with Judah. Thus were many voices speaking to many hearts....

The Assyrian camp at Lachish was a small city. Thousands of tents dotted the landscape like cattle, and smoke from the campfires billowed into a haze that drifted all the way toward Jerusalem. Proud and cruel, the army under Sennacherib had undertaken a new campaign to put to rest once and for all the rebel nations who resisted his authority.

Inside Sennacherib's royal tent, the military commanders met to discuss their response to Hezekiah's decision to call upon Egypt for help rather than to submit to Assyrian dominance in the region. Hezekiah had already paid a fortune to the king, but Sennacherib was not satisfied. He now wanted Hezekiah's complete and abject humiliation because of the appeal the king of Judah had made to the Egyptians.

Kiriam, Sennacherib's finance minister, bowed and came before the king, who was sitting on a couch in the tent. The generals were pouring over a map toward the front of the huge tent. Sennacherib was in good humor. He cheerfully invited Kiriam to approach him with his report.

"Is that the tribute of Hezekiah?" the king asked, while eating some fruit that a steward had just presented to him.

"Yes, majesty," said Kiriam. "I have the complete list. These items are on their way back to Nineveh to await your return from your victorious campaign."

"Let me hear it," said the king, closing his eyes and sitting back in the couch so he could drink it all in.

"We have from the king of Judah thirty talents of gold, eight hundred talents of silver, precious stones, antimony, large cuts of red stone, couches inlaid with ivory, nimedu chairs inlaid with ivory, elephant hides, ebony wood, boxwood and all kinds of valuable treasures, his own daughters and concubines…"

"That will do," said Sennacherib. "I have heard that this king, who is so enamored with his god, actually stripped the temple of its gold to produce the required tribute!"

"Truly you have humbled him, O king," said Kiriam.

Sennacherib stroked his beard in contemplation. Had he? This same Hezekiah who pledged tribute on one hand also was making diplomatic correspondence with Egypt. Was that the mark of a humbled man…or a crafty one?

"Kiriam, you trust too much in gold and ledgers," said Sennacherib. "I believe that Hezekiah's attempt to buy me off was only to put me at a disadvantage later on. That is why my generals and I are looking at other possibilities."

A commander entered the tent and whispered into one of the official's ears. The official approached the king and bowed low.

"Well?" said Sennacherib.

"The army awaits your command, majesty," said the official. "Your delegation to Jerusalem with your latest offer to Hezekiah…"

"Excellent, commander! Begin at once."

After the commander left, the king turned to his ministers.

"Horse, foot, chariots, archers, elephants, battering rams— more than one hundred eighty-five thousand of the greatest army in the world! This shall be quite a delegation to Hezekiah—a little diplomacy can be quite fruitful!"

The ministers laughed with their king as they heard the trumpets sounding and the orders being given to move out of Libnah toward Jerusalem.

"Look at them, Nathan," said Rugio proudly as the Assyrian army began an organized and efficient move out of Lachish. "They are proud, ruthless, and motivated. The greatest human empire in the world. And under my influence they shall destroy what is left of the Lord's people!"

Rugio stood with Nathan, his chief aide, atop a hill that overlooked Lachish. The banners of the different divisions gleamed in the sunshine as beautiful uniforms of purple and gold marched by. Archers in magnificent chariots followed by infantry headed down the highway. Behind them were the elephants, followed by the huge battering rams. On either side, the proud Assyrian cavalry with their pikes and banners escorted the army eastward to Jerusalem. Above them, in invisible escort, were thousands of warriors under Rugio's command who also seemed to be in proud formation.

"Hezekiah knows that these same troops have already reduced most of his cities in Judah," Rugio continued. "I'm sure he will not resist. So whether he fights or chooses to accede to Sennacherib's demands is no matter—either way Judah will cease as a nation."

"Lucifer was certainly correct about Sennacherib," said Nathan, a warrior who had recently been promoted to Rugio's side. "Your suggestions to him were quite effective."

"What is already in the mind of humans can easily be exploited," said Rugio. "This man was bent on conquest. I only needed to appeal to his pride."

He looked in the direction of the great tent of Sennacherib that dwarfed every other tent in the camp. "Stupid, human pride!"

"Still, it took some cleverness on your part," said Nathan.

"True," agreed Rugio. Not being noted for his cleverness like Kara or Pellecus, he enjoyed the compliment. "It was clever. But simple too. I merely appeared to him in the form of the Assyrians' chief god, Ashur, and commanded him to avenge my name that was being dishonored in Jerusalem. He was quite taken in."

They watched as the army continued to move inexorably down the road. From time to time the demon escorts would look in the direction of Rugio and cheer him. Rugio acknowledged their homage and encouraged them in their upcoming battle with Michael's angels, who jealously guarded the holy city.

"The archangel must be demoralized by now," said Rugio.

"I cannot wait to see the look on his face when once more we enter his holy place," said Nathan. "This time, however, he is at the mercy of the faith of men—not of angels! I think I shall let him escort me into the presence of the Ark personally!"

Rugio smiled at Nathan's bitterness toward Michael. Ever since the encounter on earth when Serus came to Michael's assistance, Nathan had held an unending grudge against the archangel. At last he would get satisfaction!

"The war is slipping away from him," Rugio surmised, as an elephant trumpeted loudly. "Judah will disappear. And the precious Seed is about to find itself with no nation in which to germinate. Lucifer will get exactly what he has wanted all along—a draw to the game."

The angels who guarded Jerusalem quietly awaited their next command. They understood that the enemy was headed once more for the gates of Jerusalem. Since the destruction of Israel, the Host had prepared itself for the coming assault. But unlike days past, the number of angels afforded by the people's prayers was much smaller. Off in the distance Michael could see the Assyrian army—proud and menacing.

Judah's recent idolatrous past, coupled with the collapse of Israel, had left the people in a state of numbness. Even the recent religious reforms of Hezekiah had not sufficiently captured the national heart. Thus, the strength of the angels in Jerusalem was not what it once was—nor what Michael would like it to be.

The archangel surveyed the magnificent city of Jerusalem from above. Once the home of the Jebusites, Jerusalem had been taken by David and had become the capital of his kingdom. Through the years kings had added to it—expanding its walls, creating public buildings, and erecting marvelous residences. But the greatest structure of all—the jewel of the nation—was the temple of Solomon.

Michael recalled the days when Solomon built the temple—David's unfulfilled dream realized in his son. The temple was one of the greatest wonders in the world—a marvelous structure of polished stone, whose walls inside were overlaid with pure gold, and whose mysterious inner sanctum captured the hearts of priest and pagan alike.

Most importantly, God's very Presence, which rested in the Ark of the Testimony, was evidence of the Lord's continued shepherding of His people. The temple had always been a source of comfort in troubled times—even when they had in many ways forgotten the Lord on whom they called but seldom feared. Looking down at the temple now, Michael wondered what the future held for it—and the rest of the city.

"Michael!"

Michael turned to see Crispin gliding in from above. He smiled at his old teacher with whom he had shared so many incredible experiences since the war began.

"Greetings, good teacher," hailed Michael. "What brings you to Jerusalem?"

"Curiosity," said Crispin, motioning for the archangel to follow him. The two continued down into the city, alighting upon the rooftop of Hezekiah's palace. "The king of Assyria, Sennacherib, that proud puppet of Rugio, has sent a message to Hezekiah. The envoys are just now returning with it."

"Isaiah is also at court," said Crispin. "It will be interesting to hear his counsel. Hezekiah has already ignored the prophet's urging not to become involved with Egypt. Perhaps now that the threat is at his doorstep, he will trust in the Lord."

"These human kings!" Michael said, shaking his head with disdain. "All they know is blustering threats and coercion. They are truly students of pride."

"Excellent students," agreed Crispin, with a sly grin on his face. "Of course they have had a great teacher—the best!"

"My king, this is the envoy of Sennacherib, king of the Assyrians," said Eliakim, the palace administrator.

Hezekiah motioned for the man to approach. Bowing his head, Eliakim walked to the Assyrian commander and escorted him to the king. The man, dressed in the resplendent garb of the imperial guard, made a curt bow of his head. Hezekiah looked at the man and sized him up: cruel mouth and eyes, proud demeanor—probably a relative of the king or of one of his favorite concubines. An up-and-coming young officer whose future was bright in the bloody world of Assyrian politics.

The king was seated on a couch in a small receiving room. Not one for royal protocol, the king of Judah preferred more informal settings in which to deliberate pressing issues. He said it made him deal with such matters more reasonably. Besides, he had no reason to impress this man. Also present in the room was Shebna, Hezekiah's secretary, and Joah, the official recorder for the court of Judah.

"Well, you have a message for me," said Hezekiah. The Assyrian took out a scroll from a wooden box bearing the seal of Sennacherib and read these biting words:

> *"To Hezekiah king of Judah, Let not thy God in whom thou trustest deceive thee, saying, Jerusalem shall not be delivered into the hand of the king of Assyria. Behold, thou hast heard what the kings of Assyria have done to all lands, by destroying them utterly: and shalt thou be delivered? Have the gods of the nations delivered them which my fathers have destroyed; Gozan, and Haran, and Rezeph, and the children of Eden which were in Thelasar? Where is the king of Hamath, and the king of Arpad, and the king of the city of Sepharvaim, of Hena, and Ivah?"*

When he had finished reading, the Assyrian commander lowered the manuscript and awaited the king's invitation to proceed further. Hezekiah simply looked at him and said, "Yes, what else is there to tell me?"

"King Hezekiah," he began, "know that my lord Sennacherib, whose empire is the greatest on earth, will be merciful only once. Your people are afraid and your army is incapable of defeating us. Jerusalem shall be besieged and before it is over your men shall be eating their own waste and drinking their own urine in order to survive! This is the price of rebellion. Therefore, do not resist the king."

After the man had been escorted out, Hezekiah began to tear his clothes, ripping them in tatters before his men. They remained silent as their king sat for a moment in solemn contemplation. Hezekiah looked around him. This was one of the rooms he had played in as a child, when his father was king and he was simply the heir. How simple it all was then! But because of the compromise of the kings before him in allowing Judah to slip into idolatry, even the reforms he had instituted seemed to have occurred too late to save his nation. He looked at his men.

"I want you all to put on sackcloth and send for the prophet Isaiah," he said. "The man is in Jerusalem. He is the only one who can help us right now. He will hear from the Lord. Go now!"

The men bowed to their king and left the room. Hezekiah watched them leave, thankful to have such capable men around him. He looked out a window. Below him was Jerusalem—tense, holy Jerusalem. The sun was beginning to set behind the top of the temple, creating a marvelous silhouette of the magnificent edifice. That was it! He would go to the temple and pray! He would not bargain with this dog. For now he would let it rest with Isaiah. Surely the Lord would hear his prayers after such mockery by this...this Ashur-worshiping tyrant! He called for a steward.

"I am going to the temple," he said. "When Eliakim returns tell him that I am there! And get me some sackcloth!"

"Yes, my king," said the steward, who bowed, stepped out, and returned in a few moments with the rough, prickly material.

"I'm afraid, majesty, that it is a bit filthy," said the steward ashamedly.

"Not as filthy as the king who is wearing it," said Hezekiah. "Nor the nation that he governs."

Outside the antechamber, Isaiah the prophet awaited the return of Hezekiah from the temple. Michael and Crispin stood nearby, observing this curious man of God who had conferred with the two previous kings, Uzziah and Ahaz. Having prophesied during the time of Israel's destruction, Isaiah had seen in Judah a similar fate if they themselves did not repent. His message was typical of the prophets of his time: Repentance would bring the Lord's mercy; continued sinful behavior would bring destruction.

He also brought another message, a curious promise of a future King whose vindication of Israel would be eternal and glorious—something very comforting, albeit very remote in these troubling times. Crispin had looked into the prophecies of this man, but understood little more than did the humans to whom they were spoken.

"He certainly speaks of the Seed—this King from David's line," remarked Crispin, as he and Michael continued their discussion of the prophet.

"I'm sure he is one of the more troubling prophets to Lucifer," agreed Michael. As they spoke, Crispin and Michael were joined by Gabriel and Sangius, who had been sent in view of Hezekiah's prayers that were being lifted up to the Lord.

"Well, Gabriel," said Crispin. "What news from Heaven? May we expect some relief?"

Gabriel looked at Crispin and then indicated Isaiah, who remained silently awaiting his king. "The Spirit of the Lord shall speak to Hezekiah," said Gabriel. "He has prayed for deliverance from Sennacherib and has repented on behalf of the nation."

"And...?" prompted Crispin.

"And the Lord has heard his prayer," answered Gabriel. "Even I do not know what His words shall be...exactly."

The others understood that Gabriel was not at liberty to divulge any further news, so they politely moved the conversation forward.

"Interesting times for a prophet," mused Sangius. "The others failed, of course." He sighed and looked at his brother angels, reading consternation on their faces over what he had just said. "I mean Israel was destroyed and all..."

"The prophets did not fail, Sangius," corrected Crispin. "The prophets did their duty in speaking the words of the Lord. It was the failure of the kings and priests and their own prophets to heed the warnings that brought about the destruction of Israel."

"Yes, well I'm afraid the same shall happen to Judah," Sangius remarked.

"If they do not repent," said Crispin. "I quite agree."

The angels remained silent for a moment as they contemplated the horrific possibility that the nation they had watched over for so long might become as their northern brothers had a few years previously.

"Isaiah's prophecy against the king of Tyre has certainly enraged Lucifer," said Gabriel, breaking the quiet moment. "How does it go...?"

" 'How you have fallen from heaven, O Morning Star, son of the dawn'—you mean this one?" asked Sangius.

"Well done, Sangius," commended Crispin. "But do you know the rest?"

"Of course I know it," he said. "The moment that Isaiah said these words I held them in my heart. You must recall that I was close to Lucifer once." He looked at Michael. "These words have special meaning to me."

He then closed his eyes and spoke:

" 'You said in your heart, "I will ascend to heaven; I will raise my throne above the stars of God; I will sit enthroned on the mount of assembly, on the utmost heights of the sacred mountain...I will make myself like the Most High..." ' "

The chilling words brought back the memory of Lucifer's attempt to do just that, an action that resulted in a break with Heaven and the loss of so many former brothers—now bitter enemies. Such audacity! How true rang the words of the man of God.

"Lucifer certainly tried," said Michael, sadly shaking his head. "He actually said he would be like the Most High God. What a tragedy!"

"And what nonsense," said Crispin. "That a creature should try to subvert his Creator. But this is the subtlety of pride. Every sin, every act of defiance, every attitude that is out of place—every thought that is contrary to the Lord is rooted in pride. It is the great separator between creature and Creator."

"Such an awful chasm," said Gabriel.

"Yes," remarked Crispin. "Broken permanently at Eden, I'm afraid. Humans have been operating in its deadly effect ever since."

"Do you think it possible, dear teacher, that the chasm might one day be bridged?" asked Gabriel. "Will there ever again be a pure relationship between humans and God?"

"Considering that it is men and angels who are guilty of the pride that wrought the chasm," answered Crispin, "I would say that neither man nor angels shall ever be capable of bridging that gap."

CHAPTER 13

"We must believe the prophets."

Hezekiah awaited the prophet's words. He still wore the sackcloth that he had put on when he entered the temple to pray on behalf of the nation. Eliakim entered ahead of Isaiah and announced the prophet's arrival. Hezekiah warmly greeted Isaiah and bid him respond to him.

Isaiah greeted the king, whose reforms in the land had been encouraging to the man of God. He saw in Hezekiah a man who was truly humble and who sought after the Lord with all his heart. In spite of the king's dalliances with other nations rather than completely trusting the Lord, Isaiah knew that the king of Judah was a good man.

In the room, Michael and the others awaited the Lord's pronouncement for Judah. The Spirit of God had indeed given the prophet a message from the Lord God. They stood in complete silence, sensing the Lord's Spirit within Isaiah's anointed words.

"I have an answer for you from the Lord," said Isaiah.

"Pray tell me and I will do whatever the Lord requires," said Hezekiah.

" 'Know this, Hezekiah,' " Isaiah began. " 'Your prayer concerning Sennacherib has been heard by the Lord and He has spoken against him. He shall not enter this city or even shoot an arrow against it. He will not besiege it not bear a shield against it! He shall leave the way he came for I the Lord am defending this city!' "

Hezekiah began to weep, praising the Lord God and hugging the prophet. Isaiah smiled at the king and watched as his ministers entered the room and shared in the celebration. The angels also were overjoyed in the Lord's decision, worshiping the Lord for His mercy—all, that is, except Gabriel.

"What is wrong, Gabriel?" asked Michael. "This is wonderful news!"

Gabriel looked grimly at the others.

"There is more," he said, looking out a window beyond the walls of Jerusalem in the direction of the Assyrian army. "Much more."

The sentry yawned. The night was passing slowly and his duty was not up for several more hours. The army had been campaigning for several years now, expanding the Assyrian empire in new directions and bringing glory to its commanders. But tonight was cold and depressing. He longed for his family in Nineveh and didn't look forward to what would probably be years of siege warfare against Jerusalem. He played with the red amulet his mother had given him for protection before he left on the campaign. *It will be a long war*, he thought to himself.

Rugio, who stood outside the field commander's tent, awaited Nathan's return. High above the Assyrian camp, the thousands of devils that accompanied the army were watching for any sign of the archangels, who they knew were in the city. Nathan had given specific instructions that they should keep vigilant.

When he had completed his rounds, Nathan joined Rugio. He was quite exuberant.

"Our legions are intact and ready," he said. "We have been sending forays into the city to start the panic, so when the siege begins…" He stopped. Rugio was not listening.

"My lord?" Nathan asked. "Rugio?"

Rugio looked at him as if waking from a dream. He was looking into the sky as if he were seeing something…listening to something. Nathan looked about, noticing nothing in particular. He looked quizzically at Rugio.

"Something is stirring," Rugio said. "Something I cannot quite discern."

"Perhaps it is something good, my lord," offered Nathan.

A loud shriek broke the silence. Several demons were moving about in different directions. Others looked about, trying to determine what was happening. Rugio demanded to know what the disturbance was all about. Even the humans were beginning to stir themselves! What was this?

"My lord!" came a call from the blackness. It was one of Nathan's commanders.

"What is it?" Nathan called back.

"The Angel of the Lord! He is here!"

Gabriel stood off a distance from the Angel of the Lord, who was slowly pouring into the camp. Michael was at the other end of the great army, positioning himself with thousands of the Host to throw a panic into the army from his end. It was to be a night of great destruction; and though Michael did not enjoy seeing humans die, he understood that the Lord was righteous in all of His actions—even in the taking of life at times.

The sentry peered into the darkness. Was that something moving? He looked again, rubbing his eyes. It looked like…an army! Thousands of the enemy were in the field. They were being attacked.

"Alarm! Alarm!" he called out.

Somebody blew a trumpet, signaling that the camp was under attack. Men began pouring out of their tents, weapons in hand. Commanders tried to regain a sense of order, but they themselves were thrown into a panic as they saw enemy soldiers everywhere! Loud crashes, trumpets, men shouting—all of this created a confusion that caused a once proud and disciplined warring machine to disintegrate into a panic.

The Host also moved through the camp, causing the men to strike out at anything that moved. Michael sent some angels to the edge of the camp and threw the elephants into a panic. The great beasts cut a bloody swath through the center of the camp in a wild stampede that trampled tents and started fires.

The angels under Rugio's command fought to regain order as well. With the knowledge that the Angel of the Lord was leading the attack, they managed only some brief skirmishes with some of Michael's angels. Nathan himself went after Michael, but the archangel swung a hard blow with his sword that sent Nathan falling backwards into the camp. The impact of the warrior's fall caused a huge fire to break out in one of the storage tents. The Host, in the guise of Israelite soldiers, were everywhere to be seen. Assyrians struck blindly at the phantom enemies, with the result that they began killing each other!

Understanding what was happening, Rugio took his sword out and cut deeply into one of the angels. The angel yelped and moved back. Rugio grinned a malevolent smile at the angel, whose Israelite disguise had vanished. The angel positioned himself to dodge Rugio's next blow when suddenly a light shot out from the center of the camp, blinding every human and wicked angel throughout the camp.

The light went straight up into the air like a gigantic fountain, and cascaded to earth in streams of brilliant, white, downy light. As the light fell upon the camp, humans began dropping dead where they stood. Devils scattered in every direction, screaming that "the

Angel" was going to destroy them. Even Rugio bolted from the camp, cursing the Lord as he went. Then the light disappeared.

Nothing remained but bodies. No explanation to Hezekiah's men, who investigated the next day. No clues as to what terrible thing had happened to the Assyrian army. Just bodies—some 185,000 dead Assyrians. As they rooted about, an Israelite foot soldier came upon one of the Assyrians who was undoubtedly a sentry. He had stood near a hut used by the guards posted on the extreme edges of the camp.

The Israelite saw something in the man's hand that gleamed in the morning sun. It was a large reddish amulet that had broken off the man's neck. He looked at the man—a young man about his own age. For some reason the Israelite felt compassion for the Assyrian. Turning him over, he saw that the soldier had fallen on his own sword. Something had apparently frightened him so much that he had killed himself!

Bethlehem, 4 B.C.

Gabriel recalled that bloody day outside Jerusalem. It was interesting to hear Eli's description of the battle. How different the perspectives of humans and of angels! Looking now into the sky, which was filling with angels and creating a milky haze over Bethlehem, Gabriel could only think of how many more angels were here tonight than on that bloody night when Sennacherib's army was destroyed.

He looked at Bakka, who was now seated next to Daniel. He was glad to see that Bakka was beginning to take a greater interest in his assignment. Bakka looked up at Gabriel and smiled.

"I am learning a great deal about this man," said Bakka. "His family is one of the Levites. They had been in the priesthood but left it at some point."

"Yes, I know," said Gabriel. "I told you that he was an interesting assignment."

"But I'm not certain what the assignment is yet," said Bakka.

"Keep learning," said Gabriel. "It will become evident."

Eli looked down at the two boys who were now both asleep.

"Looks like my stories were not interesting enough to help them make it through the whole evening," he said humorously.

Daniel looked down also. Both of the boys' fathers were taking their watch at that moment. The other shepherds were also asleep. Daniel looked around as if wanting to make sure that they were quite alone. He leaned in to Eli.

"My fathers were part of the reason for our nation's destruction," he said, almost whispering. "I bear that shame."

Eli considered the man with whom he was speaking. Daniel had always been an outsider among the shepherds—never entering into fellowship with the others, keeping mainly to himself. Now he seemed to be opening up as a result of the conversation that had been going on all night.

Perhaps the images of Israel's holy history in which man came so close to having a relationship with his Creator, only to throw it all away, had touched a chord in his failed heritage. If indeed Daniel's family had been in the priesthood, then the burden he carried for the nation's destruction was understandable, though without real complicity. Eli hoped to encourage the man for whom he was beginning to have compassion.

"How is it that one man's family could bring down a nation?" posed Eli in a very general way, as if he himself were trying to figure it all out. "The prophet said that we all like sheep have strayed from the Lord's fold—not just one family."

Daniel nodded that he understood Eli's direction.

"I know that my family is as guilty as any other in Israel," said Daniel. "And I know that they are no more guilty than the rest of the nation." He looked at Eli intently, tears welling up in his eyes. "But I know that one person can make a difference in a nation's history. You have spoken of such men and women this night. I only wonder why someone in my family could not have made a difference."

He stood up and turned away from Eli toward Bethlehem. He pointed at the star that loomed overhead. Eli looked at the star as well.

"Some people point to such things as that star, which has recently appeared, and say that it is a sign of great tragedy to come; or perhaps that it signifies some great event that will occur. I wonder if perhaps we should look within…maybe the answer we seek is somehow in our hearts and not in our history?"

Eli was silent for a moment.

"Daniel, you are more philosopher than shepherd," he said amusedly. "Perhaps the heritage of your family cannot be so easily dismissed—there is very much the priest alive in you."

Daniel managed a sincere smile—albeit a halfway one.

"By that I mean you are speaking like a prophet yourself!"

Daniel looked at Eli with a curious expression.

"Jeremiah," said Eli. "He too spoke of knowing the Lord through the heart and not just through custom. 'I will give them a heart to know Me,' he said. 'They will be My people and I will be their God, for they will return to Me with all their heart.' Sounds very much like what you are saying."

Daniel thought about this for a moment. How wonderful it would be to know God in one's heart rather than through men and temples and law and…Yet how could that happen? Apart from the law and traditions of their fathers there was no other way to the heart of God.

"Yet we have strayed like lost sheep," said Daniel. "And our nation is no longer free. We are a captive people. Look at Bethlehem—filled beyond capacity because of the whims of an emperor who declares a census throughout his realm. How can such a divided and conquered people hope to know the God they abandoned so long ago?"

"How indeed?" said Eli. "And yet, Daniel, we must have hope that someday the Coming One shall present the answers to us. We must believe the prophets. Like that star—perhaps one day the King will appear and bring light to a darkened nation."

"Perhaps," said Daniel sullenly. "But they did not hear the prophets. Will they now welcome the King who comes?"

Eli had no answer. He had wondered the same thing many times. He could only hope that when the King arrived, He would set things right as only He would be able to.

"I can only hope, Daniel, that when the King arrives, we shall know it," Eli said. "I hope that it shall be on a day in which we are all looking for Him. I hope that it will be as obvious as that star you keep speaking of."

"And just as bright," said Daniel, looking up into the sky.

Michael had ordered his angels to fan out in front of Mary and Joseph as they entered the town. Only a few townspeople and some soldiers were out and about. Roman officials who were assigned to Bethlehem for the census sat at a table outside a small tavern. In front of them was a long line.

Joseph left Mary and walked to the official, who was taking information from an older man. The official looked at Joseph.

"Get to the end of the line," he barked.

"I am Joseph, of the tribe of Judah. I am here to report for the census. The woman who is with me is not well," he said. "Might we move to the front of the line?"

The official looked at a soldier who came over and escorted Joseph back to the end of the long line. Mary remained on the donkey in obvious discomfort.

"I'm not sure how much longer," she said. She was beginning to perspire heavily.

"I will find us a place to stay," Joseph said. "Then we'll take care of the census."

"Hurry, my love," said Mary.

Michael remained with Mary as Joseph disappeared into an alley to seek out a place where she might have her baby. The angels gathered around Bethlehem numbered in the thousands. He had done all that he could to protect this couple—especially the woman who carried within her the hope of the world.

"Michael! Michael!"

Michael turned to see Gabriel, surprised to see the archangel in Bethlehem. He knew that Gabriel had been with the shepherds nearby.

"Gabriel," said Michael. "Welcome. What a glorious night!"

"Yes, glorious," agreed Gabriel. "Many lives will change this night. But I came to tell you something of great interest. Something about Lucifer!"

"Lucifer?" asked Michael. "What has he to do with this night?"

"He is here," said Gabriel. "And he wishes to meet with you."

Chronicles of the Host

Judah's Disgrace

The hope we had in Hezekiah was dashed by his son, Manasseh, who turned the nation of Judah away from the Most High and back to idolatry. Back and forth went this nation of proud and stubborn men. And the prophets of God continued their message—the same as they had delivered to Israel: Repent and turn from your wicked ways or be destroyed.

Even in the midst of such despair, the Lord also held out the hope of the one who would make things right—but it was lost on a people bent on self destruction. And within a very short time, during the prophet Jeremiah's ministry, the nation of Judah fell into the hands of a new menace—Babylon.

Nebuchadnezzar, a proud and powerful ruler from the east, had moved into Jerusalem two times and had placed leaders on the throne who might be commensurate with Babylon's dominance. But compromise was not enough for Lucifer; he needed the utter destruction of the nation to get advantage on the Seed.

So it was that, guided by Pellecus, who loved the wisdom and black arts of these Chaldeans, the nation of Babylon was set upon a course of complete destruction of Judah. It was a time of grief and shock—both to the men who had felt they were secure in the city that housed the Presence of God; and to the Host, who had long held and hoped that such an event might never happen. How could we have known that the salvation of God was not bound by political boundaries and the heritage of kings?...How could we have known that the end of a nation was not the end of the promise?...How could we have known that the stem of Jesse would find its fruit years later in Bethlehem?

Babylon, 587 B.C.

The temple of Marduk, in Babylon, was Nebuchadnezzar's proudest achievement. Ever since taking the throne from his father, Nabopolasser, who had founded this newest and greatest

Babylonian empire, Nebuchadnezzar knew he was destined to play an eternal role in human history. He wanted to be remembered not as a conqueror, but as a civilizer—one who brought Babylonian culture to the world and transformed the world into a Chaldean image!

Since the destruction of Assyria at the battle at Carchemish, the empire had been expanding steadily. Syria, Palestine, even Egypt were under the control or influence of Babylon. Surely his father would be proud of how things were going. All of this brought Nebuchadnezzar back to his thoughts of the great temple of Marduk.

Strolling along the balcony of his palace, the king looked over the city of his fathers. Since his first days as king, Nebuchadnezzar had set himself to recapturing and surpassing the former glory of Babylon. He had built great ziggurats that served as both temples and astronomical observatories. Most impressive of all was his recreation of the famed Tower of Babel, an enormous tower some 295 feet tall, which dominated the Babylonian skyline. The famous Hanging Gardens, a complex of concentric squares with lush palm trees and green shrubs that he was ever tinkering with as a gift for his wife, had become a legend throughout the world. He had much to be proud of. And yet....

As he strolled the balcony of his palace, Nebuchadnezzar looked south toward the ziggurat complex of Etemanki. There, beside the southern wall of that enclosure, was the great temple. He had done all he could to honor Marduk, the chief god of the Chaldeans. The temple was a marvelous structure with two outer courtyards, a number of inner chapels, and a separate sanctuary that honored the god Marduk's father, Ea. But most magnificent of all was the shrine to Marduk himself.

Located on the western wall, the shrine was entered through an intricate and beautiful façade that towered over the entry. Nebuchadnezzar had covered its walls inside with sparkling gold. The shrine housed a figure of Marduk, also made of gold and seated upon a throne made of gold. Beside the figure was a golden table. Outside the shrine were a golden altar and beside it a bronze altar, on which frankincense was offered every year at Marduk's chief festival.

Was the god pleased with his efforts to honor him? Nebuchadnezzar wondered if there was more he might do to ensure the continued favor of the god who was sometimes capricious in his dealings with humans. The high priest seemed to believe that all was well, yet the king had been having troubling dreams lately. Looking about him to make certain he was alone, the king got on his knees.

"Marduk, great god of the Chaldeans, what is it that I am to do?" pleaded the king in a whisper as he looked at the great temple in the distance. "I have conquered the world in your name. I have humbled many kings and their gods. I have built for you a great temple that is incomparable. What have I left undone? Send me a sign, great one, that I might know your..."

The sound of a thud nearby made the king look around. There beside him on the balcony lay an eagle, dead. The king looked about to see if someone had tossed it at him.

"Who is there?" he demanded.

A servant came running up the stairs upon hearing his master cry out. The servant bowed low before the king awaiting his command.

"Who has been up here?" Nebuchadnezzar asked.

"You are alone here, great king," said the shaken servant. "Nobody has passed your guard upon the stairway."

"Summon Ashpenaz, my chief advisor," said Nebuchadnezzar. "And bring wine! I will meet him in my chambers."

"Yes majesty," said the servant, who just then saw the dead bird. He bent down to pick it up, but the king stopped him.

"Leave it," said the king.

"A dead eagle, majesty?" responded the servant, quite puzzled.

"A message," said Nebuchadnezzar, looking at the dead bird.

After the king left the balcony to meet with his advisor, Pellecus and several wisdom angels with him strolled the same spot. Pellecus looked down upon the dead bird.

"A message in a bird," he said sarcastically. "Something of a poem in there: How feeble is the mind of a human king to look at such nonsense and divine a great thing."

The others laughed aloud at Pellecus's words.

"Babylon is indeed a great city," he said. "These people are fairly advanced as humans go. Their knowledge of the arts and sciences and of sorcery is unmatched, even in Egypt. Of course the sorcery comes easily when it is being manipulated by our demons, but it still impresses and captures human minds."

"So the strategy at this point…" began Drezzan.

"The strategy as always is to use this man to destroy Judah," said Pellecus. "After all, the Lord's own prophets have predicted it. Why disappoint Him?"

Laughter.

"And how do we achieve this?" asked Tinius, who had found his way back from disgrace in Lucifer's eyes. Pellecus had always liked Tinius's questioning of Lucifer; it flew in the face of decorum at Council. So he had recently courted Tinius and appointed him as one of his own aides.

"Excellent question, Tinius," said Pellecus. "Lucifer was always disturbed with your incessant questioning. I find it refreshing—to a point. But in answer I must tell you of a very encouraging report I have received from Jerusalem."

Tinius and the others looked at Pellecus with anticipation of hopeful news from the city they hated. Pellecus began:

"As you know, twice Nebuchadnezzar has entered Jerusalem to put down rebellious behavior. The first time he dealt with Jehoiakim, that Egyptian puppet who took the throne when Josiah was killed in battle. Nebuchadnezzar took many captives and brought them here to Babylon. Then he had to deal with Jehoiakin, who had replaced Jehoiakim. Again he moved in and took many captives. He then replaced the king with a man named Zedekiah, one of Josiah's brothers. Now, it seems, this man is rumbling about rebellion against Nebuchadnezzar. This time when he moves in, I will make certain that the prophecies foretelling Jerusalem's destruction will be fulfilled!"

"The problem is that with the captives he also brought the faith," said Tinius. "These exiles are the nobles and the priests. They have brought it to Babylon with them and are organizing in secret meetings. I think it is dangerous!"

Pellecus nodded in agreement.

"True, the exiles are a bit of a challenge," he said. "And yet I believe that faced with the luxury of Babylon and the purse of the king—who is willing to train them up in the culture and arts of Egypt in service to Babylon—most will be assimilated relatively calmly." He scoffed and added, "They have been idolaters for years. This would simply make it official!"

Tinius and the others laughed.

"There are some, majesty, who may not bow to Marduk," said Drezzan.

"You speak of Daniel, of course," said Pellecus. "I wouldn't worry about him."

"There is another name I hear thrown about," said Tinius. "A man who now lives in exile on the Chebar…"

"Ah, Ezekiel," said Pellecus. Tinius looked at Pellecus in surprise. "As you see, I am well-informed in my domain. That is why Kara failed in Egypt and Rugio lost Assyria. They did not respect the knowledge that was available to them. Remember that, my brothers—knowledge is the key to ruling with authority!"

"And Ezekiel?" prompted Tinius.

"Another holy man without a country," speculated Pellecus. "He too shall disappear, Tinius. I promise that once Jerusalem is destroyed, and its temple gone, the holy men shall become obsolete, their message forgotten."

"And what happens to the Seed?" asked Tinius.

"The Seed?" repeated Pellecus. "The Seed shall be stillborn. It shall die before it is ever given a chance for life."

Nebuchadnezzar sipped his wine. He always enjoyed the sweet wine that came from the region near where he was raised as a child. Now he was king, awaiting his advisor's counsel on this most recent and disturbing message from the gods. Ashpenaz looked at the dead bird, which the king had ordered brought in from the roof.

"Majesty, it is obviously an indication of a kingdom in peril," he began.

"Whose kingdom?" asked Nebuchadnezzar, as he poured himself more wine and offered a cup to Ashpenaz. "I have done all for Marduk, bless his name. Why should my kingdom be in peril?"

"Perhaps, majesty, it is not your kingdom that is in peril," offered Ashpenaz. "Perhaps this bird speaks to another kingdom that is in peril...one that is in its death throes even now..."

"You mean Judah," said Nebuchadnezzar. "I was wondering when you would get to that." He shook his head. "It is no secret that you have, as a matter of principle, determined that Judah should be completely destroyed. I will not have you turning every omen into an excuse to invade Jerusalem again. Twice I have been to Jerusalem. I believe its people are sufficiently humbled."

Ashpenaz produced a scroll that bore the seal of Nebuchad-nezzar along with that of the Babylonian governor of Syria. He looked at the king, who returned his look with a skeptical glare.

"Well?" asked the king. "You are obviously anxious to read me something else about Judah, no doubt."

"Anxious, no," said Ashpenaz. "But quite troubled. And yes, the news concerns Judah."

Nebuchadnezzar snatched the scroll from the chief of his court officials and as he read, Ashpenaz continued speaking. "It seems, majesty, that Zedekiah has withheld tribute from our col-lectors. His counselors have even gone so far as to insult our offi-cials. To their shame, they have even spoken against you, O king..."

As he read, Nebuchadnezzar was becoming visibly more and more angry. He looked up from the scroll when he was finished and handed it back to Ashpenaz.

"So you see, majesty, these people are by nature stiff-necked and rebellious," Ashpenaz continued. "I have ordered arrests of many of the Jews whom we have exiled into our own country. I believe we should imprison them..."

"No!" said Nebuchadnezzar loudly. "I told you that I want to bring them into our empire and use their skills. These are a very capable people, Ashpenaz. They are noble, spiritual people. I want you to take from the most recent exiles—those who are fast learn-ers and handsome—and bring them to the palace and let them have a taste of real culture. I tell you—once these Hebrews begin to see what we have to offer, they will enter into our service; and all thoughts of rebellion will be crushed!"

"I will see to it," said Ashpenaz reluctantly. "And as to Zedekiah?"

"I sought your wisdom," said the king. "You are a great coun-selor. Now I shall seek the wisdom of Marduk himself. He will give us indication. In the meantime—I want you to personally recruit from the Jews men as I have described and bring them to the palace. This shall prove to all my subject peoples the benefit of being a part of the greatest empire on earth!"

Pellecus awaited the king inside the shrine of Marduk. Tinius was with him, noting the human love for gold. The image itself glimmered from the strategically positioned mirrors that reflected light from behind, casting an eerie iridescence in the room. Tinius looked at Pellecus, who was seated atop the idol.

"How disturbing it must be to the Most High to be portrayed so grotesquely," he said, patting the image's head. "After all, He made it the second most offensive point of His commandments."

"Why does He not want to be portrayed?" asked Tinius. "I should think it would honor Him."

"Because, Tinius, part of His power lies in His anonymity," came a voice.

"Ah my prince, welcome to Babylon," said Pellecus to Lucifer.

"I have just returned from Zedekiah's court," said Lucifer. "Kara has those fools actually believing that they can oppose Nebuchadnezzar!" He laughed. "They will be slaughtered, of course."

"The king is about to hear from Marduk," said Pellecus. "I prophesy it shall be a very destructive meeting."

Lucifer looked intently at Pellecus.

"There is much at stake here, Pellecus," he said gravely. "We must destroy not only the nation; we must destroy the reason for the nation."

"The reason?" asked Tinius.

"Yes, of course," agreed Pellecus. "With the cream of Jewish society in exile, we must make Jerusalem become a place so desolate that there will be no reason ever to return—thus nullifying the Seed's relevance. Correct?"

"I see you have worked it all out," said Lucifer. "Yes, that is correct. Two times Nebuchadnezzar has entered the city. This time there must not be a city left to reenter. This includes everything—the palaces, the walls…and the temple."

"The temple?" said Tinius nervously. "You would destroy the temple? The Most High's seat of Presence upon earth?"

"The Lord's Presence left that hollow sanctuary years ago," said Lucifer. "We are merely expediting the symbol. Once the temple is gone the faith will follow. All former covenant with the Lord shall be obliterated. The exiles will either become alien residents and disappear into the history of other nations, or they shall be pressed into service by the king, and thus lose their position of authority. Either way, the nation will cease and the threat to us will be gone."

"And then?" asked Tinius.

"And then we will negotiate this war to an agreeable close," said Lucifer.

Chapter 14

"I can protect you only to a point."

Nebuchadnezzar took the golden censer and placed it before the image of Marduk. With him was the high priest of the temple, who chanted the necessary oblations that would conjure the god. Bending down on his knees and touching the floor with his head, Nebuchadnezzar began to cry out to the god who had thus far guided him into so many great victories.

"Great Marduk," he began, "dread god of Sumer and Babylon, chief ruler and exalted deity from on high, I beg you to come into my unworthy presence and give me the wisdom I need to deal with your enemies…"

Pellecus had remained upon the image. Near him stood Lucifer and Tinius, watching the episode in amusement.

"Well, he's waiting," said Lucifer. "Lead this fool."

"Nebuchadnezzar."

The king looked at the high priest, wondering if he had spoken, and if not, whether he had heard the voice. The high priest was lost in his low chanting and didn't even realize the king was looking at him.

"Nebuchadnezzar, hear me…"

"Yes my lord," said the king, barely able to get the words out of his mouth.

"*You seek from me direction and I have spoken to you clearly…*"

"The eagle, my lord?" he asked.

"*The rebellion,*" came the answer. "*You have allowed your enemies to become an offense to me. They have insulted the gods of Babylon. They have trusted their god to deliver them in their temple. They are an offense and therefore you must deal with them harshly lest your kingdom be taken from you…*"

"Yes, lord," said Nebuchadnezzar. "I will see to it at once."

"You must see to it that not one stone is left of the temple in Jerusalem," Pellecus said, glancing at Lucifer's nodding approval. "You must tear down the walls so that it shall never again be an offense to Chaldea. And you must humble yourself for allowing such offense to happen by declaring a fast to my name."

"That's a bit much, isn't it?" said Lucifer, smiling.

Pellecus looked back. "I was going to have him build another temple but I thought it might distract his work in Jerusalem!" He looked at Lucifer and Tinius. "And now the finish…"

Pellecus touched the censer and made it flare up into a smoky greenish light that filled the shrine. The high priest opened his eyes, and together the king and the priest saw in the strange fog the figure of a man-beast—who looked like the image of Marduk.

"*Go now!*" the figure ordered. "*And leave nothing undone!*"

"As you command, O lord," said Nebuchadnezzar, who hurriedly left the room. The high priest was still peering into the smoky haze, wondering why the god had never appeared to him so dramatically.

"My prince, I give you Solomon's temple," said Pellecus proudly.

"You mean what is left of it," said Lucifer.

Chronicles of the Host
Jerusalem, Jerusalem

The unthinkable did in fact happen—Nebuchadnezzar came into Jerusalem for the third time. The Host watched in horror and shame as piece by piece, stone by stone, the temple of Solomon was dismantled, its holy emblems taken to Babylon, and its altars profaned by lovers of Marduk.

How could this be, we asked? Howling numbers of the enemy gloated in the city's despair, feeling closer to winning the war than they ever had. The king and the remaining nobles and priests were put in chains and led off into ignominious exile. We could only hope that somewhere in the midst of the people who were led off in darkness was the Seed who would one day bring them back into the light....

Babylon, 585 B.C.

The assignment given to Ashpenaz was one that he neither relished nor approved of. He thought it a mistake to try to train up aliens in the ways of Chaldea—especially these hardheaded Jews! But he figured that in time the king would see the error of his ways and dispose of them in more practical, if not brutal, ways.

He entered the large receiving room that was covered in deep azure tiles with the famous Babylonian lion in relief everywhere. Hundreds of young men of the best families of Judah awaited him. They were fine looking young men, dressed in simple Babylonian tunics and standing at attention as if this were a military inspection. He looked them over, then stood upon a platform to address them.

"I am Ashpenaz," he began, "the king's chief administrator. You have been selected by our great king as the best of your nation. You shall be schooled in the wisdom of Babylon, taught its language and history, schooled in its culture, taught our literature. In time, some of you shall enter into the king's service. You will serve him."

Some of the men began to relax, looking about at each other. One gave a scornful look to his friend who had predicted that they all were about to be executed.

"You will eat the same food as the king eats and have the benefit of living in and around the royal palace. You shall receive special treatment and will be trained for three years. After that you will be assigned permanently. Follow the stewards, receive your new names, and begin your training.

"New names?" a few people muttered.

"And," Ashpenaz added with a hint of menace, "serve the king well."

"I was sure we were to be executed," said a young man, as they left the hall. "Instead, we are to serve in the greatest empire in the world!"

"And eat at the king's table," said another.

"Think of it, Daniel," said a young man named Joseph. "Our families will be well taken care of!"

"Will they?" asked Daniel, a young man who as a child had been carried to Babylon a few years before the most recent destruction. "Are they taking care of us—or are they buying us?"

"What difference?" asked Joseph, also relieved that they were to be spared. "This is Babylon. The greatest city in the world. Lead city in the arts and sciences. It's massive. Why, you can even ride a four-horse chariot on top of the city walls, they are so thick!"

"Jerusalem had walls," said Daniel in an almost melancholy tone. "Once."

"Leave Daniel alone, Joseph," said Anath. "He will never become a servant of the king of Babylon. His kind can only cause us more grief. Best stay away from him."

The young men pulled away from Daniel lest they be associated with him by some of Ashpenaz's agents. Daniel watched as his friends, many of whom he had grown up with in Judah, turned away from him and regrouped on the other side of the room.

"Don't mind them, Daniel," came a voice. It was Hananiah. With him were Mishael and Azariah. The three were inseparable friends and had lately befriended Daniel, sharing his special love for the Lord God of Judah.

"I don't care about them, Hananiah," said Daniel, as they were ordered to disrobe and put on the new uniforms that designated them as wards of the king. "It is Jerusalem that I am thinking about. Do you suppose it is true? The temple, I mean?"

"That is what the new arrivals are saying, Daniel," said Azariah. "They were taking it down stone by stone. The walls too are being broken in places."

"Daniel!"

"Yes, sir," Daniel responded.

The steward, an older man who didn't enjoy being saddled with these young Jews, handed Daniel his new clothing. He looked at the writing on the ledger.

"Your new name is Belteshazzar," he said gruffly.

"Belteshazzar? What does it mean?" asked Daniel.

"Belteshazzar! It means 'may the god Bel protect you,' " said the man.

The boys laughed at Daniel's new name. They stopped laughing when they all received their names: Hananiah, Mishael, and Azariah became Shadrach, Meshach, and Abednego. Each name evoked the name of a Babylonian god, imploring his protection.

"We are in a profane land," said Daniel, after the man showed them to their rooms in the palace. "We have been given profane names. We are in the land of our enemies, not our benefactors. And now we must trust the Lord God of our fathers to help us through this difficult time." He placed his hand in the middle of the group and added, "We must pledge that we shall never compromise and bow our knee to this devil god they worship—this Marduk!"

The three men looked at Daniel and at each other. Ashpenaz seemed quite definite that they were expected to serve the king with utmost loyalty. Some of the Jews seemed ready to give in completely. Others were troubled by the thought of serving a foreign god in a foreign land. And yet all they knew was now destroyed. And had not their father Abraham begun his journey from Ur in this very land? Perhaps they were only returning to the true land of their fathers....

"Agreed," said Hanaiah, who was now called Shadrach. They all took hold of Daniel's hand in pledge. "We will never compromise, though it cost us everything."

"Except our names," said Abednego resignedly.

Ashpenaz had been thinking about his mission to subvert the Jews by lulling them into the king's guardianship. How often in his own political career had he seen men coerced into compromise by offers of something better, something brighter, something safer. And now he was in charge of seeing these youths from a conquered land brought into service of the greatest empire in the world. *Such irony*, he thought.

Yet among these men who seemed overly eager to cater to their conquerors, there were a few exceptions who still held on to their faith. Even though the house of their God had been destroyed; even though their city had been ravaged; even though they had been taken captive to a strange land they remained true, preferring their own faith to the king's luxurious fare! Of all those who withstood the king's offer of food, drink, and accommodation, the most headstrong of the lot was Belteshazzar, formerly known as Daniel.

How strange to call Daniel by this new name which honored the god Bel, also called Marduk, who had the greatest temple in Babylon dedicated to him. The other young men readily overthrew their old gods in exchange for the new ones. But Daniel continued to call upon the God of his fathers.

Ashpenaz liked the young man. In spite of his subtle defiance, it was refreshing to find someone so true to his convictions that he would deny himself rather than dishonor his God. So much of the religious fervor in Babylon was contrived, if not simply political. Here was a true man of faith!

As the young men walked by on their way to a class on Babylonian history, a palace official tapped Daniel on the shoulder. He indicated for the young man to follow him. Daniel's friends looked back as they moved on, wondering what was happening.

"Looks like he's finally getting reprimanded," said one of the young men.

"He will get us all killed," said another.

The official, one of those assigned to training the young Jewish nobles, led Daniel down a side corridor and onto a small balcony that overlooked the city. Ashpenaz stood at the golden railing, looking at the great ziggurat. He turned when he heard Daniel and the servant approaching.

"Here is the young Hebrew," said the man.

Ashpenaz nodded and indicated that the servant could leave them alone. Daniel studied the man who had been Nebuchadnezzar's chief minister for years. He had a hard look about him, as one who had survived as well as been a part of many palace intrigues. His eyes were cold and his mouth severe. And yet at the same time there was something oddly gentle about the man.

"I think when we are alone I shall call you Daniel," Ashpenaz began. "It is somehow much more fitting."

He looked down on the young man for whom he had grown fond. For some reason he favored Daniel above the others. Looking around as if to make certain they were alone, he continued, "Daniel, are you certain that you will not eat with the rest of the young men?"

"Yes, my lord," said Daniel. "I cannot eat these things and disobey my God."

"Daniel, look over this city," he said, escorting Daniel along the balcony, which turned a corner so that he could see in two directions. Truly it was a spectacular sight. The temple of Marduk, Nebuchadnezzar's tower, the little boats of commerce sailing into the city down the Euphrates, the Hanging Gardens—all of these were in view.

"Daniel, hear me," he said. "This is the most wonderful nation on earth—the greatest empire in the world ruled by the greatest king. You have the opportunity to become a great lord in this place." He hesitated. "But you must do things the Babylonian way. You and your three friends are taking an admirable stand but a reckless one."

"My lord?"

"I mean your insistence that you will not eat from the king's table," continued Ashpenaz. "It is without precedent—and your enemies in the palace might use it as an offense to the king." He looked around. "I can protect you only to a point."

"Enemies?" asked Daniel.

"Petty men, Daniel," said Ashpenaz. "But powerful. They have the king's ear..." He glanced about cautiously. "And his eyes."

"Nevertheless, we must stay true to the law of our God," said Daniel. "Those men might have the king's eyes. But I have the eyes of the Lord of Hosts watching over me."

"But Daniel," Ashpenaz continued, "if you do not partake of the king's rich food, and you and your friends begin to grow thin in comparison to the others, I might lose my head. The king and I have been together for some time. But I can assure you that in this matter there would be no reprieve."

Daniel thought about it for a moment.

"I do not wish to see you in danger because of our actions," he said. "Do this. For the next ten days allow us to eat only water and vegetables. If at the end of that time you think we are looking thinner than the others, then we will do as you ask."

Ashpenaz smiled at Daniel with great relief.

"Agreed," he said. "We shall put it to the test for ten days. Now go and join the others."

Daniel bowed and left the balcony.

"I have never seen such a man after the heart of his God," he said aloud, looking at Marduk's temple. "A God that he cannot even see."

"That, Serus, is Daniel," said Gabriel.

The archangel had brought Serus to Babylon to introduce him to the man who would be his charge for the remainder of the man's life. Crispin was with them, having been dispatched to Babylon when it was learned that Pellecus was the prince over this kingdom. The three angels watched as Daniel disappeared into the palace after his talk. Walking along the same balcony, they strolled past Ashpenaz who seemed lost in very deep thought.

"I wonder what he is thinking about?" asked Serus.

"I would say that he is trying to determine just what sort of fellow Daniel is," offered Crispin. "After all, he doesn't usually experience such blatant integrity!"

"The Lord has a very special plan for Daniel," said Gabriel. "He will be one of the greatest prophets of Israel."

Serus looked at Daniel from the corner of the room where he and Gabriel had stationed themselves. "A prophet? In the wickedness of Babylon? How can that be?"

"You must understand, Serus, that just because the nation has been destroyed does not mean that the Lord's plans are altered," said Crispin. "It is the prerogative of the Creator to run His plan as He deems fit. Unfortunately it is the nature of the creature to run afoul of it."

Serus looked at Crispin.

"So then all this sputtering from Lucifer and Pellecus and the others about the war almost being over..."

"Is just that," said Crispin. "Sputtering."

They entered the palace and walked toward the assembly hall where Daniel and the others were being instructed. As they passed through the halls, several devils saw Gabriel and cursed him. The angels ignored these vile spirits and continued talking.

"So you see, Serus, what Lucifer and Pellecus and most humans have yet to figure out is that the Lord is not relegated to their opinions or expectations of Him. He is sovereign, and as such that also makes Him at times unpredictable. A dangerous trait with which to contend when one is strategizing against the Lord based upon flawed and creaturely presuppositions. Pellecus understood this...once."

"And Daniel?" asked Serus. "How does he fit into the Lord's plans?"

Gabriel looked first at Crispin and then at Serus as if what he was about to divulge carried tremendous weight.

"Daniel will be given a message that is both terrifying and wonderful; a message that shall speak both to his times and the end of the age. Most importantly, Serus, he shall speak of the Messiah."

"The Messiah?" asked Serus.

"Yes," said Crispin, "the Anointed One. It is the Messiah who will one day come to free His people. The Messiah is the Seed of

Eve—the one spoken of in Eden—who will crush the serpent's head one day. The King spoken of by the prophets—whose throne will reign for eternity from David's own house!"

"But how do you know this, Gabriel?" asked Serus. "How do you know that Daniel will be told these things?"

"Because it is I who will tell him when the time is right," said Gabriel. "But first, Daniel will be tested in many ways during his time in Babylon. And at the proper time, should he prove worthy, I shall deliver this message that is both wonderful and terrible at the same time. He shall write it down and seal it up for the end of the age."

Serus took a moment to process all that had been spoken to him. It was fantastic! The Messiah! So the end of Israel did not mean the end of the hope! He was coming after all! It was all beginning to make sense now. From Adam to Abraham to David to the Messiah—the Seed was slowly coming forward to one day be born as the prophets had said!

"I have to admit that I thought the war was almost over—if not almost lost," said Serus, with a tinge of embarrassment.

"Poor Serus!" said Crispin. "I would say that the war is neither over nor lost!"

"Gabriel? Here in Babylon? Astounding!"

"Yes," said Lucifer. "And true."

"But what is he doing here?" asked Kara.

"That is our task to discover," said Lucifer. "That simpering Serus was with him. And Crispin. It seems, Pellecus, that your administration of Babylon is not as secure as you thought!"

The three angels were standing on the king's tower, looking over the city. It was amazing to them that humans were so dull of the spirit world. Here was this bustling crowd below—enormous avenues filled with shops and people; soldiers in their watch towers

and priests in their temples—and all were oblivious to the numbers of wicked angels who inhabited their city with them!

Everywhere devils could be seen seducing the people in their
proud delusion of security and supremacy. Babylon was a world
empire at peace with itself and led by the greatest of kings—a king
who was completely unaware of the dark spirits that had saturat-
ed the very core of his nation.

"So many of our own angels here," sputtered Kara, looking
around as if at any moment Michael or Gabriel might swoop down
upon him. "It is quite obvious that this place is darkness and death
to the Jews. Their nation is finished and the temple is destroyed.
So why should the archangel be here?"

"It is certainly refreshing to see Kara losing his mind at last,"
said Pellecus. "Obviously he is on some very important assignment."

"But why?" continued Kara. He turned to Lucifer. "You said
that once the temple was destroyed our struggle would be finished."

"Quiet!" screamed Lucifer, his reddish-purple aura beginning to manifest with impatience. "Don't you see that we have
been undercut by the Lord! Thanks to Pellecus's insistence that we
keep abreast of the enemy's movements, we have discovered that
something is afoot here in Babylon. The trail, unfortunately, leads
to bigger game than we had anticipated."

"We were looking for elements of the Host and we found an
archangel," said Pellecus. "My angels in the palace have discovered some curious and potentially threatening information. Shall I
report?"

Lucifer nodded in assent, his aura fading as he calmed down.

"The archangel Gabriel is here to watch over a particular Jew
taken captive during one of Nebuchadnezzar's conquests," he
began. "Daniel is his name. Unlike his brothers, he is a man who,
while living in a foreign land, will not serve its gods. He won't eat
of the king's food, drink of the king's wine, nor partake of the

king's hospitality. And," he added with a bit of drama, "he is a man who will be a prophet!"

"More prophets," fumed Kara. "I thought we had killed all the prophets."

"This, of course, means something else," continued Pellecus. "It means that the war must continue."

Lucifer glared at Pellecus, but his stare softened to resignation and realization that this was in fact the truth. The war must continue.

"Then the Seed is still here," said Lucifer, looking down upon the city. "Somewhere among these people, somewhere among these captives."

Lucifer turned back toward Pellecus and Kara. The sun was just beginning to set over the city behind him. His dark silhouette stamped the brightness of the sun whose rays shot around the black figure.

"It means that our only hope is not simply destruction of the country, but of the people. It means that the Seed will never be secured until the last Jew is dead or completely absorbed by other nations."

He stepped out of the sun and continued.

"Of course, I would prefer they all die, but that would be difficult. Better to begin as usual with those who show the most promise in terms of their ability to oppose us."

He turned to Pellecus.

"I suggest that you make things difficult for this new prophet in Babylon!"

Bethlehem, 4 B.C.

"I see the boys are awake again," said Elron, who had returned from his watch. His son, Joshua, stood and greeted him.

"Father, we have been talking about Daniel!" he said excitedly.

Elron looked at Daniel, who had been sitting by himself that last time he had seen him. He wondered what this was all about.

"Daniel, have they been disturbing you?" he asked.

Eli laughed loudly, as did the others around the fire. Joshua suddenly understood what his father meant.

"No, no," he pleaded. "I mean we were talking about the real Daniel!"

"Oh!" said Elron. "Sorry, Daniel!"

"That's alright, Elron," said Daniel. "I only wish that I were real too."

The camp exploded with laughter—not so much at the play on words but the fact that they were spoken by Daniel. What was happening with this man?

The men settled down around the fire once more for the final hours of the evening. Elron sat next to his son, who was glad to have his father back with him.

"What have you learned about the real Daniel?" Elron asked his son.

Everyone smiled at the question.

"He was a prophet! At a time when there were no prophets!"

"Well, I didn't exactly say that, Joshua," said Eli, careful to protect his words. "Remember that Daniel lived around the same time as Ezekiel. The Lord was at work even while His people were in exile."

"But there were enemies who wanted to destroy Daniel," Joshua continued. "Men who were jealous of him and wanted him dead!"

"But why?" asked Jarod. "The king liked him, didn't he?"

Eli leaned back, and thought about his words. Now that the adults were back he weighed his words more carefully.

"Because, young Jarod, it seems that men are always jealous of that which is real and pure and true," he said. "And evil especially cannot tolerate something that is righteous. Some men were jealous of Daniel's integrity, and they wanted him destroyed."

"So what did they do?" asked Joshua excitedly.

"Like most evildoers they set a trap for him," said Eli. "They figured if they could catch him at something that would make the king mad, they could get rid of him. But the Lord was with Daniel.

"And do you know what happened to Daniel after those ten days of eating vegetables?"

The boys looked at Eli, hanging onto his words. He pointed at Beniah, a shepherd who was fairly sizeable and known for his ability to eat a great deal at a sitting.

"After those ten days they were in better shape than the others," he continued. "Like our friend Beniah here!"

Beniah grinned as he tossed another date into his mouth. Everyone laughed.

"Try as they might, the king's men could not get the better of Daniel," Eli said. "Then one time Nebuchadnezzar had a dream. The problem was when he woke up he could not remember what the dream was about! So he ordered all of his wisest men to not only interpret the dream but to tell him what the dream was in the first place!"

"So Daniel did it!" cried out Joshua.

"Let him tell it," said Jarod scornfully.

Eli laughed. "Yes, Daniel not only told the king what the dream was, but he also interpreted it for him. And such a dream..."

"Such a dream is right," said Serus to Bakka as they stood by the little gathering of shepherds. He looked about at the amazing number of angels who were now assembled around Bethlehem in the sky, on the hills—everywhere. "It looks as if another dream is to be realized here tonight. Little wonder that Lucifer is begging to meet with Michael and Gabriel."

Serus, who had been with Michael in Bethlehem escorting Joseph and Mary, had been ordered to return to the shepherds.

"I was wondering when he would initiate dialog," said Bakka. "He can read signs and prophets as well as we."

Serus looked at the star that hung high overhead.

"Signs and prophets," he repeated. "Since Eden we have awaited the time of the Seed. Lucifer knows that his time is becoming increasingly precious."

"What do you suppose he will wish from Michael?" asked Bakka. "He knows that the Child is not a point of negotiation."

"Lucifer as always will seek some sort of advantage," said Serus. "I know him, Bakka. Remember that I served him in Heaven. We view that star as the beginning of the end. He will see it as the end of the beginning."

Chapter 15

"We must have blood on this one."

Lucifer and Michael locked eyes. Two powerful angels on opposite sides of the greatest conflict ever met on the fields of Bethlehem. With Michael were Gabriel and several other warriors. Lucifer was accompanied by Kara, Pellecus, and Rugio. Lucifer smiled at the archangel.

"Well Michael, it is finally coming to an end," he said. "We have been watching Mary of course, ever since the news. Wonderful annunciation, Gabriel!"

Gabriel ignored Lucifer's reference of his announcement to Mary about the Child that she was carrying.

"Of course it was a rather delicate situation," he continued. "I mean a Child born without a father in a society that stones a person for such indiscreet behavior."

"The Child has a Father," said Gabriel.

"Oh yes," said Lucifer. "Well, I must admit that we were taken by surprise on that one. We knew that the prophet proclaimed a king who would rule an eternal throne. But I had no idea that the Lord Himself would be so...so involved with this woman."

"Don't turn something sacred into some sordid act, Lucifer," said Michael. "You speak against the Holy Spirit!"

As he finished saying these words the wind picked up around them, kicking up dust and debris and forcing the unfortunate people who were not yet registered to cover their eyes and mouths for protection from the freakish weather. Then it settled down suddenly.

"I speak no ill of the Spirit of God," continued Lucifer. "His indiscretions are of no importance to me…"

"What do you want, Lucifer?" said Michael firmly.

"We wish to discuss the Child," said Kara. "Naturally."

"Ah yes," said Gabriel. "Well the Child is quite safe, and not one of your angels has been able to penetrate the shield we have placed about Him."

"So I heard," sneered Kara. "No matter."

"We are here to discuss the future," said Lucifer. "Once the Child is born there shall be much destruction such as this people have never witnessed."

"You are forcing this war into a bloody conclusion," stammered Kara.

"These people will never listen to this or any other prophet," said Pellecus.

Michael smirked at the demons who stood before him. Crispin, who had been standing with the archangels, moved to the front to speak.

"Since Eden and even before, you have opposed this," he said. "You have done all that you could to stop the Seed from arriving. You have introduced idolatry that profaned God's temple and saw its destruction; you have inflamed pagan nations to occupy the holy city; you have dispossessed these people of their nation while possessing their minds; you have brought sickness and war and plague and murder to the people of God. You have contested us in every way—and still you cannot stop the plan of God. You foolish demons! From whence comes such pride that you should oppose the living God?"

"We shall continue to oppose," said Lucifer. "This Child shall fail like the prophets before Him. The one advantage that we have always been able to exploit is the one factor over which even the Lord Himself has no control—the free will of humans."

The angels with Lucifer nodded in agreement at the remark.

"True," said Crispin. "Free will is an unpredictable and dangerous thing—as all of you have discovered to your own disgrace. We shall see if the Child born here shall be able to capture the hearts of His people in a way different from the prophets."

"Whatever His message, it shall not be received," said Kara. "And all this will have been for nothing!"

"How frightened you all must truly be," said Gabriel. "The Seed is closing in on you. The One who shall crush the serpent's head shall soon be upon the earth. You're finished, Lucifer."

"I will never bow to this Child," said Lucifer. "Any more than a human shall truly listen to the Most High. In the end He shall be another prophet with another message who came and was forgotten. That shall be the legacy of the Messiah!"

Lucifer vanished. The others gave an arrogant glance at Michael and Gabriel.

"Farewell, Archangel," said Kara. "We shall see you on the other side of this event. And then you will see how we deal with this Child-King!"

Kara vanished as well. Only Pellecus remained. He looked at Crispin.

"Well, teacher," he said. "The game has come to this, hasn't it? Not many moves left, hmm? The Child shall be born after all. But the game must be played out in the hearts of men. Eve played in Eden—and I'm afraid she didn't fare well. I am comforted by this. Men shall never be able to live at peace with God."

"Of course you're correct, dear Pellecus," said Crispin. "Men shall never be able to live with God. Perhaps that is why God must live with men."

Chronicles of the Host

Daniel

In spite of the efforts of Pellecus and Kara to discredit Daniel to his king, the Lord's blessing rested upon him. The Lord had given Daniel favor with Ashpenaz, so that he was able to promote Daniel to the king. So Daniel, like Joseph with the pharaoh of Egypt, became close to the king of Babylon.

He was respected for his wisdom that humbled the king's greatest men, and for his ability to interpret dreams and other mysteries. His was a glorious witness to the Lord Almighty, for he never claimed power unto himself, but always gave glory to the Most High God. Thus did the Lord reveal to Daniel many terrible and wonderful things that should happen in the future, because Daniel was a man of integrity and holiness.

Realizing that an attack on Daniel was useless as long as the king of Babylon was enamored with him, Pellecus decided upon a strategy that would eliminate Daniel's friends who were also faithful to the Lord. In doing so, the cunning angel believed he would isolate Daniel and make it easier to dispose of him later on.

Thus did the demons contrive to place in Nebuchadnezzar's proud heart a plan that would bring more glory to himself by having the nation bow to a golden image created in the king's name. The word went forth, fanned by devils throughout the empire and brought high and low through the kingdom by the king's couriers, that all should bow to the image of the king or face imminent death.

So it was that a dark plan was birthed in the hearts of envious Chaldeans to take advantage of the integrity of the three

Hebrews who had been singled out in their minds by Pellecus. This trio—Shadrach, Meshach and Abednego—would be the first of many to die, and would eventually lead to Daniel's destruction....

Babylon, 580 B.C.

The two men sat quietly at the table, waiting for a third to join them. Up until now they had not met together on this issue. In fact, they didn't realize that anyone else was a part of this discussion until Arbo-kan had called them together. And so they sat, cordial and silent, until Arbo-kan arrived to further explain why they had been summoned.

One of the men, Divis, was a temple warden at the Marduk complex. He was charged with the purity of ceremonies carried out there to honor the great god of Babylon. Divis was an ardent worshiper of Marduk, and he felt that the introduction of foreigners in Babylon was an offense to the gods.

The other man, Bellesor, was a commander in the king's own guard. A military man of great decisiveness, he too longed to cleanse Babylon of the alien captives and hoped that one day Nebuchadnezzar might change his mind about them. Perhaps tonight's meeting would implement such a plot!

Arbo-kan came into the room, startling the two men, who thought that perhaps they were being arrested for meeting under such clandestine arrangements. Arbo-kan smiled at their discomfort.

"I'm sorry, my friends," he began, sitting at the table with them. "Seems we are all a bit nervous these days."

Unseen to the men, three creatures appeared behind each of the chairs—all of them the figures of men but with the hideous features of the god Marduk. Pellecus had made sure that the men's demons were at this meeting to ensure its outcome. They stood behind the men to whom they were assigned, speaking murderous thoughts against the Hebrews, which they had been thinking for so long.

"I believe you all understand why I asked you here," said Arbo-kan, unfolding a document. "The fact is that the Jews are becoming problematic. Not all of them of course. In particular, I mean Daniel."

"Daniel," muttered Divis in disgust. "He has bewitched the king!"

"He's a devil," agreed Bellesor.

"Whatever he is, he must be dealt with," said Arbo-kan. "And quickly."

Bellesor took a drink of wine that had been provided for them when they first arrived at Arbo-kan's house near the palace.

"But how?" he demanded. "The king won't hear of it. Ashpenaz favors him. How can we possibly destroy this menace?"

"Legally," said Arbo-kan, indicating the document that lay on the table before them. As they read they recognized the proclamation that the king had issued regarding the worship of the image. Bellesor looked at Divis and nodded his head in approval.

The three figures behind the men also nodded in approval at the introduction of this scroll. Bellesor's demon said, "Best keep things legal, hmm?"

The others laughed aloud.

"These simple humans," said the demon behind Arbo-kan. "What stupid games they play in order to justify their wickedness!"

"So long as they carry it out, what matter?" said the other. "Pellecus will reward us for this!"

"Only if we draw blood," said the angel that was now speaking into Arbo-kan's mind. "Only if we draw blood..."

"Blood, my friends," continued Arbo-kan. "We must have blood on this one."

The three men pored over the declaration, and were satisfied that it was quite clear in the matter of a death sentence being appropriate for offenders. The low glow of the little lamp cast an eerie light on the faces of the conspirators.

"The law is quite clear," said Arbo-kan. "If the music commences and a person does not fall and worship at that precise moment, then the offenders are subject to being thrown into the great furnace and burned alive. As you know, last week when the music sounded, all over the city people fell and worshiped. But these unrighteous Jews refused to bow to the king!"

"Where was Daniel during this?" asked Divis. "Surely he did not bow."

"Daniel was out of the city on the king's business," said Arbo-kan. "An unfortunate circumstance—or we would have all four of them dangling. But we do have the three main instigators of this...this offense."

"And we have witnesses?" asked Bellesor.

"Of course," said Arbo-kan. "And they will testify that as they bowed low the Jews remained standing and defiant. The king will be furious!"

Divis took a sip of the wine.

"When will the charges be brought?" he asked.

"Next week," said Arbo-kan. "I have sent Daniel on a mission that will take him out of Babylon for a month or so. While he is away we shall move against his friends. If we do so while he is near the king, he might be able to persuade the king to mercy. We serve a great king but one of divided heart at times."

"Very well," said Bellesor. "Let us drink to the death of these three Hebrews."

"And to the ultimate destruction of Daniel," added Divis.

"We shall recapture the purity of Babylon in this," said Arbo-kan. "I assure you."

The demons in the room began to laugh.

"What a noble sentiment," said one. "Arbo-kan is only look-ing out for the nation he loves. There is nothing personal about this!"

"He's a proud brute," said another. "Jealousy will find a way!"

"Let's report to Pellecus," said the demon who guided Arbo-kan. "He will be interested in how things are developing!"

The three vanished as Arbo-kan extinguished the lamp on the table.

Gabriel could hardly understand Serus in his agitated state. He asked him to repeat once more what he had just said.

"They are holding Shadrach, Meshach, and Abednego!" he said, a bit more calmly than before. "They have been charged with treason by Arbo-kan!"

Gabriel finished giving orders to another angel, who imme-diately left, and then turned back to Serus.

"Yes, I know," he said. "They refused to bow to the king's image."

"But what shall happen to them?" Serus asked. "Are we to intervene?"

No," said Gabriel. "We are not allowed to interfere with their decision or the outcome. The Lord has spoken on this."

Serus could not believe what he was hearing. These men had obeyed the Lord. They had refused to bow to an image and wor-ship. They had chosen the Most High over an idol. Now they were in danger of being sentenced to death. And the Host was to do nothing?

"How can this be?" Serus asked.

Gabriel walked with Serus down the corridor that led to the King's Hall of Justice, where the sentence was being rendered. They passed several snickering devils along the way, who mocked them for their foolishness in trusting the Lord to deliver the humans when now it was obvious that they were to die a horrible death.

They entered the trial room where at the front Shadrach, Meshach, and Abednego were being held by palace guards. In front of them, Arbo-kan was charging them with the offense. Devils were sprinkled all throughout the room. On one side, Gabriel saw Pellecus watching the proceedings gleefully. Pellecus looked up.

"Ah, welcome, Archangel," he said. "A poor day to be in court, I'm afraid. At least if you are a Jew!"

Gabriel ignored Pellecus's comments and kept an eye on the three men. He noticed that they did not have the look of fear that most humans had when they were approaching certain death. They seemed quite calm—almost at ease—as Arbo-kan meticulously laid out his charges against them.

"And I must say that fond as I am of these young men, I cannot abide an offense against my god—much less my king! I therefore must insist that the law be carried out and these three offenders be thrown into the furnace as an example to all who would oppose the king's authority."

Nebuchadnezzar was beside himself. He wished Daniel were there to advise him. But he had to make a decision that was not vacillating. He looked at the men and was troubled.

"We await your justice, great king," said Arbo-kan.

"I know what you are waiting for, Arbo-kan," said Nebuchadnezzar. "Be still."

Arbo-kan bowed low and seated himself.

The demons in the gallery were chattering loudly, boasting that the king would put an end to these three troublemakers and that Daniel would be next! Nebuchadnezzar stood from the chair on which he sat and walked to the three men. His heart was torn.

"Is it true that you refused to bow to the image and worship like everyone else did?" he asked the men. "Listen. It is not too late to save your lives."

Arbo-kan turned his head as he heard these words. He could hardly believe what he was hearing. Was the king going to give them a second chance? He looked at Bellesor and Divis, who looked equally puzzled.

"I shall have the music played once more," continued the king. "If you will only fall down and bow before the image and worship, I will spare your lives. But if you refuse, then I will have you tossed into the furnace and burned alive. Your God shall not be able to deliver you from my hands."

Gabriel watched as the men gave their answer. He wondered what the men might do. Pellecus enjoyed the consternation on Gabriel's face.

"I don't think they will bow, do you?" he asked in a saracastic tone. "I believe they are too proud!"

The men looked at the king and then answered him:

"Our God is more than able to deliver us if He chooses to do so," they said. "But even if He chooses not to save us, we will not bow down to your image."

Pellecus winked at Gabriel and said, "Excuse me while I infuriate a king."

Appearing behind the king, Pellecus began to speak a raging spirit inside the man who only moments before had wanted to be merciful.

"*How dare they insult the king to his face...and in front of his nobles?*"

"You dare offend me like this?" said the king.

The men remained silent.

"The furnace is not made that burns hot enough for these dogs!"

"Bind these men and hold them," he ordered. "And heat the great furnace to seven times its normal heat! Now!"

A cheer went up from the devils in the room as guards moved in and took the men to a holding room while the furnace was stoked. Gabriel was sad for the men but very proud of their stance against the king. He looked down at Serus.

"They did the right thing, Serus," he said.

Serus nodded that he understood.

"Yes, the right thing," sneered Pellecus. "But at the wrong time."

Gabriel had ordered several angels to minister to the three men while they awaited their execution. The angels stayed in the room with them and comforted them, laying hands on them and being a source of strength through the Spirit of God who filled the room. Shadrach, Meshach, and Abednego were prepared to die for their faith. They only wished Daniel were there to see them give up their lives willingly for the Lord they all loved. They knew he would be proud.

"Daniel would gladly share this fate with us," said Meshach.

"Perhaps he might yet," said Shadrach. "For surely he will never bow to an idol."

"It is glorious to live for the Lord," agreed Meshach. "And though I do not wish to die, I somehow know that there is glory in this as well."

Arbo-kan, Bellesor, and Divis were granted the privilege of pushing the men into the furnace. They came into the room and ordered the guards to bring them along.

"After you have been reduced to ashes, we shall see that Daniel follows in short order," said Arbo-kan. "And then all the outrages of the Jews will be dealt with! Bring them along!"

The men descended into a great room underneath the palace where the great furnace had been heated to seven times its normal capacity. Even before they had gotten to the bottom of the stairs they could feel the heat.

"Just a taste of what you shall soon experience firsthand," said Divis, pushing Meshach along.

The king watched from a small alcove that served as a safe gallery from which he could see everything. The three Jews were hurried along and paraded in front of the king, who was fanning himself because of the heat. Arbo-kan bowed low before the king and then took the three men toward the roaring furnace. He ordered Bellesor and Divis to use the large grips to open the door.

"Great king, behold the justice of Nebuchadnezzar!" he said, and the door was opened. "Behold the justice of our god!"

The second the door opened up, the intense heat shot out at the same time the three Hebrews were shoved into the furnace. Arbo-kan, Bellesor, and Divis barely had time to scream in horrible pain as the fire leapt out and consumed them, burning them up in front of the king. The men fell in a crumpled, smoldering pile before the furnace.

Gabriel was watching from the side along with Serus and a few other angels. Pellecus too was on hand. He laughed aloud as Arbo-kan fell dead.

"Shall we see if they are done yet?" Pellecus asked, to the laughter of the demon angels who were with him. They crowded around the furnace.

But as they looked into the fire they suddenly backed off in horror. The figure of a fourth Person stood inside! It was not just a man—and it wasn't an angel. It was the Lord of Hosts Himself! Pellecus leaped back in fear, looking at his scattering demons who exited at the appearance of the Most High.

Nebuchadnezzar also saw inside the furnace. There was someone else in there! He could hardly believe his own eyes. Perhaps the intense heat was playing tricks on his mind. He asked if they had not thrown three men into the fire.

"Yes, great king," said Ashpenaz, who had come to plea for the men one last time. He had arrived just as the men were thrown in. "Three men, majesty. The others died when the door was opened."

"Then who is that fourth Person I see in there?" he asked.

Ashpenaz looked but saw only three men—walking about the furnace as if they were not even hurt at all. How could this happen?

"Yes, there!" said the king. "There is a fourth man...with the appearance of a son of gods! Don't you see Him?"

The king jumped up and got as near to the furnace as he could. He then called to the young men to come out of the furnace. Gabriel bowed low before the Lord's appearance. But his heart was joyful—the Lord had delivered after all! Pellecus cursed the Lord and vanished.

Chronicles of the Host

Deliverance!

What a blow to the enemy when the three men stepped out of the burning furnace! When the astonished king examined them, he found that not even their clothes were singed. They did not even smell of smoke as everyone else in the room did. The king looked at Ashpenaz sternly and issued an immediate decree that the God of Daniel was never again to be offended in any way. He also appointed the three Hebrews to important positions in the kingdom....

Soon after that the Most High God began to disclose to Daniel through wonderful visions what must indeed transpire in the future. Daniel was hard-pressed to understand the cryptic scenes that played out before him, but the angel Gabriel assured him that his task was not to understand the mysteries but to record them and seal them for a future time when their meaning would be revealed.

Babylon, 539 B.C.

"Daniel!" muttered Kara, glancing at a map of Nebuchadnezzar's empire. "How far he has come since arriving in Babylon. How far shall we allow him to go?"

"He is becoming as difficult a distraction as Moses was," said Rugio. "I should like to thrash him just once."

The demons were in the king's study, discussing the latest reports about Gabriel's visits to Babylon. Kara scoffed at Rugio's bold threat.

"Thrash him?" he said. "He enjoys not only the protection of the Lord of Hosts but also of the lord of Babylon. Nebuchadnezzar will never turn on him. I would say that the captive has become the captor."

"True," said Rugio. "These Jews are perplexing types. And their prophets are equally vexing. Ezekiel and Jeremiah have been preaching hope in the midst of exile. These people cling to their faith like…"

"Like we do," interrupted Lucifer, entering the room with Pellecus.

"Faith, my prince?" asked Kara.

"Of course, Kara," said Lucifer. "We must have faith that we can persevere in this war and ultimately achieve a satisfactory conclusion. We cling as desperately to hope as the Jews do."

"As for Jeremiah, I wouldn't worry too much about him," said Lucifer. "He has fled to Egypt with some other exiles. They have made a nice little community for themselves on Elephantis."

"And Ezekiel?" asked Kara, knowing of a recent prophecy that had unnerved Lucifer. "What has he been spouting lately?"

Lucifer glared at Kara, who sheepishly tried to reframe the question. The others waited for Lucifer's reaction. He surprised them all when he smiled back at Kara.

"Ezekiel is quite a man," he admitted. "Bizarre to be sure. But clever on the whole. You speak of course of his prophecy against the king of Tyre?"

Kara looked very uncomfortable.

"I was speaking generally, my prince," said Kara. Pellecus grinned at him with a "you are such a fool" sort of grin.

"How early you dig your grave, Kara," said Pellecus. "Don't you recall that we still have hope?"

"Yes," continued Lucifer. "The Lord is tantalizing at times. His veiled description of this haughty earthly king of Tyre is clever, but shallow."

"And quite revealing," mused Pellecus almost absentmindedly. He caught himself and then added, "For a human, I mean."

Lucifer bowed in acknowledgment to Pellecus—more courteous than sincere. He then ordered a demon into the room, one of his scribes, and asked him to read the portion of Ezekiel's prophecy that had become the subject of the current discussion. The demon, whose former position in Heaven had accorded him the privilege of recording the sacred testimonies of the Zoa, now read for Lucifer the words of Ezekiel:

> "You were the model of perfection,
> full of wisdom and perfect in beauty.
> You were in Eden,
> the garden of God;
> every precious stone adorned you:

ruby, topaz and emerald,
chrysolite, onyx and jasper,
sapphire, turquoise and beryl.
Your settings and mountings were made of gold;
on the day you were created they were prepared.
You were anointed as a guardian cherub,
for so I ordained you.
You were on the holy mount of God;
you walked among the fiery stones.
You were blameless in your ways
from the day you were created
till wickedness was found in you."

The demons in the room were deafeningly silent. Rugio could only manage a snort of dismissal. Pellecus merely waited for the dialog to begin once more. Kara looked around wishing that someone would say something. Then Lucifer broke the spell.

"The Most High has His petty ways of digging in," he said. "Not content merely to reveal His word, He must also revel in it. No matter."

"Of course the description is quite revealing," said Pellecus. "If it were not for Ezekiel, you might not appear at all in Heaven's chronicles!"

"You make light of something far more dangerous than you realize," said Lucifer. "These words—these revelations—are not for the simpleminded fools who are captive in Babylon. They are for those who one day shall read the words of these prophets—and establish a school of thought that is both dangerous and far-reaching."

Lucifer's eyes began to glow a white light that looked at first like small dots and then began to fill the room with their intensity.

"However, the Lord is not the only voice for prophets," said Lucifer. "Place these words in the *Prophecy of the Morning Star.*" "They will affirm our destiny and give rise to our own cult when earth is finally ours."

He then rose above them all in the center of the room and began uttering:

"Record these words for the book divine,
The prophecy unfold, in time:
The prince will rise in much distress,
His earthly cover now to best,
The prince of Tyre now called me,
The prince of death I'll always be,
And so Messiah, ever-told.
Whatever prophecies unfold;
Willing deathly place to be,
Anointed One His price to me,
Bloody end will be His place
A thing of scorn and of disgrace;
And when the Seed of woman dies
Another, greater seed arise."

"Inspiring!" said Kara.

"Your sincerity is always gratifying," said Lucifer, always suspicious of Kara's praises. "And in this case, it is true. Nevertheless, I am anxious for your report, Rugio. How go the Medes?"

"They are on the march, my lord," said Rugio. "Like Assyria before them, I have guided their leadership through their gods and they have created an army unmatched on earth! They will be here tonight."

"Well done," said Lucifer. Of all his leaders, he trusted Rugio most of all. He was not ambitious like Kara, nor clever like Pellecus. Rather he was intensely loyal—something rare in Lucifer's hierarchy.

"I have decided that you shall be the prince over Persia," said Lucifer. "You, Rugio, will guide the Persians into world empire and bring them on to Babylon."

"Why should Rugio be accorded this responsibility?" sputtered Kara. "He guided Assyria and they are no more! At least my Egypt still exists."

"It is obvious by now, Kara, that in the affairs of humans, empires come and go," said Pellecus. "Assyria, Babylon—even the Medes one day. The point is to take advantage of a nation's strength while it is thriving and then move on, once it has run its course."

"But why Babylon?" continued Kara. "Why should it be overturned?"

"Because these kings have grown too close to the Jews," said Lucifer. "Another nation with more appetite might be able to dispense with them."

"Besides all, Daniel prophesied the end of Babylon," said Pellecus. "Only moments ago he interpreted some words that the Lord Himself had written on the wall while that fool Belshazzar was giving one of his parties."

"Writing on the wall?" asked Kara.

"Theatrical but effective," said Pellecus. "Daniel told the king that the words meant his kingdom was to be overthrown by the Persians. There is always a prophet nearby when disaster looms."

"At any rate, Rugio shall be prince over Persia," said Lucifer.

"I have studied their king," said Rugio. "Cyrus is benign and tolerates other faiths in his domains—as does Darius, his soon-to-be-ruler in Babylon."

"That is certainly discouraging," said Kara.

"But," continued Rugio, "there are some ambitious men within that government who I believe will be very useful in dealing with Daniel and these other prophets."

"And when will Cyrus arrive with his army?" asked Lucifer.

As he finished speaking, an alarm went up in the city. Shouts of panic were relayed through the great streets. Lucifer glanced outside at the commotion. Tower signals were being lit. Trumpets sounded. People within the palace began rushing about. The city was under attack...and the gates were being thrown open to the enemy!

Lucifer walked back to the table with the map of the empire. Next to the parchment, on the table, was one of Belshazzar's wine cups, half-filled. Lucifer knocked it over, spilling the red wine across the map of Babylon from north to south.

"Well, Rugio," said Lucifer, smiling, "I would say Cyrus has indeed arrived!"

CHAPTER 16

"A simple exile will never do."

Chronicles of the Host

Persia

In the end, the kings of Babylon were judged by the Lord and found to be wanting in the balance, and Babylon was overthrown by the Medes, whose king was Cyrus and soon after, Darius. The city was taken without an arrow being fired, and Belshazzar was one of the few men killed in the collapse.

Ever faithful to his prophet, the Lord Most High gave Daniel favor with the new king, and Daniel was appointed as an administrator over much of his domain. Sensing an opportunity in this promotion, Rugio, with the assistance of Kara, moved quickly upon the hearts of Darius's closest ministers to engineer a jealous and hateful spirit. Within the hearts of these men they created a dark and unholy plot that might see Daniel overthrown once and for all....

The gathering of newly appointed administrators for the new kingdom had been a glorious event. Darius, who was ruler now in Babylon for the Medes, had overthrown the previous government and established 120 districts, each ruled by a capable man called a satrap. The men bowed low as Darius greeted them in Nebuchadnezzar's reception hall.

Taking his place on a dais provided by his chief minister, Darius congratulated each of the men for their service to the kingdom and for having the king's confidence. He then made an announcement that took some of the men by surprise:

"And I must say," Darius continued, "that Daniel, formerly called Belteshazzar, has proven himself time and again to the kings of this land. For this reason he shall be the third man in this trio of administrators who shall govern over you all. He will do well by you, as he has for the kings of Babylon and for his present king."

Daniel stood silently as 120 men nodded to him in homage. As the assembly broke up, the 120 satraps came by and congratulated Daniel one by one. Most of the men were sincere in their praise of Daniel—but there were several who were quietly enraged.

"There," said Kara, pointing out a man in a deep blue cloak who had just spoken with Daniel and was now meeting with a small group of men on the other side of the room. "That man— who is he, Rugio?"

Rugio smiled.

"You have a good eye for discontent, Kara," said Rugio. "That is Kezzar-mar. He is an ambitious man of subtle nature. Quite bent on advancing in Darius's government. But he has an obstacle to promotion—the prophet Daniel."

"Ah yes," said Kara. "The human lust for power. Soon we'll turn that ambition into hate."

"The hate is there already," said Rugio. "I visited him last night and made him dream of bowing low before Daniel in front of all the important men in the kingdom. He woke up infuriated!"

"Has he some accomplices?" asked Kara. "It will take more than one voice speaking against Daniel to bring him down."

"Of course," said Rugio. "I have not been idle these few months since Darius has been in Babylon. I suggest we look into the conversation he is having right now. I believe he is talking with some of the other like-minded men."

Kezzar-mar smiled and nodded as one of the satraps walked by. He then turned his attention back to the three men to whom he was speaking.

"These are not satraps," he continued. "They are cattle—cattle led by a religious zealot who has imprisoned the king's mind."

"Might I suggest that we discuss this elsewhere?" said Berza, whose satrapy was near the old city of Nineveh. "It might be more prudent."

The others agreed.

"Very well," said Kezzar-mar. "Tonight at my apartments we will meet to discuss this rather delicate problem that is facing us. At that time I will relate to you a very interesting dream that I had."

The group of men broke up and each left separately. Only Kezzar-mar remained behind. He looked up at Daniel, who was still receiving the congratulations of the other satraps. How could so many be beholden to one man? It must be sorcery. And yet Daniel would never bow to another god, much less a king. If only some sort of charges could be brought up against him, he muttered under his breath.

"*Charges,*" came a voice. "*Now that might prove interesting.*"

Kezzar-mar smiled as a thought came into his mind. In his mind's eye he saw Daniel on the docket, with the great men of the kingdom leveling charge after charge of corruption against the man.

"Of course Daniel is a man of integrity. The charges must be unique..."

Kezzar-mar felt hatred for Daniel rising in him as he thought about the possibility of trapping the man legally. Yes—that just might work! But how?

Daniel will never be brought up on charges of corruption or abuse of power, he thought to himself. *One must be cunning...subtle...but Daniel is above reproach.* "There are no charges that can be made," he caught himself saying.

"Then you must find charges against this holy man that have to do with the law of his God whom he worships, not with the law of men which he respects."

A sly smile came over Kezzar-mar's face. That was it! What he could not do outside the law, he could manipulate within the law! He walked over to Daniel and congratulated him once more. Daniel looked deeply into his eyes and thanked him. Kezzar-mar bowed his head, and excused himself, thinking that very soon Daniel would be meeting his God face to face!

"Excellent work, Kara," said Rugio, after Kezzar-mar left the room.

"I'm sure that Gabriel will be particularly shocked when Daniel's integrity is the basis for his destruction," said Kara. "I merely hinted to Kezzar-mar that when one is undermining a holy man, one should take advantage of his holiness."

The meeting in Kezzar-mar's apartment was attended by humans and devils. The humans had come to hear Kezzar-mar's plans for dealing with Daniel. The devils had come to make sure the proper atmosphere was established to ensure compliance on the part of the others. The men seated themselves around the low table in the center of the room. Kezzar-mar dismissed his servants and then turned to the others.

Kara and Rugio remained off to the side, listening with interest to the intricacies of the human mind when involved in something sordid. Pellecus had joined the other two demons for the meeting when he heard that Daniel would be the subject of the discussion.

"Reminds me of those grand days in Heaven," said Kara, "when we too dreamed of greater days...meeting in Lucifer's house...speaking of the future..."

"Yes," said Pellecus with a sneer. "I only hope that their plans turn out a bit differently than ours have."

Kara glared at Pellecus.

"I should wonder what Lucifer might think of such talk?" said Kara self-righteously. "After all, Pellecus, we are Lucifer's greatest rulers."

Pellecus looked at Rugio's vacant stare and Kara's usual stupid arrogant smirk.

"That, my dear elder, is what frightens me."

Just as Kara was about to respond, the devils realized that the men were beginning to discuss frankly the issues revolving around Daniel and the need for his immediate, albeit discreet, removal. Kezzar-mar began by underscoring his utmost loyalty to Darius and the kingdom.

"I love our king as all of you do," he said. "But he has a blind spot when it comes to governing these foreigners. He is much too compassionate and accommodating." He stood as he continued speaking. "But our kingdom was won with blood and not with compassion. Brothers—these Jews view Cyrus as a liberator. But why shouldn't they? He has turned over the artifacts from Solomon's temple that were taken by Nebuchadnezzar and given them to the Jew Zerubbabel for the rebuilding of the temple!"

"Astonishing," said Berza. "We send the Jews back better trained and with greater knowledge that when they arrived years ago."

"We will have to fight them eventually," added Sheshbar, sipping his wine. "Why send them back to fortify that rebellious city once more?"

"I had hoped that Darius, who rules in Cyrus's name here in Babylon, might show a different spirit," said Kezzar-mar. "But that hope was lost when he appointed Daniel over the rest of us."

"Thus our meeting," said Berza. "And the question: What to do with Daniel?"

"The question, Berza, is not what," said Kezzar-mar, "but how?"

The silence in the room was chilling. Even Kara was impressed with the tension that hung as the talk shifted from politics to murder.

"Zerubbabel," commented Kara. "He's the one who has taken it upon himself to organize these animals as they prepare to return. I hear he has even appointed a high priest!"

"A lot of good that will do them when they get to Jerusalem," said Rugio. "Once they see the total destruction they will lose heart."

Pellecus only shook his head in disbelief.

"What you two forget is that this was prophesied by Isaiah," he said. "And now it is happening."

"Don't worry about these Jews," said Kara smugly. "Berenius is already in Jerusalem organizing some very discouraging enemies. Zerubbabel will find himself with tremendous opposition from the people who live there. They want nothing to do with the Jews. But then, who does?"

Kara and Rugio laughed.

"Considering that it is from these people that the coming King will be born, I would say that we all had better have something to do with them."

"Then we are agreed," said Kezzar-mar, filling the cups of all three men once more. "We shall present the king with this law requiring all of his subjects, over a 30-day period, to pray to no other god or man, save the king himself. Once he signs, it cannot be repealed—according to the custom of the Medes and Persians!"

"And the penalty?" asked Berza.

"Death, of course," said Kezzar-mar. "This is high treason. A simple exile will never do. Besides—all of these Jews are exiles!"

The room burst out in laughter.

"How is he to die?" asked Sheshbar. "Lose his head?"

"You have a merciful streak, Sheshbar," purred Kezzar-mar.

"Impaling," offered Berza. "That makes quite an impression!"

"How about burning alive?" suggested Farsin.

"All of those are credible suggestions," said Kezzar-mar. "But I prefer something more traditionally Persian—and more terrifying to Daniel as he breathes his last." He held his cup to the other three and said, "We'll throw him to the lions!"

Chronicles of the Host
Murderous Plot

Darius considered the decree before the great men of his court. Kezzar-mar, who seemed particularly interested in its success, built a marvelous and eloquent case as to why this edict needed to be prepared and implemented. Among other considerations, he told the king that this would help unite the kingdom and drive out any hidden enemies. Darius was not opposed to other people practicing their particular faiths. But could they not practice their faith while showing loyalty to their king? Thus did Darius agree to the decree that for 30 days nobody could pray to their own gods—only to the king—on penalty of being thrown to the lions.

"Gabriel, have you heard?" came the voice of Serus.

"Yes, just now," Gabriel answered, a serious look on his face. He and Serus were in Daniel's house awaiting his arrival. "Daniel read the published edict earlier. You can be sure Lucifer's hand was in this."

"Nevertheless, what are we to do?" asked Serus. "Daniel will never pray to another god. He will die first."

"Perhaps that is the Lord's will," said Gabriel grimly. "Until we know the Lord's heart in this matter we cannot assume anything, except to continue to encourage Daniel's faith during this test."

Daniel's footsteps could be heard coming up the stairs to the room in which he lived. The old prophet was accustomed to opening the window that faced the direction of Jerusalem and praying three times a day. When he opened his window, Serus protested to Gabriel.

"Will he still pray so openly?" he asked.

"Daniel is a man of faith, Serus," said Gabriel with admiration. "He will not allow a breach of integrity in his life."

"Faith kills, sometimes," came a voice.

Gabriel and Serus turned to see Kara and Rugio standing outside the window that Daniel had just opened.

"I'm happy to see that Daniel is so predictable," Kara continued.

"When will Kezzar-mar arrive?" asked Gabriel with disgust. "I'm sure he would not want to miss out on true devotion. Perhaps he could learn something."

"Kezzar-mar is far too clever to come himself," sneered Kara. "But he has sent some men who will spy on Daniel. Don't worry."

"And then you will see this Daniel praying that the lions finish him off," said Rugio grinning. "Ah, here they are now."

Gabriel looked down at Daniel, deep in prayer and totally oblivious to the conversation going on around him. Surely the Lord would deliver him from this trap! Berza's scarred face appeared in the window. Behind him Gabriel could see Kara's gloating face. Berza pointed Daniel out to Sheshbar and Farsin who also peeked in. The men acted shocked to find Daniel, a man of renown, breaking the law! Then just as quickly the three men left.

"The trap is set," said Rugio.

"Correction, Rugio," said Kara. "The trap is sprung."

The two demons vanished from the window. Even in the midst of such darkness, the room was filled with the light of sweet devotion to the Lord. Daniel stood from his prayers and seemed to drink in the Spirit that had filled the room. He walked to the window and shut it, praising God out loud as he did so.

When he turned from the window, Daniel stopped in the middle of the room and looked about as if listening for something or someone. Looking in the direction of Gabriel and Serus, he stared for a moment—then smiled to himself and left the room.

"Did he see us?" asked Serus.

"No," said Gabriel. "He didn't see us. He saw something greater."

Darius was beside himself. He could not believe that Daniel would do such a thing. Was there a mistake? Daniel was a man revered and respected by everyone in the kingdom! Could he have been simply meditating or reading or...?

Kezzar-mar looked quite distraught. He stood with the other men—Sheshbar, Berza, and Farsin—who looked downcast. Berza held in his hand a copy of the decree.

"Majesty, I could hardly believe it myself," said Kezzar-mar. "When these devout men went to see Daniel on a matter of business, they were completely shocked to find the man engaged in fervent prayer."

"Perhaps Daniel had not yet seen the decree," offered Darius hopefully. The king wanted desperately to extricate Daniel from this perilous situation. He knew that, having signed the decree, he could not undo it. He clung to hope.

"Alas, majesty," said Kezzar-mar. "But I personally read the decree to Daniel so that he would be able to serve you in the matter."

Kezzar-mar glanced quickly at Berza, who was holding the decree in his hand.

"As you know, majesty," said Berza, "the decree calls for the offender to be thrown into the den of lions."

"Yes, yes, I know," said Darius. He tore at the purple cloak he was wearing, infuriated that he had signed such a thing. He looked pleadingly at Kezzar-mar. "Is there no other way?" he implored.

"Majesty," said Kezzar-mar with deep conviction, "if we relent in this matter, we will only encourage more insolence. These are a newly conquered people, and they must see that the king's justice is both swift and without favoritism." He stopped for a moment as if to collect himself. "Majesty, Daniel must die."

Darius buried his head in his hands for a moment. Kezzar-mar ordered a steward to bring a drink to the king. Berza and Sheshbar assured the king that there really was no other way. Finally the king, looking as if he had aged several years, gave in.

"See to it, Kezzar-mar," he said. "Arrest Daniel and bring him to the palace. But he is not to be killed just yet."

Lucifer was getting tired of Darius's continued support of Daniel. He had joined Kara and Rugio to watch the charges being laid out. He looked at Rugio, who seemed a bit nervous at how the trial was going.

"This king of yours is weak," said Kara. "I thought you had guided these Persians differently!"

"Who can know the mind of men?" said Rugio defensively. "I have done everything I could to set these kings upon the Jews. They are not like the Assyrian kings, these Persians."

"I suggest that you do something before this idiot creates a new decree and allows Daniel to live," said Lucifer firmly.

Rugio nodded in agreement and looked at Kara.

"Allow me," Kara said haughtily.

Kara moved next to the king just as Michael entered the room. All the demons looked at the powerful archangel, whose presence was rare in Babylon. Michael had been supporting the Jews who were returning to Jerusalem. But on the strength of Daniel's fervent prayer, he had come to Babylon to personally look into the matter.

"Well," said Lucifer. "Two archangels in Babylon. Now that must set some sort of precedent."

"I came because of Daniel's prayer," said Michael resolutely. His bluish aura was manifesting the righteousness of his cause. "He is at peace with whatever happens to him. You cannot win even if he were to die."

"Oh, he'll die," said Kara. "I am just about to see to that!"

Michael watched as Kara moved from accuser to accuser in the room, feeding their minds and stoking the hatred in their hearts until they virtually surrounded the king with their accusations:

"The decree stands and cannot be repealed!"

"Daniel pays no attention to you—this Jewish exile!"

"He is still praying three times a day!"

"Enough!" cried Darius, holding his ears to shut out the noise. They had been talking to the king throughout most of the day—and now the sun was setting. Darius had had enough. "Arrest him! See to it personally, Kezzar-mar. I only hope that his God will rescue him!"

Kezzar-mar and the others bowed low before the distressed king as he left the room. They smiled at each other in secret congratulations. After the king had left, Kezzar-mar produced the warrant for Daniel's arrest, already made up.

"Take some guards and arrest him," said Kezzar-mar, handing the warrant to Berza. "One day the king shall thank us for this. One day all of Persia will thank us!"

"I certainly thank him," said Lucifer. "How about you, Kara?"

"Indeed," said Kara. "From the bottom of my darkened heart!"

The demons burst out laughing and looked at Michael. The archangel ignored their mockery. Rugio locked eyes with Michael, as if he might spring upon him at any moment. Kara watched the two angels whose rivalry had begun in Heaven so long ago.

"Prayer brought me here for Daniel's sake, Lucifer," said Michael. "I believe that his prayers will also deliver him."

"It's easy to pray when one is outside the lions' den," said Kara.

Daniel accompanied the guards into the massive vaults beneath the palace where the lions were kept. The big cats had access to the outside through a tunnel that led up to a yard where they were a featured part of the king's personal collection of animals. As Daniel passed by his accusers, he looked at each one of them.

All of them averted their eyes except Kezzar-mar, who held in his hand the warrant for Daniel's execution. He looked squarely into Daniel's eyes. In the gallery above, Darius awaited Daniel's arrival with apprehension. He motioned for Daniel to come to where he sat. Daniel smiled at the king.

"I can only hope that the God to whom you pray will see fit to deliver you, Daniel," said the king. "But if He does not, know that I am bound by the law not to rescue you."

Daniel gave a comforting look to the king that somehow reassured him that, come what may, all was right.

"Daniel, called Belteshazzar," said Kezzar-mar solemnly, "you have been discovered to be guilty of high treason by way of praying to your foreign God. You did this deliberately and in full knowledge that this action was criminal and that it carried with it the sentence now about to be imposed."

He gave a quick nod of his head and some guards rolled a large stone that covered the den's opening. Kezzar-mar smirked at Daniel.

"May your God have mercy upon you!"

Daniel entered the den, climbing into the pit. The lions were on the outside of the gate leading up to the zoo park. They could be heard growling in the background. Daniel reached the bottom of the pit and looked up at the faces peering at him.

"Once you are dealt with, the other Jews will give way in short order," whispered Kezzar-mar so that the king could not hear him. "Then we will deal with that rabble that is trying to rebuild the temple in Jerusalem!"

Then a large stone was rolled in over the opening. A seal was placed on the door and Darius himself, along with the other nobles present, used their signet rings on the seal so nobody would disturb it. Darius then left, unwilling to stay and see what might happen. Kezzar-mar and the other men who had brought charges against Daniel ordered the gate opened so that the lions might find their way to Daniel. Then they left to celebrate the success of their conspiracy.

"Pray, Daniel," Kezzar-mar called out as he left. "Prayer got you into this trouble. Perhaps it will get you out!"

The men laughed and disappeared into the palace.

Daniel could hear the gate on the far end of the tunnel opening. The lions would be coming shortly, but he was prepared to meet his Lord. What an honor to die for the Most High God! He prayed that, whatever happened, the Lord would receive glory for it all. Then he waited to die.

Inside the pit Lucifer, Kara, Rugio, Pellecus and a number of other demons awaited the final bloody moments of Daniel's life. They couldn't care less if he died in honor of the Lord—so long as he died.

"I think I hear dinner approaching," said Kara lightly.

"You mean something is approaching its dinner," responded Pellecus.

Daniel watched calmly as first one and then another and another lion emerged from the tunnel—six lions in all. They looked at the man in their den. One of the lions, a young male, began pacing back and forth nervously. Another licked its lips. The devils watching the spectacle urged the lions on, ready to see Daniel torn apart.

Suddenly a bright light entered the den, causing the lions to back up toward the tunnel. It was the figure of a man with a sword, which he pointed at the lions. Six separate pulses shot out and became chains of light, wrapping themselves around the mouths of the lions so that they could not even make a sound, much less bite something. Daniel watched in amazement as the light began to diminish and he saw standing before him an angel of God! It was the same angel who had visited him before with the terrifying words about what must happen to Israel in the future.

"Gabriel!" cried Lucifer. "You cannot interfere with this!"

"This man's prayers have overwhelmed your darkness, Lucifer," said Gabriel. "Now get out of here!"

Upon his words, the place shook violently and the demons were tossed back. The archangel's words carried with them the weight and authority of the Lord—for God Himself had sent Gabriel to deliver Daniel from the lions.

"The Most High is not yet finished with this man," Gabriel said. "He is to become even mightier as a prophet, and the Lord will deliver even greater words into his heart before he is taken up to Heaven!"

"I am not finished with this man either," said Lucifer bitterly. "But I sense the power and presence of the Most High here in this place. So I shall relinquish the day. Have your prophets and your lions. I shall still have this war!"

Lucifer vanished, and the other demons with him disappeared as well. Daniel could only stare at the angel who had rescued him. He didn't attempt to speak to Gabriel. Instead, he simply fell asleep and slept a very peaceful night's rest. As for Gabriel, he was relieved that the Lord had further plans for Daniel, who had become a favorite among the Host.

CHAPTER 17

"My king, may you live forever!"

The king did not sleep well that night. Darius was visited by fitful thoughts of the death of one of the truly noble men in his kingdom. Still, he was king, wasn't he? The law had to be upheld, didn't it? These foreigners, while tolerated, also had to be shown that kingly authority would be respected.

At the first light of day, the king could wait no longer. He rose from his bed and hurried down to the den of lions. At first he listened for any sounds that might come up from the pit—some sign that perhaps Daniel had survived the ordeal. Finally, he brought a torch down low toward the pit and called out:

"Daniel! Daniel! Has your God delivered you?"

Daniel was fast asleep, near one of the lions. The king called out again, but Daniel remained asleep. Gabriel thought he had better awaken the sleeping man of God, and called out his name:

"Daniel! Wake up!"

Daniel opened his eyes just as the king cried out in desperation one more time. Hearing the king, Daniel stood up and called back:

"My king, may you live forever!"

Darius was overjoyed beyond belief. He immediately ordered the stone moved and Daniel pulled from the pit. Darius peeked into the hole, looking at the rousing lions, which were still bound by Gabriel's authority and could not open their mouths.

Daniel looked down at Gabriel and waved. The king looked at Daniel, and then down at the lions in the pit. Perhaps the evening had been a bit stressful after all. He would give Daniel an extended rest. Gabriel smiled and waved back, then disappeared. At that very moment, the bonds loosened, and the lions began working their mouths, yawning and making low growls.

Darius inspected Daniel and saw that not even a thread of his clothing had been torn—the lions had not touched him! The sound of footsteps descending the stairs echoed through the chamber. Darius looked up to see the astonished expressions of Kezzar-mar and Berza, who could not believe their eyes. Was this a ghost speaking to the king—or had Daniel actually survived the ordeal?

"Look, Kezzar-mar," said Darius. "I told you that Daniel's God would deliver him and so He did. Isn't it marvelous?"

Kezzar-mar was dumbstruck as Daniel explained to the king that God had sent an angel to shut the lions' mouths; and that he had been wrongfully and maliciously accused by Kezzar-mar. The king was incredulous at hearing these words.

"Great king," continued Daniel. "The God I serve saw fit to deliver me because I respected His law rather than the law of men. In His eyes I have done no wrong. But these men wickedly conspired to kill me because they were jealous of your promotion of me in the matter of the satraps."

Darius looked in the direction of Kezzar-mar. The men who had brought charges against Daniel now stood accused by him. Before they could even begin to defend themselves, the king ordered them thrown into the lions' pit. Kezzar-mar pleaded for his life, but before he even hit the ground, the lions were on him and Berza, tearing them to pieces.

"See to it that the others are arrested and brought down here as well," said the king, angry at the betrayal of Daniel. He then turned to Daniel.

"I have issued a terrible decree," he admitted. "And now I shall issue an honorable one. Henceforth, in this kingdom, the name of Daniel's God is to be revered—for He is the living and eternal God whose kingdom shall never end!"

"So be it, majesty," said Daniel, as they left the chamber together.

Bethlehem, 4 B.C.

Jarod jumped on Joshua, snarling like a lion and pretending to attack Kezzar-mar. The men laughed at the boy's playful energy—particularly so late in the evening. Eli looked up at Elron, Joshua's father.

"That story will never wear out. It's as good now as the first time I ever heard it from my own father."

"Wonderful story," agreed Elron.

Elron stood and surveyed the little town below them, with fewer and fewer lights in windows as people retired for the night. He looked into the fields and rubbed his eyes. It seemed almost hazy out there in the darkness—a milky, translucent haze. *It must be caused by the new star*, he thought to himself, although he could have sworn he actually saw some figures walking about in the darkness.

"Some day the prophecies of Daniel shall be fulfilled," he said to nobody in particular. "Some day Messiah shall restore this nation."

"Do you really believe that?" asked Daniel the shepherd, who was sincere in his question. "Do you really believe that Messiah will remember us?"

"Daniel," said Elron. "Messiah has never forgotten us."

Serus and Bakka listened with great interest to Daniel's question. It was obvious that something was happening this night to the man's heart. He had started the evening so bitter—so morose about anything smacking of the Lord. Now he seemed truly interested in the Messiah and had listened to Eli and the others recounting Israel's glorious past. Gabriel arrived from his meeting with Michael.

"Well, so is the war over?" asked Serus humorously. "Did Lucifer surrender?"

"Hardly," said Gabriel. "He is shadowing the Child. Michael is personally watching over the mother. They are trying to find a place to stay for the night."

"I think Elron can see us," said an angel named Romus to Gabriel. "He was looking very hard into our company."

"Don't worry," said Gabriel. "Sometimes the Lord allows a human to see us. But when the time is right they all shall see us!"

"How do humans act when they see us?" asked Romus, who was new to earthly assignments.

"Usually they are frightened—at least until we can reassure them that we mean them no harm," said Gabriel. "Of course the enemy also will appear to humans, posing as holy angels or friendly spirits, only to deceive them. The human mind generally will see what it wants."

"You have appeared to many humans," said Serus, "delivering the Lord's words or interpreting dreams and visions."

"True," said Gabriel. "The Most High has accorded me that honor. I was deeply moved to be able to speak to Mary regarding the Child. In fact, I appeared to most of that family during the course of events. But my greatest contest came when I appeared to Daniel during the waning years of his life."

"Ah yes," said Serus, "the prince of Persia."

"Yes," said Gabriel, remembering it vividly. "The prince of Persia..."

Babylon, 536 B.C.

Daniel awoke in a cold sweat, his bed dripping from the perspiration that had overtaken him in his dream. Or was it a dream? He got up from his bed and lit the little oil lamp on the table beside him. Looking down at the bed, he scratched his head and sat down. The Lord had spoken something horrible to him—a vision of bloody warfare. But what did it mean? How should it unfold?

Though the images were fresh in his mind, he did not understand their meaning. What was the Lord trying to tell him? He decided that he must fast and pray until he received the interpretation from the Most High. So he began that very moment to seek the Lord in this matter.

Gabriel appeared before the Great Throne of the Lord in Heaven. It was his turn to do homage to God by raising His Most Holy name in prayer and praise. All higher-ranking angels had assembled before the Lord, as was customary. The praises were a sweet incense, filling the Temple with a fragrant aroma. The angelic choir, too, in thousands, sang praises to the Most High God, whose Throne would forever endure and whose justice was ever honorable. In their place, circled about the Throne, the 24 elders also raised hands in worship to the Most High.

But as was also customary, Lucifer arrived to put in his appearance to accuse the Lord's people. The Host never understood why he was given that special privilege, since his authority in Heaven had been removed. Nevertheless, his appearance, though unwanted, was not unexpected.

Following Gabriel's leading of praise, Lucifer walked boldly to the place where he was allowed to position himself and began bringing charges against God's people and plans. The angels held their tongues in respect to the Most High's obvious allowance of this accusing angel.

They listened as Lucifer harangued one prominent person after another—Zerubbabel, who was leading the people's efforts to rebuild the temple; Zechariah and Haggai, whose prophetic ministries were being stirred; and other notable men of God. One by one Lucifer brought sordid and unrighteous accusations before the Lord, who merely listened in silence. Finally, Lucifer brought up the name Daniel, and began to rail against him with a ferocity unseen before even in Lucifer.

As he spoke, however, a smoky, bluish haze began to ascend around the Throne of God. All angels bowed their heads in anticipation of what was happening. Only Lucifer did not understand the meaning of this fragrant smoke. Then the Lord spoke, a thunderous voice that shook Lucifer to the ground:

"Lucifer, thou fallen angel! These are the prayers of my servant Daniel, who seeks the meaning of a vision I have sent to him. Behold that I the Lord hear the prayers of my servants. Daniel is a man whom I hold dear, and I will not hear your accusations any further. I shall therefore send Gabriel to him with the meaning of the vision, that he might seal it up for the latter days..."

Lucifer looked up to see all the angels, including Gabriel, prostrate before the Lord. He crept out of the room and immediately returned to earth. With only a few moments to contest the prayers of Daniel, he had decided that only one warrior in his kingdom could face the archangel.

Rugio was at Susa where the Persian kings were building a splendid palace. Having been given lordship over this nation, Rugio had decided that the best course of action was to fill these insolent kings with a pride for personal luxury. Perhaps then he could maintain power over the occupied countries through tribute and taxation and thus keep them downtrodden and controllable.

"Rugio!"

"Here, my prince," he answered.

Lucifer came in from the west and began explaining to Rugio the situation that was about to occur.

"Daniel is even now fasting and praying to the Most High for an interpretation that he must not receive," he said. "It is apparently a revelation of the latter days and it is critical that there be no understanding or recording of this."

"Of course, my lord," said Rugio, a bit perplexed. "But how can this stop the prophecy from happening in the latter times?"

"Because," said Lucifer, losing his patience, "the Lord cannot fulfill a prophecy that has neither been heard nor understood. You are prince of Persia. You have the authority to stop Gabriel from entering your territory. It is a right and an honor—and it is quite necessary if you want this kingdom to survive!"

Rugio suddenly understood the importance of this contest. *If only it were Michael*, he thought to himself. But he was certain that he could stand against Gabriel. He nodded in understanding and vanished. Lucifer hoped that Rugio could indeed stand against Gabriel. He smiled to himself. After their humbling with Darius it would be quite delicious to see Gabriel humbled in return!

After learning from the Most High the meaning of the vision, Gabriel hurried to find Daniel and deliver the interpretation. As he neared Babylon, where Daniel was in fasting and prayer, he suddenly began to feel a resistance, as if he were being held by an invisible grip. He stopped in the air above the city and heard laughter all around him.

"Welcome to Babylon, Archangel," said Rugio, who appeared before him.

"Give way, you wicked angel," said Gabriel. "I am on the King's business."

"I too am on the business of a king," said Rugio.

Again, laughter as devils began to appear in the air all around the two powerful angels. Gabriel looked about at the scowling, harassing, cursing demons who were mocking both him and the Lord.

"Give way! Give way!" one of them repeated in Gabriel's voice.

"He's on the King's business!" said another.

Gabriel looked at Rugio sharply.

"What is this, Rugio?" he asked finally. "You cannot prevail against the prayers of Daniel. They are what brought me here!"

"Perhaps," said Rugio. "But they shall also send you away from here. After I have resisted you long enough he will stop praying and you shall have to return without delivering your message."

Gabriel looked at him in surprise.

"Oh, yes," said Rugio. "We know all about the revelation you carry. It is deadly to us, and you shall not be permitted to carry it to this or any other prophet!"

With those words, Gabriel drew out his sword and brought it down upon Rugio. Rugio moved just in time and drew his own sword. The two angels fought throughout the day, sword crashing against sword, neither angel gaining the advantage. The howling devils encouraged Rugio in the fight. Sometimes the two went to wrestling, arms locked, desperately fighting to gain ground.

All the while Daniel continued in prayer, unaware of the great contest that was occurring overhead. Whenever Daniel became tired, Gabriel's strength began to wane. When Daniel roused himself to continue in fervent prayer, Gabriel gained the advantage. But throughout the battle Gabriel could not overcome Rugio, who fought valiantly to keep the archangel from completing his mission.

"I can go on like this forever," blustered Rugio. "How about you, Archangel?"

"I can go on as long as Daniel continues in prayer," said Gabriel. "And he is a man who does not easily give up!"

"We'll soon find out," said Rugio, who signaled Nathan, his aide. Nathan disappeared into the city. "Nathan will find out just how dedicated he really is."

Nathan found Daniel just as he had imagined him—seated at a table, weary, tired, weakened from the fast—and praying fervently. The man was crying out to God passionately, but he was weak of voice. Nathan saw Serus standing near him.

"Ah, Serus," said Nathan. "How is our man of prayer?"

"Praying," said Serus. "As always."

Serus moved to protect the man should it come to it. Nathan looked at Serus and laughed at him.

"Don't be a fool, Serus," he said. "I am not here to attack the man. Merely to speak to him."

"It won't do you any good," said Serus. "He has the Lord's mind in this."

"Let's see if he can lose his mind," said Nathan, who then began to whisper into Daniel's mind.

"Daniel, you must not resist any more. You have done well and now, someday, the revelation will be given to you. Therefore rest from this..."

Daniel looked up, perceiving the voice that was speaking to him. He then continued in prayer. Nathan looked at Serus, who only smirked back.

"Daniel! You are esteemed in my eyes. Therefore, you must stop praying for, behold, I shall answer thee in another time..."

Daniel looked up once more. This time he started to address the voice. Nathan looked confidently at Serus, when suddenly Daniel burst out with, "You are not the Lord! I know the Lord would have me pray until I hear from Him. Now begone in the name of my Most High God!"

Nathan was suddenly blown out of the room as if a sudden gust of wind had picked up a piece of cloth. Daniel immediately sensed the presence was gone and continued with his praying.

Both Rugio and Gabriel also sensed something breaking forth in the heavenlies. Something had happened. Had Nathan gotten through? Had Daniel indeed given up? Rugio began to smile, and the devils howled louder than ever.

"Well, Archangel, it looks as if one of us will have to leave the contest," he said.

"My thoughts exactly, Rugio," came a strong voice breaking in from the sky.

It was Michael.

Rugio looked at Gabriel and Michael with fear in his eyes. The devils in the sky scattered quickly at the other archangel's appearance. Michael only had to step into the battle and it was over. Weakened from the previous 21 days of warfare with Gabriel, Rugio was knocked away easily by one thrust of Michael's sword. The prince of Persia disappeared into the ground.

Gabriel found Daniel by the banks of the Tigris, still praying as he walked with a couple of servants. Daniel, whose eyes had been low, looked up and saw a man towering above him. The man was dressed in linen with a belt of fine gold around his waist. He had eyes of lightning, and his arms were like bronze.

Daniel's servants did not see the vision, but they sensed something uncanny and fled into the woods. Daniel continued looking at the man and then, what with the fast of 21 days and the shock of this visitation, suddenly felt very weak. He fell to the ground in a faint.

Gabriel looked at Daniel and touched him, waking him up. Daniel sat up and saw that the man was still standing there. He rubbed his tired eyes in disbelief. Then the angel spoke.

"Daniel, you are esteemed of the Lord. Now listen carefully, for the Lord has sent me to you to give you these words..."

Daniel swallowed hard and stood up, trembling all the while. He looked about to see if anybody else was nearby—but they were alone.

"Do not be afraid. Since the very first day that you began to pray I have tried to come to you. But I was resisted by the enemy, the prince over the land, for these twenty-one days. And then the Archangel Michael came and supported me so that I might come to you. And now I shall explain the meaning of the vision that concerned you..."

Daniel bowed low in the face of such a visitation, but he was crippled of tongue and could not answer. The angel touched Daniel's mouth and he summoned the courage to speak.

"This vision, my lord," Daniel began. "It is frightening. I am overcome with grief because of it. And my strength is gone. How can I bear it?"

The angel then touched Daniel once more and imparted to him strength. Daniel felt a rush of energy and vigor flowing into his body, coursing into him like a warm substance. The angel then stepped back and began speaking:

"Daniel, I must tell you what is written in the Book of Truth. I must tell you what the vision meant..."

Thus Gabriel began explaining what the vision meant; what the future held for Israel; of the wars of the king of the North and the king of the South; of the Abomination of Desolation; of a great leader who would oppose the Throne of God; of the destruction of nations; of times of great distress and great deliverance.

Gabriel spoke of these events and then told Daniel to seal up the revelation, for these were for later times, and not his own. Daniel then looked up and saw two more angels—one on the opposite side of the river and one on his own side. One of the angels called out to Gabriel, saying:

"How long will it be before these astonishing things are fulfilled?"

Gabriel, who had spoken with Daniel and was now rising above the river, lifted his hands to Heaven and said:

"It shall be for a time, times and half a time. When the power of the holy people has been finally broken, all these things shall be completed!"

Daniel, now completely himself, ran down the riverbank calling out to the angel. "But what will the outcome be? How shall it all end?"

The angel looked down at Daniel and said:

"Go on, Daniel. Live a blessed life. The words are closed up and sealed until the end of time. But when the Abomination of Desolation is set up, there shall be only one thousand two hundred ninety days remaining. Go now and live the remainder of your days in peace!"

Daniel never fully understood the words of the angel. He only knew that at the appointed time—in the endtimes—something both terrible and glorious would occur. He glanced up and down the riverbank and saw that once more he was alone. So Daniel lived out his life in Babylon, respected, blessed, and assured a great inheritance one day.

CHAPTER 18

"This Christ shall die a humiliating and bloody death!"

Bethlehem, 4 B.C.

"That terrible seal has yet to be broken," said Gabriel. "Those and other words spoken to Daniel have not yet been fulfilled. Those things cannot happen until Messiah has come. The message to Daniel is like the words I spoke to Zechariah—of a vision of the Angel of the Lord who encouraged the people to continue building the temple that Ezra had begun. I said that they should not be discouraged that Messiah did not appear immediately when they completed it. Messiah could not appear until the times were full."

Bakka looked at Serus and Gabriel, realizing suddenly the significance of this evening; the importance of his mission to Daniel; the momentous event that was unfolding in Bethlehem.

"Tonight is the night," he almost whispered. "The Child that Micah spoke of. This is the Coming One…the Seed of the woman!"

Gabriel looked at Bakka with compassion.

"Yes, Bakka," he said. "Tonight is the night. That is why the Host is gathered. Soon we shall announce to the world that a Savior has been born to them in Bethlehem."

Joseph found Mary where he had left her, near one of the inns that had rejected them. He was having trouble finding a place to stay, because so many people were in town for the census. She was becoming more and more discouraged; and the labor was becoming more and more intense. They needed a place, and fast.

"Mary! Mary!"

Joseph came bounding excitedly to his love. He pointed behind him as he ran to where she sat on the donkey that had brought her on this long journey.

"The man over there at the inn," he panted, out of breath from running. "He said we may use the stable area. There is clean straw and we may bed down in it. He said we might even drink fresh milk if the animals will give."

Mary was relieved. She smiled at her husband and indicated that they had better be moving along. Joseph grabbed the rein and led the donkey through the little street to the back of a small inn. The stable was more cave than building, but it would do nicely at this point and Mary was grateful to get off the animal that had romped her around for so long.

Joseph gently lifted the girl off the animal and set her down in a soft bedding of clean straw. He found an old cloak that would serve as a cover and Mary lay down upon the straw bed. The moo of a cow, who was disturbed by the activity, caused Mary and Joseph to laugh at their situation.

"Here we are," he said. "You are about to give birth to the Savior of His people and you have to share the room with a fussy cow! I'm sorry it could not have been somewhere more fitting."

Mary smiled.

"Anywhere that the Savior is born is fitting indeed."

"The woman's time draws near," said Lucifer, as they looked down upon the little stable area.

Kara and Pellecus were with Lucifer, looking at the innumerable holy angels in and around Bethlehem. Nobody seemed to pay any attention to Lucifer—all focus was upon Joseph and Mary.

"I have not seen so many angels gathered together in one place in a long time," said Kara. "Not since the days that I was an elder in Heaven."

"Yes, well, those glory days are over," said Pellecus, who then proceeded to set the bait. "But you led us well in Heaven."

"Thank you, Pellecus," said Kara, surprised by praise from a usual critic.

"Yes," continued Pellecus slyly. "You led us right to disaster here on earth. Now this accursed Seed is about to become a reality!"

"I did my best in Heaven," said Kara. "It was I who persuaded the elders to have Lucifer named steward of the earth. I did my part in this plot. If you seek out blame, look to yourself! You and your obvious disdain for the Academy. It was your blatant opposition in the classroom that opened us up to suspicion in the first place!"

"Enough!" screamed Lucifer.

Several holy angels nearby looked in Lucifer's direction following his outburst.

"We already look like we are defeated," he said. "Must we also look like fools?"

Pellecus looked at the stable below. "Whatever the outcome— below, in the womb of that woman, is the future thrust of the war," he said. "Eve's curse."

"Eve," muttered Lucifer hatefully. "I shall bruise His heel; and He shall break my crown. Provided He lives so long."

Mary's labor had passed the point of soon—the baby was now imminent. Joseph had helped deliver his cousin's baby, but helping with his own child made him a bit nervous. The angels in the room comforted him and Mary, laying their hands on them and helping them along.

"The Child is about to be born," Gabriel announced. "Glory to God!"

The angels in and around the stable began to proclaim praises to the Lord as Mary, the betrothed of Joseph, became Mary, the mother of Jesus. The Child was delivered. Joseph cut the cord that was attached to the baby and picked him up. He held the boy up in his hands and shook Him gently so that He started to cry, taking His first breath—Heaven's own Son breathing the very air He had created.

Michael and Gabriel stood together, looking at mother and Child. The baby, now wrapped in a swaddling cloth, was still beside his mother. She smiled at her husband, Joseph, who was giving thanks to the Lord for bringing the baby into the world. Mary could not help but remember all the events that had led up to this moment—and now it had come. But she didn't want to think about her son's future right now—she only wanted to enjoy Him.

"Gabriel, go and announce to the shepherds," said Michael. "It is time!"

The archangel looked at the Child once more and disappeared into the night sky. He came over to where the angels had encamped around Bethlehem and told the news to them. A great shout went up over Bethlehem as the Host cheered the news that the Savior had been born!

Gabriel looked down at the little group of shepherds. He had always loved the shepherds of Israel—ever since the time of David. Now he was going to deliver to them the greatest news a shepherd would ever hear.

Eli was about to lie down for the night. The long conversation had ended and the few men who were still awake awaited their time in the fields with the sheep. Only Daniel remained intensely alert, for he had been praying ever since Eli had stopped. He stood up, looked toward Bethlehem...and began to pray.

"Most High God of my fathers," he said. "For several generations my family has not served You as they should. I am a Levite and yet I have been shunning my priestly duties, as did my fathers before me. Yet I know, O Lord, that You are a God who hears a contrite and sincere prayer. I have heard the stories of Your deliverance of Daniel; the defeat of Goliath; how You built up a nation of priests and even in its rebellion, You destroyed it while giving it a hope and a future.

"Now, O Lord, I see that I have allowed the bitterness of the past and the shame of my family to separate me from Your will. I ask, O Lord, that You will allow me to enter once more into Your service; to serve You as a Levite; to do honor to Your name all the days of my life until the Messiah should come and I serve Him as well."

As Daniel concluded his prayer, he began weeping. Bakka walked over to him and placed his hand upon him, comforting him. He then spoke so that Daniel might hear him:

"Daniel, behold, the Lord will hear your prayer!"

Daniel felt himself being turned in the direction of the camp. He saw a man dressed in white, with a gold belt, entering the open area where the shepherds lay. Daniel looked around to see who had spoken or who had turned him—but saw nobody. He hurried to the camp, rousing the men.

Eli and the others looked up and saw the angel Gabriel standing before them. The glory of the Lord was all around them. The two boys jumped back in fear, their heads filled with the stories of the evening. Was this Goliath back from the dead?

Suddenly the angel spoke, and the men became still and no longer afraid.

"Do not be afraid, shepherds of Israel. I bring you good news of great joy that shall be for all the people. Today, in the city of David, a Savior has been born to you; He is Christ the Lord!"

"Messiah," whispered Eli aloud.

"And this shall be a sign to you. You will find the baby wrapped in cloths and lying in a manger."

Suddenly it was as if the very heavens opened up and thousands of angels appeared in the sky above the shepherds. They could not believe their eyes. It was like the stars themselves had descended to earth! Everywhere were angels! The angels began to cry out in a great chorus:

> *"Glory to God in the highest!*
> *And on earth peace,*
> *And good will to men!"*

Then just as suddenly the angels vanished and all was dark and still again. The shepherds looked at each other. Had Eli's stories gotten into their minds? Or did they truly witness this spectacle?

Daniel understood immediately.

"Messiah has come!" he said. "He is there—in Bethlehem!"

"Indeed it is the Messiah!" said Eli. "Just as He promised our nation through the centuries! He has come! The King has come!"

Eli danced about the fire with a vigor he hadn't shown in years. The other shepherds joined him, and the men celebrated and praised God for His visitation. Only Daniel held back from the others. He sought the Lord alone—in prayer.

"Thank You, Most High Lord," he said, weeping, "for allowing me to be a part of this life. I shall never forget the night that You pulled me back from my darkness and into the light of Your Messiah. I will ever serve You!"

The shepherds decided to leave the sheep and go to town where they might have a look at the Child. As they hurried down the gently sloping hill, Joshua tugged on his father's cloak.

"Yes, my son," said Elron.

"But Father, why should a king be born here in Bethlehem in a stable? I thought kings were born in palaces."

"Because, Joshua, He is not like an earthly king to be born in the splendor of wealth," came a voice from behind. "He needs no human palaces or cities of gold in which to establish His throne. He needs only the hearts of men. A heart like yours—tender, innocent, hopeful...and open."

Joshua turned to see who had spoken these words. It was Daniel.

The evening passed and morning came. And the first day of the new life of the new Savior came and went. In Jerusalem, on the roof of the new temple being constructed by Herod, Lucifer met with his Council. He looked at the angels who had thrown in with him: Kara, Pellecus, and Rugio—as well as Tinius, Nathan, Berenius, and the others.

Once more they looked to him with hope. Once more they hung on his words, looking for an answer—believing that as always Lucifer would have another tactic, another ploy, another way to keep the war going. Lucifer spread his arms out wide, indicating the city below them.

"Jerusalem, my brothers. Jerusalem. Look at it. It isn't large by human standards. It is of no commercial consequence. Joshua, Egypt, Babylon, Persia, the Greeks, the Ptolemies, Antiochus, the Maccabbees, and now the Romans—all have held this city and others shall in the future. A city of little consequence and yet the city in which the final battle of this war must occur."

He looked over the high point of the temple to the streets below and turned back to the demons.

"We have seen through the years, from Abraham down through Moses and the prophets—that all roads of destiny have led to this place. We fought a good fight but we failed to prevent the Seed's arrival. And now He is here. And we will one day bloodily contend with Him as well.

"We have never been able to make peace in this city—nobody has. And I believe that will be to our advantage. These people never have respected a prophet sent to them. This Messiah must make peace with Jerusalem—and I prophesy that it shall never happen! But I realize something else…that this war has taken on a new dimension. Once more, and as always, the Lord leaves a door open for us to take advantage of!"

The demons muttered among themselves.

"A new dimension?" asked Pellecus. "And what is that?"

"Think of it, Pellecus," continued Lucifer. "Our enemy for all these years has been safely hidden among the people. He has always been talk, speculation, a dream tucked away in a future womb of someone of the house of David. We have never been able to defeat Him, because we could never find Him. Well, now He is out in the open where He can be destroyed."

"But He is too well covered," said Kara. "We shall never get to Him."

"True, Kara," said Lucifer. "But I am gambling on these petty, proud humans to do what we might never be able to do."

He looked at the demons, his eyes inflamed.

"I am gambling that these people will destroy their own Savior!"

The demons began to reason among themselves for a bit.

"Think about it," Lucifer said. "They hold nothing sacred. They respect nothing of the Lord, be he priest or prophet. They kill prophets, you know…and with some suggestion on my part, I believe they will kill this one as well."

"Your part, my prince?" asked Rugio.

"Yes, Rugio," said Lucifer. "That is the other part of this new war. It occurs to me that before the Seed was here, He and I could do battle by proxy—through Israel. Now that He has arrived, I shall move against Him personally."

Lucifer cupped his hands and held them in a contemplative manner, resting his mouth upon his clasped fists. He then continued.

"I see no other way. It will come down to Christ the Anointed and Lucifer the satan. It will be classic, my dear brothers. And it shall be bloody. I will approach Him with every vile thought and temptation possible. We will inflict diseases upon His people as never before; we shall cause men to go insane and women to have barren wombs. All that the demons assigned to you can do to wreak havoc around this Man—you shall do.

"And when it comes to the final battle, I shall see this Man dead and bleeding. I promise you this. This Christ shall die a humiliating and bloody death—one that all the world shall be ashamed of. This Man—this Seed—this Messiah—shall pay the price of this war that began in Eden with His own blood!"

He stared off into the sky and repeated the words under his breath.

"With Your own blood!"

Chronicles of the Host series
by D. Brian Shafer

BOOK ONE: CHRONICLES OF THE HOST

Lucifer, the Anointed Cherub, whose ministry in Heaven is devoted to the worship of the Most High God, has become pessimistic about his prospects in Heaven. Ambition inflamed, he looks to the soon-to-be-created Earth as a place where he can see his destiny realized. With a willing crew of equally ambitious angels, Lucifer creates a fifth column of malcontents under the very throne of God. Hot on their heels, however, is a group of loyalists, led by Michael and Gabriel, who are suspicious of Lucifer's true motives. In detective-style fashion, they slowly start to unmask the true nature of Lucifer's sordid plot. *Chronicles of the Host* is a fantastic novel of the beginning of all things. Follow Lucifer's deceptive plans to rule over Earth and his inevitable fall from grace.
ISBN 0-7684-2099-7

BOOK TWO: UNHOLY EMPIRE

The prophetic clock is ticking. Lucifer and his army of "imps" search frantically for the prophetic "Seed of the woman." The memory of God's promise that this seed would rise up and bruise the serpent's head stirs them to shadowy demonic activity. *Unholy Empire* chronicles the duel between God and the fallen angels as both focus their attention on the Seed. The devils watch for any and every sign of the Seed in an all-out effort to stop, delay, compromise, or otherwise destroy this impending prophetic nightmare. If they fail they are all doomed.
ISBN 0-7684-2160-8

BOOK THREE: RISING DARKNESS

The Chronicles saga continues as Israel establishes herself in the land of promise, in spite of the unholy efforts of Lucifer. A satanic shift in strategy occurs as Lucifer forsakes the simple elimination of one family that *might* carry the Seed. Now he is determined to bring down the whole nation. He is obsessed in his efforts to prevent the appearing of this mysterious Seed. Kings, priests, prophets, and pagan nations are deceived into unwittingly becoming cosmic chess pieces in this calculated war between light and darkness. From Jerusalem to Babylon and on to Rome, Lucifer believes he can destroy Israel in a deadly and delicate game of power politics…and he must do so or the nightmare will only intensify: a nightmare that will eventually be realized one starry night in Bethlehem.
ISBN 0-7684-2177-2

Available at your local Christian bookstore.

For more information and sample chapters, visit www.destinyimage.com

Additional copies of this book and other
book titles from DESTINY IMAGE are
available at your local bookstore.

For a bookstore near you, call 1-800-722-6774

Send a request for a catalog to:

Destiny Image® Publishers, Inc.

P.O. Box 310
Shippensburg, PA 17257-0310

*"Speaking to the Purposes of God for This
Generation and for the Generations to Come"*

For a complete list of our titles,
visit us at www.destinyimage.com